Applesauce

Applesauce

by
June
Arnold

McGraw-Hill Book Company
New York · Toronto · London · Sydney

For Kate, Roberta, Fairfax, Gus

Eloise

Just after Lila died—Lila with her huge, deep, utterly empty brown eyes like those usually set on each side of a gentle mare's head—Maisie had called Dr. Solomon and handed Gus the phone. Gus had just told Maisie a dream he'd had the night before because he thought it would make her laugh, or because it made him laugh, or because he had to do some of the talking when she came over and the only thing he had to talk about was his thoughts and he didn't want to get into an analysis of them again because she was alive and he wasn't, so she won all the points and left him right where he was, only beaten and not knowing any other game to play.

"Hey, this is funny, this'll make you laugh," he said brightly, trying to make a ceremony out of mixing her drink, which was vodka neat. "I dreamt that I had a dictionary and was looking up the word *nipple*. It said, 'nipple, see apple.' I turned to *apple,* and it said, 'apple, see nipple.' Nipple, see apple. Apple, see nipple. Hahahaha."

She reached for the telephone.

"What are you doing?"

Her finger held at zero, for suspense, to make him wait for the clicks that would follow and from which he would try to guess the digit she'd picked. "Most people see the thing behind the word, but you just see the word," she explained carefully. "That's a very schizophrenic thing to do, and I'm calling Dr. Solomon."

"Mr. Ferrarri?"

He didn't even hear the voice the first time, and waited.

"Mr. Ferrarri?"

The second time he heard it clearly enough, but it was impossible to get a picture of the man from just two words, and not even real words but more the equivalent of a formal beep tone. Just as people have a signature and a handwriting, they have a mechanism that says Mr. Ferrarri, and a voice. He waited again.

"Mr. Ferrarri. Mr. Ferrarri. Are you there? Hello? Hello Mr. Ferrarri?"

"Yes," he said, barely audibly. "Yes," Gus said. "This is Gus Ferrarri. Is this Dr. Solomon?"

"Yes, this is Dr. Solomon." Relief poured through the receiver in such a deluge that Gus shifted the phone to his other ear.

"Hello, Dr. Solomon. Did you want to speak to me?"

"Well, yes. That is, I thought you wanted to speak to me. Your wife . . ."

"My wife is dead."

"Oh. I'm sorry. Please forgive me."

"All three of my wives are dead. I killed three wives. The lady you talked to earlier is a friend. I don't think she wants to become my wife, either. Do you blame her?"

"No. I mean yes." Dr. Solomon hastily tugged at his voice and tried to pull it smooth. "Perhaps if I knew the circumstances I could help you."

"Dr. Solomon. That was an unforgivable thing to do; I hope you'll forgive me. It was very unfair of me to take advantage of your commitment to listen and force you into a silly response. Of course you don't blame anyone, do you? Certainly you don't blame me for killing three wives, and I hope you don't blame yourself for appearing ridiculous."

Maisie snatched the telephone from his hand. "Dr. Solomon, I'm very sorry about Mr. Ferrarri's behavior. I shouldn't have called you . . ."

"Don't let her blame herself!" he said into the mouthpiece.

Maisie left him with the problem of whether he would finish her drink, together with his own gin and water, or pour it back into the bottle in case she ever came back to see him.

Gus had known for a long time that his own core had been cut out, as neatly as if he had been an apple. And what had happened then?

A boy held it in his hand, and nibbled away the bits of apple which still clung there. And then he took the core itself between his thumb and finger, the core already beginning to turn brown as if the air were a flame which burned so swiftly and yet so subtly that at first the tiny discoloration seemed a mere illusion of staring eyes. But by the time one blinked the brown was permanent. The boy held his prize aloft and called to a group on the playground.

"Apple core!"

The group turned. "Baltimore!" said one.

"Who's your friend?"

"Harry!"

As hard as he could, then, the first boy threw the core at Harry, who tried to dodge.

Suddenly Gus stood up. What was it that was thrown at the cockroach in Kafka's story, the apple or the apple core? He searched the bookcase. Was it the apple in its pristine temptation (what a prissy god to have thought of such a thing) or the jaded core, already turning brown, its heaver in the full knowledge of digestion?

"Good evening, Mr. Gus," said Hattie, walking up to him

with an apple-cheeked lack of pretext. She looked like the drawing his nine-year-old daughter had made of her, brown and bursting with the color of fireworks as the child imagines them in the morning of the Fourth (before the disillusion of the actual sanity-flattened ceremony), her core pushing through at every bulge and hillock—a picture which contrasted horribly with his own attenuated form (it was a family group). "It sure is a fine day for a walk. Some folks have the opportunity to take walks and don't, while other folks what would like to take walks don't often get the chance. It's a funny world, the way God made it."

"It's easy enough for you to say that, Hattie, but you don't seem to understand. I decided I won't do it because I can't do it; I didn't decide I couldn't do it because I didn't want to."

Hattie planted herself firmly in front of him. She looked like she could dig holes for her feet in the rug, project roots, grow—if she wanted to. "It ain't easy to say the same thing every day. It ain't easy at all, and I don't understand why some folks think it's easy. I only hope that the day you decide that you are going to take a walk that it really will be a fine day for a walk and not a miserably rainy day like today."

"Well, you don't have anything to worry about any time soon, Hattie."

"I ain't worried about soon, since spring's just around the corner."

Suddenly he caught her in a trace of anxiety—she had planted herself in front of him and would not budge; at the same time she wanted to check around the corner for evidence of her bold prediction. He felt her silent sight as she realized that, given him, it made no difference where spring was. "I'm a long sight more worried about past. It's the most miserable winter we've had since thirty-six, and every day

I've had to come in and say it's a fine day for a walk, and hope that if you did decide that yes it was a fine day for a walk, you wouldn't notice that it was really such a day as to make a dog sick. Miss Dinah wants to know if you want a piece of the pie she just made."

"What kind of pie?"

"It's apple."

Ferrarri lunged for her, grabbed her around the trunk, yanked her up by the roots, and threw her from the room.

"The apples come from a can, just a can, that's all," she said from the hallway in righteous, adult, coreful protest.

By the window (the streaks from last night's snow showed up the dirt of which) Ferrarri cried from eight forty-five until ten, looking into his own back yard and the adjacent and opposite back yards measured like a spine down the block. Or like an egg carton. His own eggs were not in sight.

One came up behind him and tapped him on the shoulder.

"Why are you crying, Daddy?"

Tender as a young colt, Bobby was three, and had the same velvet brown eyes as his dam set wide in a white face.

"I'm crying because the machine which makes tears went berserk this morning and I found myself overflowing with tears and there was nothing to do but let some of them spill out."

"You're Mommy. Aren't you?" Bobby said.

"*NO*. Your mommy is dead." Gus knelt to the child's height and touched his shoulder. "Understand that. Do you understand that?" The blank, animal stare came too close, was going to grab him. Abruptly he stood up. "You have to understand it. All the mommies are dead. I am a monster who makes all the mommies die; I am a mommy-murdering monster, do you hear? *STOP CRYING.*"

"You yelled at me."

"Because you have to hate me." Gus knelt down again, without touching Bobby. "Listen. I'm also a liar. I lied to you when I told you the tear-maker went berserk. I don't even have a tear-maker any more. Tears are made from a person's core and I don't have a core. When the present supply of tears is gone, there won't be any more. I won't be able to cry. And you can't love someone who can't cry. He's a monster."

"Remember the apple tree in the country?" Bobby's black-brown eyes centered their innocence on Gus's face. "My mommy had long hair—down to here."

"Your mommy was as golden brown as a chestnut mare glistening in the sunlight. She was as silken and swift as a thoroughbred. She was as beautiful as any mommy in the whole world. She was Lila. But she is dead. I am Daddy. Understand?"

"How did she get dead?"

Gus stood up and went to the door. "Hattie!" He turned back to Bobby. "You know perfectly well how she got dead. She fell out of an apple tree and broke her leg."

"Did that make her dead?"

"She broke her leg so your father had to have her shot," Hattie said, looming in the doorway. She placed her bulk between Gus and the child, shaking her head in impotent reproach. "Good morning, Mr. Gus. It sure is a fine day for a walk."

"Hattie, you're absolutely right for once, it certainly is a fine day for a walk. And I'll bet Bobby would like to take one. Why don't you take Bobby and take a walk. Take two walks. Take a break. Take your time. Take everything in. Take off."

"Goodbye,—Daddy," Bobby said as Hattie finished buttoning his coat.

"Goodbye, son. Take it easy," he called after them.

Gus leaned out the window and watched Bobby and Hattie slide down the street, laughing and exchanging warm snowballs with the other streetwalkers who laughed back as they plied their trade of love. The four very bad Hofmaster boys grinned when they were hit. Hoopy too? Hoopy, the oldest, offered cigarettes which had a sliced-down razor blade concealed just under the paper so the smoker's lips would be sliced at the first drag (he had been patient with that trick; the first several victims had seized the cigarette so that the blade was horizontal and only cut their fingers). Today Hoopy was in a snowball fight, as well-adjusted as Campbell's soup. He held the little Hofmaster on his shoulders like the great men of the past do civilization and let him throw all the snowballs and that much farther. And—Gus listened a second time to make sure, and it was true—Hoopy laughed a straightforward fourteen-year-old laugh. "Somebody put something in the air," he said, "and they're all getting high on it. It isn't me. Hoopy's happy, and he's a monster." Gus leaned out the window and took a huge drag of the air whose dry-ice harshness cut his throat like a razor blade and he pulled himself coughing inside. "Hoopy's managed to get his damn devil-slicers into the air itself."

He sat by the back window. The noise of a typewriter came through the wall from the apartment next door. Someone was an efficient typist; the sharp metallic clicks came swiftly and precise. Suddenly he imagined that he was a sheet of paper and there was a giant typewriter whose keys were fitted with pinpoints on their inked end, and the giant's child practiced THE QUICK BROWN FOX JUMPS OVER THE LAZY OLD DOG over and over—*bing!*

He went up another flight to his room. When they had first moved to New York from the southwestern country, he had looked into that mirror while he was getting dressed to go to the tailor's and have a suit made. He grew an immediate picture of himself seized, stripped, legs tied outstretched, with KICK cut into the inside of one thigh, ME into the other, with tailor's scissors.

He hadn't been out of the house since.

He left his room and went downstairs to the living room. There was a couch, in the middle. He sat down gingerly and listened. It was quiet. He closed his eyes. No pictures came. He sighed and lit a cigarette.

It is insufficient not to do something. Flip it over, he said to himself. Whatever it is, make it the "to do" of the other side. Then . . .

A noise made him turn. It was his fifteen-year-old daughter, Dinah, shining blondly down the hall. She came into the room surrounded by her own attractiveness, and began playing Mozart on the flute.

"It is marvelous how you can know that I am sitting here hoping some sunlit apparition will appear out of nowhere and play the 'Dance of the Blessed Spirits' on the flute for me at this exact moment." He stabbed out the cigarette and stood up.

Dinah made a wild round movement with her eyes which strangely duplicated the round mouth and which meant that she could not possibly listen because she obviously couldn't answer *and* play the flute.

"I am blessed to have such considerate children."

The wild round movements grew more intense until she suddenly snatched the flute down in disgust. "I'm whistling. I'm still whistling, did you hear it? Good God! Whistling."

"I didn't hear any whistling at all. I didn't hear even a single suppressed whistle." He reached for a chair and pulled it up in front of her. "Dinah, do you want to know what I'm going to do, what I've just decided to do? It just came to me as I was sitting here, and it's a marvelous idea."

"Sure."

"I'm going to build a room, a complete room, every single inch of it, a marvelous room built just the way a room should be."

She leaned forward; he leaned back instantly. A reflex. She lunged when she leaned, as if she were a Southwest Conference guard compressed into a girl. "On the roof? Are you going to build a room on the roof? Oh, that's a great idea, Daddy! Can I have it?"

"The idea?"

"*Daddy.*"

"No, not on the roof. In my room."

"You're going to build a room in your room?"

"Yes. I'm going to build a room inside my room, an inside to my room, a lining, so that it will actually be the same room but it will be a different room."

"Why?"

"Look, I feel that if I build a room, every single inch of it myself—floors, walls, ceiling, and all—if every bit of it passed through my hands and I could look at it bit by bit before it went up, then I would *know* the room and would feel comfortable in it."

"Don't you know your room now? You've lived in it for a year."

"I don't really know it, no."

"God, Daddy, it would be a lot easier to *get* to know it than to build it all over again, wouldn't it? How well do you want to know a room, anyway?"

"Look, baby. You can never know something as well after it's already there as you can if you knew it before it was there. It's like having children. I don't know everything about you *now,* but I watched you become what you are now and that's a very different way of knowing someone than if you met them after they were grown."

"Okay, Dad. If you want me to help you when I get back, holler. I've got to go now, though." She turned at the top of the steps and held the flute like the bar of an aquaplane board. "I don't see how children and rooms are the same thing, at all."

He decided not to call Maisie until he had gathered together everything he would need to line his room, and to do this he would first have to make a list so he could order the supplies and equipment. To make a list he needed a table, a kitchen table and something to eat. In order to eat he had to have something else to do, and making a list was just the right sort of thing to do while eating. In order to make a list he needed something else to do, and eating was just the right sort of accompaniment to making a list.

A sandwich would be perfect except that I would get mayonnaise on my fingers and have to deal with a messy list. Marks of mayonnaise marring the list. List! and hear the whispers about soup on old men's ties, ice cream on the bulging fronts of pregnant women, egg on the mouth of the boy.

The shrill blast of the telephone made him jump backward and simultaneously slam the icebox door—which, since he had pulled out the vegetable bin, would not close and bounced back against his nose. He slammed in the vegetable tray now, so angrily that he dislodged it from its runners; he grabbed for it as it fell and knocked over an open can of peaches.

"Hello?" he demanded, turning his back on the sticky syrup as it trickled into the tomatoes and lettuce from one stream, onto the floor from another.

"What took you so long to answer the phone? I was just about to hang up. Were you going out?"

"No, I wasn't going out. Certainly not. The phone only rang three times—I answered it in the middle of the third ring."

"It rang five or six times, at least. Five at least. I was just going to hang up when you answered it. Were you out in the back yard?"

"No, I wasn't out in the back yard; you know perfectly well I wasn't. I was in the icebox, if you must know."

"In the icebox? You mean refrigerator. What in the world were you doing in the icebox?"

"Mother, for heaven's sake, I wasn't *in* the icebox. I was looking in it to find something to eat, and I got tangled up trying to get out to answer the telephone."

"You never have wanted anybody to know what you're up to or what you're doing and you have a perfect right to be as secretive as you choose. But you can't blame your own mother for being *interested*."

"Mother, look, I'm not up to anything, least of all a conversation like this. I was just looking in the icebox to see what I could find to eat."

"Why don't you fix yourself a sandwich? You like salami, but you always have to eat it on rye."

"Because I don't want to get mayonnaise on the list."

"Are you going to have a party?"

"No. I'm going to build a room."

"Well, that's nice, too. Doing something with your hands, it gives one a sense of accomplishment."

"Like picking pockets?"

"I meant that for someone forty years old to suddenly start building things isn't much else than something to do." Like a flash (he could see it) a new lilting excitement came into her voice. *"Where* are you building, in the back yard?"

"In my room. I'm forty-five, Mother."

"You are? Well. In your room. Listen, I ran into Maisie the other day . . . who was that who just came in?"

"Nobody came in, Mother."

"I heard a door open and someone come in."

Gus turned around to look, and saw that the peach juice

had formed its puddle in front of the icebox and was now following the list of the floor and flowing into the grease-infused dirt underneath the icebox. "There is no one here but me and the peach juice."

"But I heard a door open and someone come in."

"Maybe someone came in your apartment."

"Wait a minute. I'll look. No, there's no one here. It must have been someone coming in your house."

"All right, wait a minute and I'll look." He opened the door into the hall and the one into the dining room. "No, Mother, no one came in here."

"But I'm positive that I heard a door open and someone come in. And a minute ago I heard it again."

"You heard me opening the door to look and see if someone came in."

"I heard it twice."

"Because I did it twice. I opened the hall door to see if someone came in that way, and I opened the dining-room door to see if someone came in there."

"They didn't come in here, so they must have come in there."

"They didn't come in anywhere, Mother."

"How could I hear them if they were just standing outside?"

"How could you hear who? There isn't anybody."

"I know there isn't anybody *here*."

"There isn't anybody *anywhere*."

"*Well.* Now, listen, I happened to run into Maisie the other day—in the beauty parlor, wasn't that a funny coincidence?"

"Yes, considering that she lives next door and you live on Eighty-ninth Street."

"So I wanted to see her. But that's not the point. The point is that she was worried about you and asked me if you were thinking of seeing a doctor. Of course I had to tell her that I had no idea what you were thinking about. But it wouldn't be a bad idea—you must be pale, staying indoors all the time —your skin can't breathe. Are you thinking about seeing a doctor?"

"No, Mother."

"I heard about a wonderful doctor that several of my friends know, they say they can't recommend him too highly . . ."

"I'm not thinking about seeing a doctor."

"Well, there's nothing wrong with *thinking* about . . ."

"Did I tell you I was thinking about building a room?"

"Yes, you did."

"Well look, why don't you come over Sunday afternoon and stay for supper and then we'll talk."

"All right. I'm sorry if you think I'm interfering in your business, but you can't blame a mother . . ."

"I don't blame you at all, Mother. Of course not. I'm very glad you called. So I'll see you Sunday, right? Good. So, then. Goodbye, now."

By the time he had opened the icebox door again, the telephone rang again.

"Why did you hang up on me?"

"I didn't hang up on you, Mother. I thought we were through talking."

"I wanted to ask you if you were going to ask Maisie too on Sunday, and you hung up. Why don't you like Maisie? I think she's a fine person."

"I do like her and I'll call her right now and ask her for Sunday. And I'm sorry you thought I hung up on you."

"Thought? What do you mean *thought?* The phone didn't hang itself up, did it?

"No, of course not. I meant, hung up on *you.*"

"You were talking to me, how could you have hung up on anybody else?"

"You're right. Look: you hang up first this time."

"All right. Goodbye."

"Goodbye, Mother."

"Hello?"

"Yes, Mother?"

"Are you getting enough to eat?"

"I'm going to get something right now. I was just going in—I mean I was just looking in the icebox—refrigerator—to fix a sandwich."

"A salami sandwich?"

"A salami sandwich."

"Why don't you try it on white this time? It lets the flavor of the salami come through much better than rye."

"I think I will, for a change. Maybe I'd better go do it right now."

"Yes, do that. Goodbye."

"Goodbye, Mother."

"See you Sunday?"

"See you Sunday. It'll be fun."

"Yes, I hope so. Goodbye then."

"Goodbye."

"Mother?"

"Yes?"

"You're supposed to hang up first."

"Oh, yes, I forgot. Well then, goodbye. See you Sunday? Oh, I said that. Goodbye."

"Goodbye."

"Don't forget to call Maisie."

"I'll call her as soon as you hang up."

"Okay. I'm going to hang up right now. Goodbye."

"Goodbye, Mother."

"Bye."

After a second or two he heard the click at the other end and gently laid the receiver back in its cradle, smoothing it with his hand, staring at it without moving to see if it would scream out at him again, and then quietly moved away.

He locked the door of his room. There was a bottle of gin, but no ice. In a hot dusty car in Tennessee, twenty years ago, he had drunk from a bottle of gin which had been cooking on the rear window ledge, and discovered that he liked this taste better than any martini. It was a dividend to learn, later, that anyway gin had fewer calories than whisky. (Eloise tended to gain weight.)

He equaled the gin with water from the hot tap, took the glass to the bed and reclined. The first swallow sent him into a fuzz like that produced by the steam of a Texas beach in August; *that* sun expanded his skull so his thoughts floated loose and unchanneled, melted his bones.

He could make a list without eating. He could build a room without a list. He could give up the rules of the world altogether, change its surface. The inside of this room—the new inside—would become the inside of his own skin. How big would he be? He got up just as the desire to melt reached its threshold and pushed it back.

Carefully he measured the room's dimensions. The floor 20'2" by 15'; the distance from floor to ceiling, 7'8". If he put the new walls just inside the present walls, allowing an inch or two in case the existing walls were irregular, he would reduce each dimension of the floor by a foot, making it 19'2" by 14'. If he put the new floor planks on two-by-fours, the new height would be about 7'3". How big would he be? His base (his feet, so to speak) would be 268⅓ square feet, his total volume 2145⅓ cubic feet. Big enough? There were days when the inside pressure on his skin was so great that he felt he would choke even that much space. And then he would wonder whether he could not, instead, put the new floor planks directly over the old, which would give him almost 68 additional cubic feet of body.

He drank another swallow of gin but remained standing. No. The floor would have to be raised, and the new planks spaced about one inch apart; otherwise where would the dirt go? Raising the floor gave him a four-inch depth for dirt, a volume of ⅓ of a foot times the area of the room minus the area needed for the two-by-fours themselves. He had decided to let this serve as the hourglass of his life. When this space was full, he would get out. How many years, counting by dirt, did he have left to live? (It's an experiment, not a problem.) New York cut his life span in half.

So much for his inside skin. It was settled: it was to be sheetrock covered with plaster on the sides, two coats of paint above, a slatted floor below. Every inch made by him.

As for his outside skin, there he was even more wildly satisfied. It would be utterly invisible, snugly fitted into the existing room, totally hidden. He would be forever a stranger to all except mice, cockroaches, little things like that. He would, in a human sense, have no outside at all.

"Liza, you are the apple of my eye," his grandmother had said over thirty years ago. (He had been a little girl then.) He had squirmed, and regarded himself as an apple. Why was it intolerable? Because, it seemed then, she called all those other things apples too. There was a large basket of apples in the corner of the kitchen, at least a hundred apples. No matter which one you took out, you called it an apple. If you looked closely, the apples were not the same: each one had a different shape, coloring, size, different splotches; nevertheless, they were all called apples. He would rather be peeled than be the object of such promiscuousness.

Gus took his warm gin and stood at the window. It was Saturday afternoon next door, and the first day of spring. Maisie and Ben were in the garden with the von Vons from next door. The two women sat in chairs like graceful shrimp; von Von (his reputation went back three generations) preferred to lean, since there was a tree, and Ben sat on the low brick wall where he could look up at von Von. It was this way every spring.

Gus watched.

In a few minutes, Ben offered everyone a drink. Von Von shook his head. Still slanted against the tree, he studied them with their highballs, letting the women talk. Then he said something to Ben. Ben disappeared into the house; shortly returned with an apple.

Von Von reached for the apple with grace, curved it into his mouth, held it there with metallic fingers, structured for the first day of spring. He took a hearty bite. His jaws moved up and down on it with the strength of fine white teeth; he half-closed his eyes in an expression of wholesome enjoyment. He held the apple itself with humor, down and out to the right, just as a Vermont philosopher would have done. He took the second crackling bite. Before the third, he raised his right foot and placed it on the low brick wall, leaned his body forward, and rested his right forearm across his horizontal thigh. The right hand holding the apple was casually between him and his audience. In a moment he would say something, and the apple would punctuate. It was perfect to gesture with—a half-eaten apple held by a lean intellectual. A few small deliberate shakes of it would bring just the right amount of conviction to his statements. His ideas were not original; they needed to be frank.

In a few minutes, he had spoken. He smiled and allowed his foot to return to earth while he nodded at their replies. Suddenly he stopped smiling. He looked down and out to the right. There was an apple in his hand, still, with only two bites gone. Quickly, almost angrily (it would seem he had been seized with sudden greed) he bit off a third hunk, chewed it sharply. A flash of hate came over his face; he glared at the apple, still there, only three bites gone. But only a flash. He put his head back, smiled into the skies, and, raising his right arm over his head, leaning back with his whole loose elegant body, he heaved the apple over the wall. He sat down now. It was always an existential conflict, to one who was once a boy, between the apple and the ball.

"Jamie, you should have come another time. I'm drunk. I'm going to stay drunk until tomorrow noon, when Mother comes over for lunch, which is the last thing Mother comes over for. Come in. Sit down. Have a drink."

Jamie's gray eyes, encased in folds of flesh, fixed Gus as he walked up and down the length of the room, and carefully sighted him, leading him a bit more and then a bit less until they had the correct time proportion, then speared him just as he entered the third quarter of the room.

"I'm told I have piercing eyes," Jamie said to his impaled friend.

"Let me go, you idiot."

Jamie lowered his eyes and began picking his splayed gray teeth with the little fingernail of his left hand, grown to a Mandarin point for this purpose. He gave up, took the drink Ferrarri handed him and sloshed large gulps of Scotch through his teeth like a whale drawing in animalculae strained through seaweed. Some of the Scotch clung to the black hairs of his beard and he sucked it off. "I can't paint. I haven't painted for three years."

Ferrarri ran his fingers through his limp, gray-brown hair, twice, again; it was too long and the same inturning strand hit him in the eye for the third time. He turned his glass upside down in his pressing palm, wetted the strand back into the others on top of his head. "For two years and ten months. It's because you don't eat."

"I haven't eaten since yesterday."

"Jamie, you bastard, you haven't eaten in years. You send a couple of hunks of flesh out around a food-bit and incorporate it, that's all." He moved the bowl of fruit in front of Jamie. Six bananas and a few browning grapes.

"I can't eat bananas and drink Scotch."

"You're the only man I know who can."

His sudden grin opened a spread of black gaps and gray with little pretense of white. Jamie momentarily straddled the coffee table in his lunge for Ferrarri, hitched up his sliding pants, made it across and put an electric arm over Ferrarri's shoulders. Red and gray swam out of focus as black pupils shot to the surface of his eyes and froze. "Christ, Gus, they *all* said I was great, you know? They used to bang on my door and beg to carry my stuff on their backs if only I'd let them give me a show. But I wasn't ready, I had to go further, and then they laughed at me. They said I'd gone too far. Ha. I hadn't gone far *enough*. We don't want to show you now (you've gone too far this time). I won't let you show me (I haven't gone nearly far enough, not nearly far enough)." He stepped back across the coffee table to his side and picked up a banana. "So we agree, Gus. That's the shit of it."

"Look. You're right, you haven't gone far enough. You've got to go so far that you break out the other side. You've got to go so far *in* that you get out the back door. If you start painting because they won't let you play in shit, and then you don't need to play in shit anymore, now you've got to get back through painting to shit again. Follow it all the way if you have to slant the whole world around you."

Jamie ate two bananas, rapidly, in mouthfuls of pillows. The folds and unplanned mounds of flesh covering his face and neck rippled and bulged in capricious but, for an instant, seemingly patterned waves of which Ferrarri tried to catch the underlying beat.

"You can't listen. Take your drink and go in the bathroom for half an hour or so. I want to show you what I mean."

Ferrarri took the couch and dragged it to the lower end of the room, or the end to be lower, the end from which the bathroom erupted, the end opposite the windows overlooking the spinal egg cartons, the end which, as the house stood, was the north end. He put the armchair next to it. The two ladder-back chairs he hung on doorknobs. The coffee table sat on the mantelpiece, the fruit, ashtrays, bottles in the fireplace with one lamp, while the other lamp (the tired one) rested on the couch. The pot with the aspidistra plant he shoved into the bathroom after Jamie. "If you get bored, you can water it. You know, with water preferably."

Across the window sills, three feet from the floor, he laid a four-by-four and nailed it to the window sill. It should be sawed into a diagonal calculated by the angle the hypotenuse makes with the southern vertical. (A timid man, Ferrarri loved to do drunken mathematics.) It took him thirty minutes to discover that this would be an 88.7-degree angle (because he found he had forgotten how to take square roots and kept having to multiply back). He plugged in his electric saw, rotated his world around 2.3 degrees, stood quietly at this tilt until he got used to it, until it seemed as thoroughly vertical as the upright position had come to seem over the past forty years, and sawed what was then a horizontal line down the four-by-four which stuck its sharp edge slightly up into the normal plane.

His floor planks had been cut to 242 inches because he had originally assumed they would lie flat; now they would be 3.3 inches short. Then his base line, instead of being 242 inches, would only be 238.7 inches, which would make the southern angle less—how much less? He refilled his glass and recalculated. The angle should be 1.3 degrees smaller. Could he, from his present accustomed horizontal tilted 2.3 degrees from the usual, retilt himself to allow for the shorter base and reshave the four-by-four accordingly?

No one but a psychotic could possibly think it could matter, he heard echoing out of the bathroom. What insane tangent are you planning to catapult yourself out on that you have so carefully to fix your position now? Your body's still on earth, you know, and you haven't even considered the direction of your error.

"Jamie?"

Ferrarri leaned over the plant blocking the doorway and saw his friend lying in the bathtub with his knees up and his sweater balled beneath his head, his eyes fixed on a crack in the ceiling (ceiling cracks from which Ferrarri's imaginative sister used to weave patterns of fancy). "What do you see when you look at cracks?"

"Cracks," Jamie answered.

"Did you say something to me a minute ago?"

"What?"

"About what kind of a psychotic I am?"

Jamie's flesh was past the age where it could be called resilient, was now merely fluid, filling the contours of whatever object pressed on it from below. With difficulty he pulled some of it up to the sitting position his bones assumed.

"Of course not. Just hand me the bottle, will you."

Ferrarri pulled up the floor planks and nailed their south end (it was now) to the crossbar over the window sills, ignoring the air space acquired from his error (but noting that it occurred at the top of the crossbar and seemed as near as his tilted eye could judge to be about 1.3 degrees, so the human error made so much of by Jamie was nonexistent, his eye was in practice, and his body was not still tied to the ground in that Gulliverian sense). He spaced the floor planks one and a half inches apart, for trash.

"I don't know whether you've lenghtened or shortened my life span—you know, by inspiring me to slant the floor, because when the hollow beneath the floor fills, I cut. In the beginning I had it figured for an area of dirt 20'2" by 15' by 4", minus the combined area of six two-by-fours. That gave me 100 cubic feet of days. I think I'll have much more than that this way."

Ferrarri reached into the fireplace and pulled forth a bottle of Scotch and poured them each half a glass. "Jamie, 100 cubic feet of days was all I wanted. That's a lot of days."

Jamie came out of the bathroom. "When Adam delved and Eve span, who was then the slanted man?"

"Jamie, say that again."

"When Adam delved and Eve span, who was then the slanted man?"

"God."

"Right."

Gus laughed. "Sit in the chair on the downward slant, Jamie, so your back will be toward the downslant. With a paunch like yours you can't cross your legs in an ordinary room; here it's done for you. Rest your glass on your belly, and when you want a swallow, it practically slips into your mouth and down your throat by itself. Now what do you see? You don't see the same room at all. You don't see the same world at all. You see everything just like it is because now you're slanted the same way everything you look at is slanted and you don't have to strain your eyes to see around bends any more."

Ferrarri sat on the couch opposite Jamie. The slant made it much easier to reach his glass on the coffee table, harder to get the glass back to his mouth.

"It's my slant, not yours, though. You need a plexiglass sphere that can rotate in all directions. Because there are no connections between anything. There is no more pattern or plan as you see the world than there is in the soft diaper-spread feces of the infant. Play there: make a connection, leave it meaningless, rub it out, make a new one. Homogenized spread cast free from one's inner core. You would paint then because you would have the meaningless beginning chaos itself in your hands and you would have absolutely no restrictions whatsoever because chaos is uncommitted absolutely, even to itself."

"You're talking like a woman, now, Liza. I would be restricted by the material, shit." Jamie closed his eyes and let his head fall back.

Gus got up and looked into the mirror in the bathroom. There were faces which did not in themselves belong to either sex, weren't there? Or which shared themselves so equally between the sexes that, depending upon which line or curve the viewer concentrated on, the face would look more or less male or female. There were optimum ages for this particular kind of ambiguity: babies up to two years, later latency (nine and ten), old age. But even within the sexual years themselves, when the face's owner was not actually screwing, there was a group of faces which did not commit themselves. One placed them by circumstantial evidence—names, dress, etc. Or one was prejudiced in advance by a mutual friend's choice of pronoun. Often the owner simply came right out with it: "I am Miss Jane Doe," someone might say, and the company present abided by her decision.

"I am Gus Ferrarri," he said to the mirror. A square forehead, imprecise eyebrows, set and solid flesh looked back at him in agreement. "I am Liza Durach." The mouth became fluid, the cheeks soft, the eyes almond-shaped in complicity.

"You're insane." Jamie laughed softly from the floor.

"You think that's a compliment," Gus said, looking at the mirror. When the faces talked, the chance of misunderstanding their gender was decreased. He said it virilely; he said it softly. He said it in the middle.

"Jesus Christ," said Jamie. "Are you going to say everything four times?"

"I am simply trying to discover who I am—in an abstract sense."

Gus looked at his watch. It was now five-thirty. Would he or would he not be down for dinner? Until the room was finished there was no reason not to be, except the reason that he should not too abruptly disappear from the children's routine. A gradual withdrawal of himself was easier for them, and he had been down for dinner the night before.

"Come in."

Bobby looked the room over carefully from the door, his critical eye measuring the quality of the carpentry and the esthetic effect simultaneously. "What are you trying to do?"

"I've done it, Bobby. I've made the room into a sliding board. Do you like it?"

"You didn't get the boards very close together, though. Somebody might fall through if he was little."

"You won't fall through, Bobby, because you're pretty big. Do you want to slide?"

"Is it slippery?"

"No."

"No."

Bobby picked up a nail, found a hammer and, seeing an orange which had rolled out of the fruit basket and lay near the fireplace, sat sturdily down and began hammering the nail into the orange, his bent head as round and yellow as an enormous grapefruit, his black-brown eyes unseen beneath his already heavy, drawn-together brows directed at the perfect completion of the task of driving a nail into the orange at hand. He hammered quietly on, one leg bent toward him on the floor, the other knee-bent into the air, his back rounded in the curve of Discobolus, his neck exactly divided by the median dent. The first nail was in. Bobby straightened up, examined the orange and its nail by turning it slowly all around, saw that the nail had neatly entered and had not gone through to the other side, reached across his leg and picked up another nail and, assuming his former optimum position, began hammering the second nail into the orange. When Bobby had finished hammering in the fifth nail, he stood up, leaving the hammer but holding the orange, walked over to Gus and held out to his father the hand with the orange in it.

"Hattie wants to know if you're coming down for dinner."

"No. Tell her, no, not tonight." Huge black-brown wells of eyes topped with heavy virgin lashes waited for him to say more. "Thank you for the orange, Bobby."

"You're welcome." Bobby turned and left the room.

Gus looked at the orange in his hand sticky from the leaking juices. "I'm still clinging to downstairs. I haven't really given up yet. I mean not *really*. I am passive and waiting for the next thing to happen."

"The sixth nail." Jamie mumbled so inaudibly that even he seemed to know that no one could have understood, because he repeated, "The sixth nail," and then, in an untypical gesture, he explained himself. "When do you think they'll put the sixth nail in?"

"The sixth nail in what?"

"The orange, fuck it. You. You're the orange waiting for the picador's thrust, right?"

"What am I afraid of, then—that it won't come?"

Jamie got up, stood for a few seconds, and then turned around once in the middle of the slanted floor and lay down, his feet up the slant and head down, groaned and cursed and then reversed his position so his head was up, with its top turned toward Gus.

"You mean I have to drive in the sixth nail myself."

A week before he had sat in Dinah's room, watching her while she combed her hair and experimented with various added attractions—a necklace around her throat, a long string of beads, dangling earrings, daisy earrings, a tiny loop, no earrings, long string of beads off, a diamond pin, two strawberries, nothing at all. She was wearing a piece of chiffon which she had constructed around her body to make it look like she was dressed—gray chiffon utterly unsuited to her blonde, tennis-court personality. A lipstick smear decorated one shoulder, left there from a last-minute check of the smell of her armpits. She saw it, spat on a Kleenex and rubbed it off.

She stopped working on her perfection and stared into the mirror. "I hate my hair." She turned her head first this way then that, as far around as she could and still see into the mirror from her eyeball caught in the eye's corner. "There's *nothing* you can do with straight blonde hair. It just *hangs*. Even if I rat—I mean, backcomb—the top of it still just hangs, and if I roll it up it just gets frizzy. And I look *innocent*. Like a *child*." Her head stopped turning, and she stared into the mirror, first at herself, and then, beyond her reflection, at his face reflected. "You think I am vain, don't you, Daddy?"

"I think you are wondering whether you are beautiful, or merely pretty. I think you suspect that you are beautiful, but you can't be sure until someone comes who can make you feel it."

"Daddy, that sounds so square."

"Unlike your name. Did you know that I wanted to name you Mary and your sister Jane, but your mothers would have none of it. 'Those are such common names,' they both said. 'Our daughter will just be one of a dozen.' 'They are common names,' I agreed. 'Therefore, by the time the child gets to high school, there won't be another Mary or Jane in existence.' "

"I used to want to change my name to Marigold, and have a horse named Merilegs." She turned around on the stool and faced him. "Can I have a sip of your martini?" She held her sip in her mouth for sixty seconds or more, until she forced herself to swallow it. "The first swallow is like drinking pee," she protested.

He stayed in her room after she left, staring at powder on the dresser, discarded ornaments spilling out of the jewelry box, hair spray brought in from the bathroom, newly washed comb and brush with tenuous pale hairs caught in the bristles. The whiff of her perfume he smelled as she kissed him goodbye was lost now among the half-dozen battling odors of her cosmetic equipment. Her own smell, whatever it might be, was abruptly aborted early each day.

Her mother had come to Houston at adolescence, fatherless. She had an Irish setter to run with her and sleep by her bed, but still she felt unprotected. Jock will protect me, she insisted to her mother. She liked to get up very early and run through the dawn and think of other people sleeping clenched tight against alarm clocks. Her mother thought she was getting too big to be out at peculiar hours.

"Getting too big where?" Liza said, forcing her arms to stay perfectly still by her side.

"Darling. I meant you were getting too old . . ."

But Liza knew exactly what she meant. For years she was too little to run out by herself because something might happen to her, until she was too big because the other thing might happen. "And by the time I'm big enough to run where I please, I won't be able to run at all because I'll be too old!"

Upstairs in her room, she looked out at the neighborhood. Houses arranged in blocks, sidewalks with driveways lying across them at intervals. It wasn't because she was too big at all; it was because they lived in a neighborhood. It embarrassed her mother to have her running when everyone else slept. And there were other things: since it was summer most of the time in Houston, all the girls wore shorts just like Liza

did, but with Liza one could tell that she didn't change to a
dress at five, or in winter, or even want to, as if she wore
shorts because they were right for her, irrespective of heat or
laundry. Her legs were too tan, too muscular; they didn't
look naked at the tops the way the legs of girls who belonged
in skirts did. And her run didn't have the greed of the rarely
allowed run of caged legs, either; she ran as if she were used
to running. It was like her clothes: sometimes her clothes
were too tight, because she ate a lot and suddenly, but one
could tell that she was not accepting fat by the very fact that
they *were* too tight. Fat was an aberration, a temporary
weakness, and had nothing to do with her view of the way
things should be. Far different with girls who were too fat
and yet their clothes fit.

Liza took Jock out for a run at six o'clock the next morning. The light was mimosa-colored and feathery, and the dew
had not yet been sucked up into the sky. The milkman and
the paper boy were tattooing the block front and back with
white. Jock jumped to her shoulder, breathed on her cheek.
"Come on, let's go!" she said, and they ran the length of the
block as fast as the wind. The milkman waved as they
passed. He was an old man, and probably fancied her as the
daughter he'd like to have. She ran past him and away in
graceful controlled leaps, heels up. At the end of the long
block she stopped and hugged Jock with both arms and
claimed him as her friend. They sat on someone's St. Augustine and breathed. They crossed the street and studied the
other side. On this run, she decided, she would be the Little
Colonel, haughty and precise.

The paper boy on his bicycle was using the sidewalk, too,
and for them all safely to pass without changing courses
would take signals, intelligence. She declared the lawn lane
for herself and Jock. The paper boy was already in the street
lane. Her intentions were clear. None could misunderstand.

Nevertheless, the paper boy wavered, looked at her approaching, seemed not to know which way to pass. She was forced to break her stride, slow down to a near walk, become confused. What an idiot he was! People simply couldn't be efficient. He passed, wobbling his bicycle as if a wavering crisis had sprung up from nowhere, and yet half a block away he could have seen. . . . She glared at his unformed face as they passed, communicating scorn.

But he wasn't looking at her face, he was looking at her shirtfront. "Let's go, Jock!" she said in clear anger, and raced furious past all the houses.

But her breasts had grown to monstrous melons and flapped across her path as she ran. She tightened her shoulder muscles, gripped her arms against her body, quickened the response of her toes so they would land fluid and there would be no jerks from there. The flapping melons contracted to tennis balls but the bounce—rhythmic, controlled, was still a bounce and the dancing weight of the two pulled at the surrounding skin of her chest until she could not bear it. She would *have* to run until she reached her own house, because she would have otherwise—otherwise but for doughface. But those insane rubber balls bouncing in time like a metronome. . . . Stop it! Five doors away, she stumbled slightly, limped, and stopped. She took off her shoe, shook it, rubbed her foot, and didn't look around. Holding the shoe, she walked five houses to her own, one hand on Jock's back.

Under her own mimosa tree, catching her breath, she hugged her knees and stared with contempt at the *neighborhood*. So that was who she was. Judy Two-Breast. Girlie— she had been girlie before, as if she were only her sex. She had been Sister for no reason, and one humiliating lunch hour at the shipyards, she had been briefly Fatty. But now——! She stripped a flower-twig from the branch in front of her and bit viciously along its stem. She had had a friend who was always Red—who was never anything but Red, although she too was a girl and had a brother and ate too much, and Liza had resented it that *her* friend should be always, only, and never anything but the color of her hair. It was bitter. "How can you stand it?" she said. "Suppose you lost all your hair. You'd disappear. You just wouldn't be any more. You'd vanish like you'd never been born and Baldy would appear in your place." Liza giggled. She'd been glad her hair was brown, but now she thought that if she were Red she couldn't be . . . Judy Two-Breast. Little Judy Two-Breast. She jumped and seized the mimosa bough that stretched shoulder-height in front of her. "Pee on you all!" she shouted, shaking the tree with adolescent fury. "Fuck you all!" Jock's furious barking echoed every shout. The tree shook and let down a spray of drifting feather-petals from its pink umbrella. "*Wake* the neighborhood!"

Seven years later Liza was introduced at a party to a man whose exterior was sufficiently unambiguous that on any streetcorner he would be taken for a man. And yet she saw, or thought she saw, or hoped she saw, that inside there was still space—for her.

Both qualities were absolute requisites. She looked at him carefully, and didn't hear his name.

"I'm Eloise," Liza said. He was certainly solid on the outside. "Hello, Gus. Could I inhabit you?"

"Why do you call me Gus?" he said.

She looked at him through round, tilted eyes. "I don't like the sound of Sug."

"Neither one is my name." He winced.

"Oh." She winced in agreement. He stared at her chin. She stared at the top of his head. They made a parallelogram.

"Would you like a drink?" he said.

She nodded, forsaking geometry.

Several drinks later they sat curved in the valley of the second hole, fighting mosquitoes on a dark golf course, while the party went on. He had just realized that she was beautiful—in a structural way that was obscured by the moles dotting her face and neck, her monotonous homogeneous coloring unrelieved by makeup, and a high-pitched silence at parties (to her, apparently, groups of more than two). She had come to this party with a photographer.

"Are you in love with him?" he asked.

"He takes my picture."

"Why do you call me Gus?" he said.

She looked at him through warm, jellied eyes. "It has us in it."

"So does Aloysius."

She laughed. "Do you think so?"

"Liza, please tell me. Who is Gus?" He reached for her hand.

She snatched it back, and abruptly rose to her knees. "I'm not Liza; I'm Eloise." The laugh had left no traces. "I just can't think of anything else to call you except Gus, that's all. I don't know *why*."

"I'm *sorry,* for Christ sakes!" He got to his knees. They were angry supplicants. "Look . . ." Her face in the moonlight was shieldless and his irritation melted. "Eloise," he said. It was a statement. "Gus is fine." He held out his hand and she smiled.

"What is your name, really?" she said as they reached the clubhouse.

"Rumpelstiltskin," he whispered. Her face flickered in one last smile before it was covered with the wax of social imperviousness.

But if he was caught by her gross shyness and its promise of compassion, he was unprepared for the thing he came to love her for: the lively wit of her watercolors. The clean and brilliant colors of her palette, alive with sex, enchanted him and he changed his manner toward her from what had been a gently encouraging handholding to a vigorous challenge. Eloise responded with a rush of joy.

"This is me." In the wide spacious corridor upstairs off which the numberless individual bedrooms of the family exited, the progress of the family members was posted in photographs nailed to every free foot of wall space. "As you can see, I was ready to cry. It's my favorite of all pictures of me." It was the round face of a child of eight or nine, pliant flesh caught in a pre-cry quiver, round pale eyes wide with betrayal. A younger boy stood just behind her, in the conventional pose of the era (he would have been told to lean forward so as to be in the same plane as the seated sister, then to relax so the photograph would not show the strain of his closed-up position). "That's my brother, Dick." Eloise stared at the face behind her own, then turned her real face to him, its flesh as fluid as the child's and eyes bare and crystal-gray. "That's not the reason, though. Everybody has a younger brother in some sense.

"Here I am in a play, a dance recital, a horse show, commencement, modeling in the Junior League children's style show, at the Country Club on June Teenth—I won a medal for diving, I think—going to camp, visiting an aunt and uncle in Oklahoma (it's a newspaper slick), graduating from boarding school, honoree at a costume ball, presented by Allegro" —she stopped in front of the white diaphanous debutante, frozen in a stylized pose, an utter stranger. "The public Eloise. The highlights of my life recorded by anxious parents and skilled photographers. Nailed to the wall like Luther's theses. Attacking what, for heaven's sake?

"You see the moles have all been retouched away. And so has the pain. That's what I don't understand. Sometimes I look at the pictures and there isn't a trace of sadness. There's not much else either. So I wonder, Gus—you know?—I wonder if the sadness was really there at all." This time the eyes that sought his were far away with bewilderment. They were fragile as the thinnest possible glass, and he felt that he was looking through them at the raw palpable tender core itself, so skinless that a grain of sand would scratch it and make it bleed.

"Enough." She turned away. "Come in my room now, where the me that I know lives."

He stepped forward to follow her and his body jerked in an awkward off-balance. A muscular spasm tightened his chest to iron. As his blood rushed now to loosen it his chest was seized with a wild pounding heat and a moist sweat chilled his forehead and wrapped his throat. Eloise! he cried. I love you. The steel box of the hall's architecture stretched high above him, drawing its walls together like blocks of ice to press him to death. He made her room and shut the door behind them.

He assumed her room was structurally as pure Bauhaus as the rest of the house, but there was practically no structure to see. A bookcase completely covered the slit-wing corner window, and the other rectangle opening onto the front was overlaid with a sheet of brown paper, on which a huge-butted figure—baby or child or adult or all three—comforted itself in the haunched position of babies, its comical back turned to the room. From the exposed beams in one corner hung a blue plastic thing like the spokes of an umbrella—a bathroom contraption for drying clothes; each blue plastic clothespin clasped the top of a strip of flypaper that extended to the floor, and at close intervals on the flypaper were stuck unframed watercolors—her own, some split and curling at the corners, some new and crisp.

"I am going to rape you, Eloise. The only question is when. Go into the garden of hours and pick the right thyme."

His hands clasped her shirted shoulders, his eyes found the well-behaved bones of her face (just under the skin).

"I'm overcome."

"A direct descendant of Emerson's Oversoul, the Overcome is what we all want to join."

"Descend means come down."

"Fall?"

"Spring."

"Eloise. Now."

Stripped down to his shorts and shoes and socks, he had Eloise's shirt off and was leaning over with his mouth against her breasts, in the position of one waiting to be goosed, when a knock sounded at the door and her mother entered.

"What are you doing, dear?" Mrs.——— glanced with familiar despair around the room. "I don't understand how you can so utterly change the character of this room. Self-expression is important, but you have destroyed the meaning of the room altogether. It doesn't belong to the rest of the house at all. Well, I guess you know what you like." She sighed and removed her eyes from the flypaper mobile. "You're Gus, aren't you?"

"Yes, ma'am." He stood as tall as possible, and extended a hearty hand. "I'm very glad to see you again, Mrs.———. You look beautiful in pink, like an apparition from fairyland. We were just rehearsing a play, as you can see."

"Oh, really? Eloise, the Dickensons are here. I want you to come down and speak to them—when you're dressed. And you too, of course, Gus. Perhaps you could get dressed too? Eloise, I wish you would wear a brassière." She turned and went out the door. They were staring at each other with the primal pleasure of being discovered when the door opened again. "Don't mind me, children; it's just Mother again. Eloise, don't forget to thank Mrs. Dickenson for the cigarette

lighter. It's gold, you know. Now don't be too long," she said
as she shut the door again.

"You are fantastically beautiful," he said between laughs
as he hugged her. "You are most fantastically beautiful."

The family accepted him as one of its members, and Mrs.
——— treated him with the same abstracted indifference
that was her manner toward Eloise, the same adequate number of questions about his work and his opinions on the
running political scene as she did Dick, Eloise's younger
brother. (The questions were three if she merely passed him
on her way to a piece of business; five if she found him sitting
on the porch or by the pool and paused for a social inter-
change; ten if it were a long thing like dinner or cocktails. In
the three group, Mrs. ——— allowed fifteen seconds for
each answer; in the five group, usually about thirty; in the ten
group, an important social experience for her, she would
leave a two- to ten-minute space between questions, and even
tried to listen to the answer.)

She accorded him the same pats the cocker got when he
was in patting range, the same order to the houseman to
bring him *his* drink (in Mrs. ———'s world one owned the
drink one asked for on the first visit and there was no way to
avoid responsibility for this particular drink in the future.
Mrs. ——— *knew* whose it was. Variety was possible only if
one were clever in trading with other dissatisfied owners),
and seeing to it that he always got his two a day however impatient dinner became. He had his corner of the pantry,
which she kept supplied with at least three but not more than
five of his favorite goodies, a service she extended to the
whole family, including the servants.

One afternoon she asked him for a goodie list (although
not directly, of course). She got her information when she
saw him sitting on the porch and needed to ask him five ques-

tions. This was the only time she ever substituted food questions for men questions. But then, when he thought about it, food questions *are* men questions in the South.

"Oh, Gus. You are certainly right to relax on the porch on such a hot day. You have to be a southerner to know how to take these summers, don't you agree with me? Of course all you young people are so healthy—sometimes I think we gave you too *many* vitamins," she laughed. "But I'll bet *you* know what to eat during these hot days to keep from becoming sluggish." She sat in a chair across from him, crossed one stockinged and spectator-pumped leg over the other, and, smoothing her skirts briefly, leaned slightly forward. "Do you drink much fruit juice in the summer?"

"Yes, ma'am. You have to, you know; that's the secret of summers. I particularly like tomato juice, although most people think it's too thick." He started to add that one summer he had drunk so much tomato juice that he'd gotten allergic to it and now it gave him hives, but he'd already taken his whole thirty seconds.

"I don't know what the psychologists would say about me," she laughed quickly and leaned slightly back in her chair, "but I've found that almost everybody has a particular sweet, something they liked as a child, that becomes an important part of their life when they're grown—unless they just won't eat sweets at all." She looked at him sharply to see if he were one of *those*. Apparently reassured, she continued: "I think it's important to keep those things, those special things from one's childhood, don't you? Nobody needs to be *all* grown-up, do they? I know *I'm* not. Of course I wouldn't want to overdo it. There are *some* things from childhood that are better left there." She frowned, and for a wild moment he thought he could ask her, quick, what? "But some things are nice. Now William just has to have his pralines, the kind his godfather used to send him from New Orleans, and Eloise her chocolate wafers (although I myself find those the dryest of all cookies), and Dick"—she frowned again—"Dick will stick to Mr. Goodbars, I can't imagine why. It's not just that it seems a silly kind of candy for a grown man to eat, but it's also—well, you know where he got the idea from? From a laundress we used to have when he was seven and eight or nine. She *taught* him to eat Mr. Goodbars." She stopped, remembering this indignity all too vividly. Then she leaned forward slightly, not too eagerly, just eagerly enough. "Tell me, what does your mother keep in the house just for you, Gus?"

"Juicy Fruit," he said quickly. "We used to have a laundress, too, named Viola, and she was never without a fresh wad of Juicy Fruit in her mouth. I'll never forget the way she smelled—the Juicy Fruit smell, I mean. She reeked of it. She was enormously fat and carried huge purses stuffed with packages of Juicy Fruit, which she gave me to get me to mind her. Mother couldn't *stand* Juicy Fruit, though. She disliked all chewing gum, but occasionally condescended to such flavors as Beechnut, so naturally I . . ." He saw that he had gone way beyond his allotted time and the next question had already been asked, perhaps a bit ahead of time. "I'm sorry, Mrs. ———. What did you say?"

"What about nuts, or pickles, or olives?" Her face was set and she was leaning neither slightly forward nor slightly back, but sitting rigidly in the polite vertical plane she used when a social situation threatened to slide off on some unseemly diagonal.

"Nuts, yes. Cashew nuts." He leaned forward abruptly, quite far forward, and smiled his most sonlike smile. "Mrs. ———, you know you don't see this sort of thing any more, I mean a woman taking a real interest in what a man eats. You don't see it at all outside the South, as a matter of fact. Look, I just remembered; I don't like Juicy Fruit at all any more. I much prefer marshmallows."

"Marshmallows?"

"Marshmallows. Definitely marshmallows."

"Marshmallows!" She leaned back slightly, smiling at the sweet squishiness of the word. "Marshmallows." She leaned forward slightly, and her eyes twinkled into his. "I *adore* marshmallows myself. Tell me, do you like them toasted on graham crackers?"

"I love them toasted on graham crackers."

"With a square of a Hershey bar in the middle?"

"Absolutely. As Dad used to say, that's real eatin'."

"Marshmallows! Gus, I knew we were soulmates the first time I saw you." Beaming with utter openness, she uncrossed her legs and prepared to get up. "Now just in case something happens and there's some terrible strike or something—not that I'm against labor but it *does* seem that someone's always striking nowadays, usually just for more money. What do you suppose they want with all that money, Gus? No, never mind. I wouldn't understand, I suppose. But just in case, do you have any other things that make you feel at home?"

"I love pickled herring in sour cream. Do you?"

"I don't think I've ever eaten it!" She leaned forward slightly, confidentially. "Isn't it—er—mainly a Jewish food? Not that that would matter if it's good, of course."

"Yes, as a matter of fact; I think you're right. You are certainly right. I had an Army buddy who was Jewish, and he taught me to eat herring. He taught me to eat all sorts of things. I went home with him one weekend, you know, and his mother cooked his favorite dishes for him, marvelous things, all Jewish—but pickled herring is my favorite."

"Yes, I have heard they're good cooks." She looked momentarily distracted, as if she thought she should be able to give a sociological reason for this fact. William would have, and he always managed to say it so like an objective truth that it didn't sound like prejudice. Her own remarks were too emotional. One of the children always told her so with *"Mother."* She leaned slightly forward, preparing to get up. "Well, I have to go to the grocery store and get by the cleaners before it closes." She laughed, the laugh a finch would give if birds gave laughs—clean, yellow, thin like the upper air. "I don't know why I'm telling you what I have to do; you don't want to sit here talking to an old lady anyway."

He watched her perfectly shaped legs walk smoothly across the oversized red tiles of the huge porch. "Mrs. ————, you're marvelous," he called after her. She turned at the door and gave him a brief smile.

The big Chrysler thundered around the corner into the driveway and ground to a halt in the gravel, twenty feet from where he sat hidden by Mrs. ————'s pyracantha, tall full bushes that were usually covered with bugs wrapped up in dark-gray cocoons instead of the traditional red-orange berries. Nobody drove like that but Eloise, but nobody got out. He waited. In a few minutes he opened the porch door and walked over to the car.

Eloise lay with her head down on the right side of the front seat and her hips standing exaggeratedly on their side behind the steering wheel. Her eyes were closed, her mouth turned down, and her hands were gingerly stroking her breasts (right hand on right breast, left hand on left breast). He opened the door. Metallic, air-conditioned air slapped against his nose, and "Ivy" came like white sugar-syrup from the radio.

"Go away. I'm Ivy."

Her hips standing tall and the steering wheel blocked him from her face. He shut the front door and opened the back, and leaned over the back of the front seat and touched her shoulder. "Eloise."

"I am a child who needs to be loved and I have beautiful breasts. They're soft and smooth and they feel like mounds of vanilla ice cream look. They comfort me. I am my own mother. I love and accept and forgive myself, and I comfort me. I've been out drinking beer with Mr. Tavish and I'm immersed in a cocoon of foam. I feel marvelous." Right and left hands moved rapidly in appreciation. She laughed and sat up, behind the steering wheel.

Halfway to Piney Point he told her to stop the car, and led her through the pines away from the road to a clearing. He wanted nothing clearer except the air; what she had told him about Mr. Tavish was transparent as crystal and he was twenty-five and saw no power over crystal except smashing a fist through it.

Her art teacher, a man of almost fifty, one-time classmate of her mother's, homo or non or multi or amorphosexual, to him pastily ambiguous, knew how to turn sublimation back into its beginnings with his tentatively opened young female students. Eloise listened to his instructions on how to paint the female body, watched his brush describe the color and curve of a breast, saw his eyes stroke, heard his voice hold a surface, highlight it, his hands gently round it, and his huge perfumed body hover near her own like a gardener now slowly pulling open petal after petal until the center was exposed, rubbing his thumb lightly over the pollen-tipped stamens, caressing velvet surfaces until she trembled, violently in love with her own body, and yet shivered too, chilled with being prematurely opened and left exposed. He said, "You are nineteen, Eloise. You need a lover. Youth is for love. Don't waste it."

In the clearing Gus lay her down, gently stroked her cheek, lightly her breast, held his nose against her hair. She wanted the petaled erotic handling of the creator; she asked *him* to be the snake that stung her. "Eloise," he said. "You are thinking of him." "Gus, you have to," she begged.

"Eloise, I love you. Now isn't the right time." "I can't bear it, then."

They lay on the dry gun-powdered dust of June Texas, softness ½ inch thick through which a rock stuck up into his ribs. Dust covered the ground surface of Eloise's arms like a sudden sunburn. A noise sounded. He looked toward it. She seemed not to have heard.

He brushed his hands down her throat, shoulder, breasts, across the curve of her throbbing hips, knowing she felt only Tavish's touch. He kissed her, his lips like restrained steel holding barely back to keep from crushing her, felt her own harden and vibrate beneath his mouth, sought with his tongue to push away Tavish, with his arms to force him out. The pounding of his chest deafened him as his body covered hers like a churning surf and he could not hear her heart beat through his own.

He licked the tears from her cheeks and tasted his own sweat. "We have been for a dip in the ocean, baby. Don't cry."

"I am not a baby," she said, sitting up, her eyes the cold glass of a gray sea. "You fucked me, and it hurt. You killed everything."

He lit them each a cigarette and leaned over to pull a fork of pine needle from her hair. "Eloise. I haven't killed anything, yet. I've hardly started. Take a look, sometimes, at all the things in the world that have to be killed!" he shouted after her.

She had stood up, thrown away her cigarette, and turned squarely toward the car. She turned back, went over and ground out the cigarette with her heel, turned again squarely toward the car, and walked away without looking back.

They sat by the side of Memorial Drive in the air-conditioned Chrysler. Outside, the air was five-thirty and without color. Cars with one man each rolled down the lane leading away from town on a close-together and steady assembly line, new with the shine of a clean and wealthy city.

"Eloise . . ."

"Shhh. I'm writing a poem. About cars. Cars are monstrous. Look at those hideous things. Bulging eyes, blunt noses pushing through the air without feeling it, stupid round wheels rolling over the highway foot by foot like the only reason highways were there was to let their blind rubber roll down them until it wore itself out. Cars. They're horrible shapes. And colors! Their colors flap against your face like pigs' bladders. . . . God, like colors that are so unspeakable that they make you want to go blind rather than be slapped in the eyeballs by that gross painted metal."

He watched her dirt-streaked face with moles glaring through, her shiny large-pored nose, her fleshy thighs flattened to huge width by the car seat. She was soft where he wanted her solid, and solid where he wanted her soft. On the outside, she played at being a little girl forced to do a dirty thing by big old man. She was on her way to making the first two dozen times first times. But where he wanted her soft, inside, where he wanted her to give herself to him, to melt into him in yielding trust, she was as defiant as a block of granite, as staunch and sturdy as the little toy soldier itself. And his musket molds in his hands. He lit himself a cigarette and looked out the window. "They're just cars taking people home from work. Do you think it would be more sensitive for everyone to walk five miles through ninety-degree dust like ants?"

"I feel like my insides are outsides."

He turned toward her just as her lowered head leaned towards him, so that his arm hit her on the forehead. "I'm sorry. Did I hurt you?" Her head, now anchored against his chest, shook in a faint negative. He thought she was crying, thought too that in a minute she would let him know for sure by moving a wet cheek in closer contact with a square of shirt. "But Gus, it's horrible. All the center pieces are ripped loose and lying on the surface, like the intestines of a cat that's been hit by a car. They're gray and squishy and thrown up on the highway and left there like pulp. It's the air. They shouldn't have been touched. They felt like they wanted to be, but they didn't. It's the air that hurts. Gus, they'll never be able to get back inside again." Her cheek moved onto her arm, moved off again as quickly she turned her face the other way. He leaned down and kissed the arm, smelling his own sweat there, as he thought. He wanted to slap her. He put his hand on her belly, smelled her through his fingertips. A flash of desire relit his loins. Her hair uncombed flew free as a child's, delicate yellow. The softness of her belly made his hand tremble and tighten. He turned her face up to his and kissed her and kissed her and kissed her until he had taken all the tears onto his own lips and evaporated them from there.

"It's that way for all girls the first time, baby. It'll get better. Eloise, you're adorable. Look, I promise you. There's nothing in the world as important as sex, and we'll prove it together. We'll get married. I don't want to leave you ever. We'll explore sex until we've discovered every living inch of it. Smile. You're marvelous when you smile. The whole world is our pallet. God, darling, I love you, I love you, I love you."

"Hello. It's the children, William." Mrs. ———— automatically rang for the butler on her efficient walk to the door of the living room to greet them. "Gus, of course you'll stay for dinner. We're expecting you. Francis, bring Mr. Gus his gin and tonic. Eloise, are you all right? You look ill. I mean you look as if you felt ill. Is something wrong?"

"No, Mother. I'll just go upstairs and clean up."

She didn't come back until he was almost through the second and last-allowed-because-dinner-was-waiting gin and tonic, stood in the doorway inside pink-flowered chintz, with a ribbon around her hair, and lipstick—merely the palest pink, but lipstick he had never seen her wear. Its paleness was meant to make her look even more childlike.

"I'm sorry I'm late," she said, still standing in the doorway balanced on both feet for a demure minute.

"You're not late, dear," her mother said. "You look very pretty. Doesn't she look pretty, William?"

Eloise crossed the room with a walk which slightly swung, and sat on the floor by her stepfather's chair, her face upturned to his like a sunbather aiming for an unshadowed tan.

"Well," he said. "Did we run out of chairs?"

"But what an idea, to sit on the floor! You're right, Eloise. What a marvelous day for sitting on floors! Yes, it is." Gus had moved so abruptly in his cross-legged descent to her side that he knocked over the ice and remaining gin and tonic on the carpet. "I'm terribly sorry, Mrs. ———," he said, picking up the ice and wiping the carpet with the cloth cocktail napkin first and then, seeing red fuzz rub off on the embroidered flowers, with his handkerchief.

"Don't bother about that, Gus. Francis will get it. But you spilled your drink!" The situation registered on her face with a wash of panic. It hadn't been a full drink, hardly even a quarter, but still he hadn't had his two before dinner. She couldn't offer him just a quarter of a drink, but would dinner wait for another whole? "Francis will have to get you another," she said, the top layer of her voice decisive.

"No, no, Mrs. ———. I was through, really."

"But you weren't!" she cried from all the under layers.

"But it was fuller than usual! I noticed that when Francis brought it in. It was much fuller than usual. So I really *had* finished it. It was just excess that spilled, and some melted ice. That's all. Excess and melted ice."

"Well, in that case," Mrs. ——— said, getting up. "I think dinner is waiting." She smoothed her skirt, and turned to him again. "If you're really sure?"

"Quite sure. Absolutely. Thank you very much, but I'm quite sure. Excess is all." He smiled, then turned his back to her to help Eloise up. "I love you inordinately," he whispered. "Let's tell them now."

"Nobody else does."

"Yes, they do. Your mother loves you, I know that, and William does too. They just mean something different by the word."

She got up off the floor, but only to sit in the chair William had just quitted. "I'm not going in to dinner." The full stiff skirt of chintz billowed up as she sat, obscuring her waist, running the gathered bodice and puffed sleeves and skirt into one huge collapsing parachute of pink flowered gloss. She was much too tall, too grave, her whole body too direct for such a dress. "Why don't you just say I'm too sensitive?" she said, getting angrily up.

"Because you'd think it was a compliment."

She laughed, and her eyes suddenly cleared. She laughed again, and caught his arm. "Come on. Let's try again."

"Papa-Will." She opened her napkin and draped it across her lap in one smooth swift practiced gesture. "I saw Hudson Lightfoot in the bank this morning. He said you were thinking about opening up a branch office on West Gray. It sounds like a marvelous idea. Are you really?"

"Well, I thought we might try it." Mr. ———'s fingers reached for his spoon, turned it on its side, and then quickly laid it flat and brought his hand guiltily back below the table. "Gus, now you're a man with young ideas. What do you think? Some of the men might like to work nearer home,

away from the crowds of Main Street, where they can park
their cars easily, find less crowded restaurants. What do you
think?"

"Some of them might not."

"Might not like it?"

"That's right. Some of them might like to work farther
away from home, though, if you can arrange that."

Mr. ———'s hand came right down on the table. The
laugh and the hand struck in unison. "Ha, ha! Son, you've
got something there. Yes, maybe you've really got something
there. I hadn't thought of that. Eloise, I think you picked a
young man with some sense this time. Yes sir, Gus, I think
you've got a point."

"Thanks for telling us what he had," Eloise said.

"What?" Mr. ——— turned to her.

"I said, 'Thanks for telling us what it was he had.'" She
tried to ignore her echo. "You said he had something there,
but we didn't know what it was until you told us that it was a
point, that it was a point that he had, so I said, thanks for
telling . . ."

"Eloise," her mother said.

"Oh," Mr. ——— said. Francis appeared bearing a large
silver serving dish on a folded napkin. "Well, well, what
savory and succulent delicacy have we on the agenda for
tonight, dear?"

Gus sat up tall to clear the hyacinth arrangement which
occupied the table's exact center. "I don't think he was at all
sure that's what I had," he said to Eloise who sat directly
across from him. The beginning of tears was in her eyes, and
she looked quickly at her plate.

"Eloise, Francis is waiting to serve you," her mother
gently prodded.

She noticed the dish then and automatically reached both

hands to the left. She interrupted the hands just after they grasped the silver handles. "What's that, Francis?"

The tall man hesitated, bent lower, and said in a whisper of agony, barely audible, "It's sweetbreads." He visibly wished it weren't.

"Oh." She released her hands and brought them back to her lap. "No, thank you, Francis."

"They're very good," her mother said. "Take *some*, anyway, dear."

"Mother, I can't stand sweetbreads. They're insides."

"But you should try them again. Maybe you could learn to like them."

Francis still stood just to Eloise's left, his face directed above Gus's head, his eyes closed and pain written in black on his face.

"*Eloise*," Mrs. ——— said.

Looking at no one, nor at what her hands were doing, she reached to the left aiming at the point where serving handles belonged. Francis lowered the dish to its position. Eloise helped herself.

"Mrs. ———, this will interest you." Gus raised his voice in confidence masking hope. "I read in a magazine the other day where a psychologist . . ."

"Ha! Mother's interested in psychology?"

"All mothers are interested in psychology. It's their natural field." Hope had thrown the mask to the ground and stood there in full face. "Right, Mrs. ———? Of course, they don't always use the book terms. But anyway, this article was discussing an experiment to see what would happen if little children, two-year-olds, were allowed to eat whatever they wanted to. You know, would they just eat candy? Would anyone go for spinach? that sort of thing. So at every meal a table was spread with a variety of foods, and the amazing thing is that the children ate what was good for them, over a period of time. You know? I mean, they drank orange juice—sometimes eight glasses in a day, and then the people in charge discovered that that child even had a vitamin-C deficiency. And then there was the story of the little boy who never ate an egg"—Gus's voice was racing now at top speed, ignoring the article which whipped past his head too fast for him to see more than a blur—"I mean he ate everything else that was good for him, except eggs. One day someone persuaded him to eat an egg—no, they put an egg in a milkshake, and although he complained about the funny taste of the milkshake he drank it, and then that afternoon he broke out in a terrible rash, and they discovered that he was allergic to eggs! What do you think, Mrs. ———? He was only two years old, yet something told him not to like eggs because they didn't agree with him. You know, it makes you think that maybe the body knows more than we think about what it should have." He paused to help himself to asparagus from Francis on his left.

"I am not allergic to sweetbreads; I just hate them." Eloise stabbed a bite with her fork and held it up to look at it. "They're disgusting, and they make me sick because they're insides, and to eat them is just like eating the intestines of a slit animal. But they're a social delicacy, and if you *can* eat them it proves you're upper class. Mother's afraid I'll go into the Ambassador and order pork chops, and that'll be a reflection on her." She forced the fork into her mouth, reached for her water goblet, washed that bite down. She took another, larger. Then another, but smaller. Suddenly she put her napkin on the table, excused herself, and disappeared into the kitchen.

Eloise leaned over the garbage can and vomited. Francis stood tall by the sink. "T'ain't fittin'," he muttered, lapsing into the speech of his childhood. "Jest ain't a-fittin'. That chile ain't used to eatin' sech things, and it jest ain't a-fittin' to make her. She's too big now to be made to do anything, nohow."

Eloise stood up and wiped her mouth. "They didn't make me, Francis. I made myself."

At coffee Mr. —— put on his rabbit look. He lowered his head, emphasizing the lines that plowed through his flesh from nose corner to mouth corner, raised his eyes which were round and black and startling like a snowman's, and pursed his lips into a triangle, letting them twitch to the rhythm of his brain trying to formulate the best possible sentences for his announcement—words chosen with care in order to get the maximum response from his wife. He was going to give her a gift, and he wasn't sure of its value. It was, after all, only a thing that money could buy. All his gifts were. The response he wanted, the reaction he always wanted and gained a delicate tingling pleasure from imagining that this he would get, was for his wife to leap up in the air like a Walt Disney fawn, crying Ooooh! or even Ahhh!, fling herself lightly into his arms across the entire length of the dining-room table, kiss him like a rapturous butterfly and snuggle then, palpitating and throbbing and mad with delight, crazily into his shirt pocket, inside his coat and just over his heart, where she would stay as long as he could maintain the fantasy, acting like a battery to drive his tired blood in gurgling bubbling rapids of fairybook joy. He loved his wife.

"Baby," he said, setting his Crown Derby demitasse into the saucer in a noiseless bull's-eye. "Your birthday's next month, isn't it?" He peered down the length of mahogany, his round eyes so bright now she could not tell if he were an utterly terrified rabbit or an uncharacteristically furious one. "So, how would you like a trip to New York, to celebrate? Do you think that would be fun, huh? You like New York,

don't you? We could take two weeks, go to all the spots—
you could wear your new clothes (which you would have to
hurry and buy), maybe drive out to see Liz and the children.
Would that be fun for you, Baby?"

"Oh, William!" Mrs. ———'s face shone like a child's
and for the first time Gus heard her rattle her cup as she set it
home. "Do you mean that? What an absolutely wonderful
idea! Oh, William, you always have the best things up your
sleeve! I am completely surprised! I had no idea you were
thinking of something like that—no idea at all! Darling!" She
got up from the table and went to his end. "I have to come
down here and kiss you for that."

He accepted her kiss, assured her it was nothing, really,
not all that (but it would be fun), and got up to lead her into
the living room. Up his sleeve, he thought. Perhaps that was
close enough to his pocket. "Do you think we will have fun?"
he asked, walking down the steps to the living room, keeping
his arm a little awkwardly around her shoulders.

Since Dick could not be counted on, the problem of a
chaperone for Eloise arose. Eloise thought this was silly, but
Mrs. ——— insisted that Dick was too apt to decide to become a roughneck in an oil field and disappear for months.
Then Eloise would be alone in the house and that wouldn't
look right.

"Oh Mother, Dick's not about to become a roughneck. He
hates work."

"Well, Dick is one person who can disappear and he
doesn't have to become anything," Mr. ——— said, with a
wry puff on his cigarillo. "Right, Gus?" He winked at Gus
and seemed ready even to slap him on the back. "He disappears all the time, right before your eyes. It's the best thing
he does." He laughed with a burst of noise and looked with
suspicion at the size of the cigarillo he held. "You don't happen to have a cigar on you, do you, Gus? A *man's* cigar?

These things look like they were made for tubercular midgets."

"Gus and I'll go get you one, Papa-Will."

In the drugstore she made a telephone call while he bought cigars, joined him with flushed cheeks and a glistening wetness in her eyes. In the car, before he could turn on the ignition, her body reached for his and she held him, trembling, tightened, running her tongue over his face, neck, lips like a grateful puppy, pressing her breasts to his chest, her tongue inside his mouth. She released him and he saw the blank face of a passerby just turning away.

"Marry me." She was looking at nothing through the windshield.

"Who did you call?"

"Marry me and I'll tell you."

"Yes."

"My cousin, Hulder. He's going to chaperone us while Mother and Papa-Will are gone. Mother's going to think of it tomorrow afternoon. He's coming by for cocktails."

"You're in love with him."

"Of course not." She turned to him with a dramatic stare and held his arm. "You promised to marry me. You've got to."

Hulder, the cousin, came by the following afternoon. He was a giant of a man, six and a half feet and built to it. He was an ideal chaperone. Mrs. ———— felt safe leaving her daughter with a man that big in the house: no one would dare come in and rape the child, even if she did walk around between bath and underwear without noticing the shades. She looked over at William, who was almost a foot closer to the ground, and began a sigh, but caught herself. After all, they hadn't been raped under his care, either. Mr. ———— voted for Hulder because he was stolid and muddy-looking. His clothes were

big, his glasses thick, his hair was straight and cut. He played
golf and talked of his responsibilities (a wife and four children, away for the summer) and referred to himself as not so
young as he used to be. Therefore Mr. ———— did not think
Eloise would try to seduce him (Mr. ———— did not want to
be called a pimp). Dick had no vote and did not appear, as
usual, but Hulder was his brother—the big cousin had taken
over the role after their father died and had taught Dick to
sail, drink, distinguish between ladies, everything except
shoot a gun. Hulder hadn't pressed that. Dick was a pacifist.

Francis, however, did not acknowledge Hulder's presence.
For the entire time the ————s were gone, he only squeezed
two orange juices in the morning, one for Eloise and one for
Dick. Since Eloise got up to fix Hulder's breakfast (he was
gone by the time Francis arrived at nine), she gave Hulder
Dick's orange juice (Dick got up when he felt like it) and
squeezed another for Dick. But Francis, although he escaped
breakfast, had to face another evidence of Hulder which
seemed inescapable. Francis made up the beds. Every morning he went into the guest room, hung up Hulder's pajamas,
and made the bed. Then he left the room and closed the
door. Either he so successfully preoccupied himself with
other thoughts during the time he was in the guest room that
he made himself completely unaware of what he was doing
or else he had some extraordinary power to forget, to shut
the door on the preceding minutes as finally as he did on the
room itself. Eloise mentioned Hulder's name to him twice;
the firm blank face she met both times deterred her from a
third.

The night the ————s left, as if they were starting on a
voyage, they had a first-night-out party: Gus, Eloise, Dick,
Hulder.

Dick said, "I haven't seen you in a coon's age, Hulder.
How's the sailing?"

Eloise brought martinis.

Hulder said, "Elly, do you still sail? Your father was more fun to race with than anyone I've ever known. He used to let me crew for him. I'll take you all if you'd like to go, at the Corinthian."

Eloise sat on Dick's lap. "Yes," she said, and went for more martinis.

When she came back, everyone was laughing, and she sat on Hulder's lap. "What's so funny? Me?" She put her hand on her cousin's cheek. "You have fantastic eyes. Cousin Hulder. Big Cousin Hulder." She laughed and got up. "I'm just trying to make Gus jealous."

"You are."

At dinner Eloise, glowing with golden radiance because the king was there, presided over the table from her mother's end.

In the days that followed she dressed to her role of court favorite. The first day she plucked her eyebrows. The second day she went to the doctor and had two moles burned off her face. The third day she appeared in a white, low-cut dress with her hair fixed like Lana Turner's. The fourth day she wore a playsuit and sandals and squinted her eyes like June Allyson when she smiled. The fifth day she gave a cocktail party and wore black crepe and would hardly talk for the first hour until she forgot she was supposed to be Jean Harlow. Gus was so much in love with her that he wondered if he were imagining that so was the whole family—Hulder, Dick—besides the boys her age who now came to the house in shifts. Her former shyness had utterly disappeared. Not a trace was left.

I did this, Gus thought, because he and Eloise had experimented further with their pine-needle adventure and she had learned to respond like a cherub, in joy. Like a cherub? Like a movie queen. Like a half-dozen movie queens. This bothered him twice. Once she insisted upon dancing for him when he wanted to hold her; he forgot it after he got to hold her. Another time she pulled away from him with a cry, found a sheet and wrapped herself in it and sat on the floor by the door to the balcony, staring at the sky. "Nothing" was the matter. He stopped asking her after ten minutes of "nothing" and suggested they leave his apartment and go out for a beer.

The first blunt intrusion of a loved one's past into a present bed, the first shutting out, Venetian blinds flicked tight where one had clear and open vision if not complete contact yet, the first moment when one has to face again the fact that we two are not one but two and only sometimes one, that is all I am feeling, Gus insisted. The chill is excessive. It had to come. He looked over at her face, serene as the moon. The chill remained, was dissolved only by the accumulated warmth of the third beer, when she laughed herself and he reached for her hand and held it.

Since he went back to his own apartment at night (even when night was dawn) out of respect for Francis' feelings, and since Eloise's outrageously flirtatious behavior seemed to him a coming into womanhood and a health for which he took some credit (enough so to make him tamp down his intermittent seizures of jealousy or suspicion) since he didn't want to see and have his credit cut off, he didn't look. She told him.

"I've been sleeping with Hulder every night. I take off my clothes and get in bed with him and lie with him and he loves me. We don't do anything but that, but he loves me."

"You tell him you've been with me?"

"Yes." She moved out of his arms and sat on the edge of the bed, with her back to him. "I kiss his feet; suck his toes. He likes that." She looked at him. "Do you like that?"

"I don't know. I wouldn't think a grown man . . . Eloise." He sat up and held her shoulders. "Are you telling me the truth?"

"Yes."

He got up and began putting on his shirt and shorts. To hide himself. His credit was where he lived. Quickly he put on his shorts, then his pants. He lit a cigarette. I made you. I thought I made you. You let me think I made you. "You're a bitch!"

"You're not my father!"

"Neither is Hulder!"

Later they talked. "Why?" he asked, in a dozen different ways. "He won't have sex with me," she said. "He says he's here on trust."

"Half trust?"

"Look, if you want to blame someone, blame me. *I'm* the one who's doing it."

"Goddammit, I *am* blaming you. I want you to stop it, but I can't make you. If you would try to explain something, how you feel, what you want, maybe we could both understand." She sat on the far side of the car seat with her shoulders drooping. "Elly . . ."

"Don't call me that!"

Gus hurled the empty martini glass into the fireplace, where it broke and stopped breaking so quickly that the noise was gone as soon as it began. Bits of glass shattered and sprayed onto the rug, where Dinah would walk barefoot. He left her room and went to his own.

Eloise. I never understood. What were you afraid of? You talked of having skin like you alone had it, skin which was a film in a high-speed camera, recording every microscopic touch with unbearable sensitivity. You said you walked down

the street and everybody touched your breasts. Everywhere
you went—Main Street, grocery store, a movie, the zoo—
every man you passed (boys too) put his hands on you.
Hands covered with bark that scratched, and you came home
and rubbed yourself with oil because you were chafed and
bleeding. How could you wear clothes? Eloise in the
moonlight—and you still smelled of olive oil and iodine left
from an afternoon sunbath. Fuck me in the water, you said.
In the back-yard swimming pool under your mother's window. But they are in New York, you said. But someone else
is there, and you knew it. Love me on the diving board, you
said. Stroke me and flex me and slip over my body with your
hands and eyes and put your finger on me here and work me
and melt me inside until I writhe and scream for you. *You
don't love me!*

Gus sat in the window and looked down and diagonal into
the back yard of next door: Maisie's. In the extra Sunday
afternoon of Daylight Saving time, they were having company, couples with children, their own children. How many
children? Maisie and Ben's three, the von Vons with two
(but he only saw one), three—no, four—others. Ben
squatted like a lean tiger at von Von's feet. A painter named
Peter leaned against the tree (the one tree) talking to a
young man, unknown. He watched them through dusk, heard
their voices sliding up his diagonal, listened only to the
sound—gentle, tentative. His friends. A graceful walk across
the garden, carrying a tray of sandwiches and milk for the
children: Maisie. A deference demanded by von Von, accorded by Ben. All of them reaching through the fringe of a
Victorian lamp, holding out a veined or stubby-fingered or
freckled hand, holding out to another hand behind its own
antique shade. The bodies are there and I look at them, the
dancers, the thickened mothers, the academic elephant, the

gross child and the graceful one—look at them because they represent a surface that encloses insides, a concrete shape of matter which moves, catches the eye, offers a stopping place for glances that otherwise would stream forever into space and be lost.

When I was a child and learned I was near-sighted, the doctor told my mother (who didn't want me to wear glasses) to have me exercise my eyes by looking at far-distant objects, to stretch the muscles outdoors. I looked at the stars. But when the night was cloudy and black, my eyes stretched into the far distance and found nothing—how far? Forever. There was no point on which to focus. Wherever they stopped, I could push them another length. Panic came. They were gone. I've looked so far I'm beyond the visible stars, beyond the universe, out in chaos where my glance will be absorbed into the senseless motion of homogeneous nothing.

My friends have each a body off which my glance can bounce, but they go outdoors. My room is lined to enclose all my glances. I know it encloses utterly. Whatever in this room is apparently lost, I know is here, will return, can't get out and therefore has to be in this room somewhere. I know it is somewhere in this room. I let it out here, therefore it must be here. The matter is only of a thorough search.

Don't you then have to be careful when the door is opened? Do you stand behind the door when someone enters or leaves? Do you avert your eyes? Close them?

Soon no one will want to come in. This room will enclose all of me so safely I won't bother to bring journeying bits of myself back to my body, as is the custom (automatic), necessity of those who live outside. The glance which travels to an uneven smear of plaster will be safe, known, easy to retrieve at any time that I desire, so I will not need to concern myself about its return. I can forget about it for an hour, and

know it can't get out of this room. But why bring it back in
an hour? It is safe there for many hours, for a day, a month.
Soon I will forget to be anxious. Perhaps it will stay there
forever. And other bits of myself will disperse themselves
into unoccupied spaces of the room, and I will not be anx-
ious. There will be no advantage to remaining inside a body
instead of inside the room. My bits will spread conflictless
and come to rest according to the laws of physics, in the cen-
ter of some dead sphere of air. My room will enclose me in
chaos without anxiety.

The kitten cried outside the door and he let it in. A
scrawny thing, six weeks old, the runt of a motherless litter
Alice had brought home with its brother to save, two weeks
ago. For one week she had fed them diligently, and the other
kitten grew fat, learned to drink from a saucer, and was on
its way to cathood. This one ate reluctantly, and when Alice
lost interest in ministering to the least of his little ones, last
week, it was as scrawny as ever. Gus picked it up and held it
in his hand, a bird, an almost embryo, a scraggly black-and-
white thing of runted bones and minimum skin.

He went downstairs and brought back a doll's bottle,
dropper, and milk. He took the kitten in his lap, where it lay,
uninterested in eating. He forced it onto its back and thrust
the nipple into its mouth. The kitten jerked its head away,
tried to wiggle free. He held the head and the nipple in its
mouth; the kitten sucked for a few seconds, then stopped. He
squeezed the bottle, pushing milk down its throat and over
his hands and lap. The kitten drank more, stopped again. It
was five weeks old and looked just born. Born without the
energy to live. Diagnosis: failure to thrive. He let it rest a
minute, holding it inside his hand with the noncrushing soft-
steel grip of a bird dog retrieving a quail. Then he insisted the

milk again, let it rest, again, until the bottle was empty. He set the little cat on the floor; it trotted away to a corner and lay down to sleep.

He went downstairs and called the number next door.

"Maisie, please come over."

"Gus." Pause. "I can't. We have company."

"I know you have company. I can see you from here, hear you from my window. Do you think I can't see? I'm sorry. Maisie, I need you."

"What's the matter?"

"Nothing. I wanted to see you."

"Gus, I can't leave now. Can I call you later? They'll be leaving soon."

"Hey, hold it just a minute, Maisie. There's someone at the door." He went to the front window and leaned out into the street. "Bill! Come on up." A dozen heads turned to mark him. He buzzed the door open on his way back to the telephone. "It's Bill, Maisie. Look, call me later if you can. Otherwise, I'll see you tomorrow."

Gus went back to his room and opened a box on the bottom shelf of the bookcase. Dust clung to his hands and he rubbed them on his pants. Dust made him sneeze, three times, as he disarranged papers already disorderly. He flipped through them, recognizing them by their top lines: This depression weighs me down like a mass of invisible air, following. . . . Do you have to behave like a spoiled child, crying every time you trip. . . . I wanted to write about Medea because I was Medea, Phaedra and Sidney's queen and the. . . . You saw yourself this morning, talking a dead man's language, tracing the map of. . . . Humiliation is a word describing a feeling whose color is red, whose consistency. . . . Primitive religious worship of the tree (three); espaliered plants; freeze. . . . Indifference indifference indifference indifference indifference. . . . When I was eight, I was one-tenth of the second grade in a Confederate school. . . .

He pulled this one and the page following it, and sat on the floor to read them. Eloise had written these things, with no particular pattern or design, on an old typewriter she'd found in her mother's garage. These two pages he had come upon right after her first suicide attempt, the day after Dinah's first birthday:

> *When I was eight, I was one-tenth of the second grade in a Confederate school. We'd never heard of Lincoln, but Lee's portrait hung in every hall and his birthday and deathday were our principal holidays. The two gentlewomen who ran the school were his nieces, I think. One of our class leaders (there were nine class leaders altogether, and me) inaugurated a game called Civil War—an obscenity in itself: the ladies' designation was War Between the States. Our play was exclusively devoted to leaving notes in the water cooler. To lower the note to faucet level, so it could be removed, one had to drink the water. Cups and cups of it. On Tuesdays, after the coolers were refilled, we floated, bloated and squishy, through classes. Imogene, whose total grand title was Imogena Seraphina Arartus Spargartus Plowden Roundtree (she was named after an aunt and was a bona fide descendant of southerners) made up this game and chose the first side. I will be a general of the North, she announced. Eight other little girls, who had been holding up their hands hoping to be chosen for the southern side before the side was filled, suddenly switched to the left hand and held it up*

*for the yankees. I was watching. Appalled, I saw
the Union army gain the pick of my classmates.
Hastily, I upped my hand. Imo, Imo, me, me, me,
waved and shouted nine of us. The less aggressive
or out-of-favor girls (those with scraggly hair)
were relegated to the Confederacy. Sides chosen,
the war raged via the water coolers.*

*The Misses Dickenson, Principals, discovered
our distended abdomens and ordered the war
halted. They had two moral principles to discuss
with us, which the game illustrated (a fantastically
progressive school, for the geography and date).
Abusing the body, and war. The latter was an evil,
and could under no circumstances be treated as a
game (Did we realize . . . ?). The former was a
debasement of the temple of the soul.*

*Why were they angry, furious, frantic? Because
the left-over side, the one relegated to scraggly-
hairs, was the Confederacy.*

*What did I learn?—to appreciate Swift's tale of
Laputa, where dogs are hosed through the anus to
detect how much they will swell before bursting.*

*And I remember because I am swollen so now,
although through no discernible orifice.*

*I have outgrown my skin, and there is no mother
around to put in gussets, or pass down my sister's
skin and transfer mine to a younger one. Skin
stretched and barely circumscribing an unstable
and bulging inside is unremitting discomfort. There
are ways to loosen skin—steam baths to expand
the covering, ice-cold gin to contract the interior,
even high altitude of jet planes to make one feel
that there is room to burst in if bursting must be.
But in the daily life, consider: a man is in love*

with me. He kisses me. This allows my tongue to exit into his mouth, leaving my skin less tight. In a moment, though, he wants to insert his tongue into my mouth. Which is bigger? My skin screams, Stop! We are too crowded already! And, although the Misses Dickenson didn't mention this, love progresses beyond kissing and there are other parts of him. Did you ever, as a child, eat too much, much too much, at Christmas dinner because you were heartbroken at your presents and gorged yourself on food—thinking it was love? Did you then pull yourself heavily onto your bed, patting a pillow around your swollen belly to suspend it in the least possible discomfort and feel that you could never eat again? And then, aching and alone and near oblivion with surfeit and withdrawal, did someone come up to you and pry open your mouth and stuff a fat wiener down your throat?

That's the way I feel about you.

"What does it mean, Eloise?" he had asked her. Her wrists were bandaged and she lay, docile and smiling like a child who is being carefully tended.

"It doesn't mean anything, baby. I told you. That was just something I wrote last week. It doesn't have anything to do with this."

"You felt crowded." She stopped smiling. "You let enough blood out to feel practically empty in there now." She turned her head on the pillow, away from him. "Is that why? Eloise, for God's sake, tell me!"

"Leave me alone! You're badgering me, badgering me!" She crashed her fist into his chest, cried out from pain, and held her wrist, sobbing. Blood soaked the bandage. He called the nurse, and left.

A year later, the day after Dinah's second birthday party, they were having a party. At six-fifteen Eloise had not come home. Francis came through the door, looking tall and crisp as magazine lettuce. "It's a hundred in the shade and you come in looking like you have a private iceberg," Gus said, with wilted humor.

"It's how you look that counts, Mr. Gus. Don't matter how you feel, it's how you look that counts."

"Yeah. Well, I don't count on either score. The bar's set up in here—" Gus went to the door of the kitchen and looked at the bar sent over by Cobb's placed on the wall of the living room nearest the kitchen. "There's a bottle of Johnny Walker Black Label for Mr. Durach when he comes and for anybody he brings with him. The others can drink bar Scotch. That includes Dick—you can tell him I said so—at least until the Durachs have gone. You'll have to get some ice."

"What time is company expected?"

"Eight. And the Rainbirds will be here at eight. I'm going to get dressed. If you need anything, just knock."

"Mr. Gus?"

Gus turned back and looked at Francis.

"Is it all right if I just go and peek at the baby?"

Gus was showered, shaved, and dressed, except for his coat, by seven, and Eloise still hadn't come home. He went to the bar, picked up the Johnny Walker and opened it, and poured himself a drink. "Francis, you and I can have a drink of the Johnny Walker."

"Now, Mr. Gus, you know I'd rather go and drink out of the bayou than have to drink Scotch."

"It's expensive, Francis. Don't you want to be a gentleman?"

"Not that bad, no sir." He poured the sugar syrup he'd just

boiled and let cool into a small glass pitcher, and set it on the bar. "I guess I'll just have to be plain old Francis if'n being a gentleman means I got to drink Scotch to do it. No Scotch." He shook his head. "Tastes just like soap. But I'll take a drink of red whisky when I get ready to leave."

Final sunshine flickered onto the brick floor in squares, indistinct through the lattice which covered the large glass pane on the west wall. Gus walked over and looked through at the scraggly pines spaced in the circle of shell which was their driveway—Eloise's pines, planted as babies and pampered up by her; Eloise's land; her childhood. He looked at his watch. Seven-fifteen.

"That baby shore do favor Miss Eloise." Francis stopped with a tray of cut limes, lemons, and orange slices. "She looks just like her mother. And smart! She turned around when I come in, and just watched me until I come over to her—watched me to see if I was going to pick her up or just stand and look at her, and she wasn't going to smile until she saw that I was going to pick her up."

"She wouldn't eat anything tonight," Gus said. "Just took a bottle. Wouldn't even eat her applesauce."

"Hit's too hot to eat, Mr. Gus. It's the weather, that's all. Miss Eloise used not to eat, and her mother and her nurse'd get all in a fuss and try to make her"—Francis laughed softly—"and there'd be a time! Miss Eloise ain't gonna do nothing if you try to make her; never has. And the more they'd push that food in her mouth the more she'd spit it out, and her in them little clean white dresses and she'd spit her dinner all over herself like she didn't care a thing for all the washing and ironing in the world. She wasn't gonna eat if'n she didn't want to. Yes sir, she sure used to give 'em a fit!" He laughed again. "I could of told 'em it wasn't no use."

The two-year-old Chevrolet, a wedding present from Eloise's uncle (her mother's brother), took the circle's outer curve in a white cloud of shell dust and stopped just as it bumped the end of the garage. Eloise came in, her face red from the heat and set in defiance. She barely spoke to either of them and went into the bedroom.

Without taking off her shoes, usually the first thing she did, she was standing in the middle of the room ripping off her linen suit with a savagery that burst one button just as Gus walked in.

"Eloise, what's the matter?"

She lost her balance getting out of the skirt, regained it but caught her heel in the hem, pulled the skirt free, ripping the hem. *"Shit!"* she cried, and threw herself across the bed. She kicked off her shoes and then stood up, tore the slip free at the shoulder straps, pulled it over her head and threw it, hurled it across the room. Too light to sail, it floated to the floor beside the bed. She picked it up and yanked hard at the material with both hands pulling in opposite directions; too expensively made, a slight tearing of threads was the only result.

"Eloise!"

She turned on him and hit the air just short of his chest. *"Get out of here!"* She ran into the bathroom and shut the door, locked it. Over the sound of the bathtub taps turned on full force he heard her sobs. He knocked insistently. "Eloise. Let me in." He knocked again. "Let me in."

"Go away."

He placed his shoulder against the door and threw his weight forward. Again. The door cracked.

"Stop that and *leave me alone.*"

He slammed his whole body against the door again, and the lock gave. She got up quickly, crowded into the space between the opened door and the bathtub. He blocked her way. Her face bursting and blotched with purple rage, she socked him on the chest with both fists. She ducked under his arm and ran back into the bedroom. She stood in the far corner, facing him as he followed her, her arms hanging down and her eyes glaring at him like an animal daring to be killed.

"Eloise, what on earth is the matter?"

She walked across to the bed and sat on its edge, shoulders, arms, face suddenly sinking limply downward. Only the heaving of her chest showed her former rage. She raised her head to look at him, her eyes washed pale and empty.

"I had lunch with Uncle Jesse," she said. "Do you have a cigarette?" She got up. "Christ, the tub'll overflow." And from the dressing room, "Oh Christ, look at the door!"

Halfway through the party (or what should have been halfway but would turn out to be merely one-fifth—one more fifth) Gus looked around for Eloise and couldn't find her.

"Francis. Have you seen Eloise?"

"No, sir. Not for, let's see, maybe ten minutes, maybe longer."

"Thanks." He started to mix himself a drink, then handed his glass to Francis.

"On the rocks?"

"No. With ice, Francis. Scotch over ice."

Outside, the air was hot and thick as cotton with the garish smell of Eloise's summer flowers—mimosa, crape myrtle, plumbago. The wet heat hit his face and he bathed in it as a child in the sweat of his mother's body. Hot and damp, hot and damp—but Eloise's words for sex were warm and wet.

The old riding ring stood fifty yards from the house, its original shell overgrown with crabgrass, the scraggly prairie bushes kept cut by her uncle (not Jesse but Uncle Shorty) now growing blatant and pointless across the center area. He walked outside the circle of lights from the house, away from the spots Eloise and her architect had installed to light the countryside (not because it was pretty but because it wasn't the city).

He was drunk. The sweat of the glass ran over his fingers and he rubbed it on his forehead. Too much humidity in the air left it there; he wiped it free. His fingers pressed against the upper bone of his eye sockets. He was drunker than he meant to be. He usually was.

He leaned over the rail of the riding ring and looked at the clear meaningless stars in somebody's painted dome overhead, then closed his eyes. The dresses at the party swam through his vision with more clarity than the faces of the women—red and pink and yellow and flowered and crazily patterned and laced and dotted and crossed, and everyone looked her best; and the men wore tan or baby blue or pale plaid and it was shantung or silk or sharkskin or fishnet. Eloise wore a golden shimmer of skin and thrust herself into the eyes of Cousin Hulder.

Gus thought he should go back and check whether Hulder had also disappeared.

He walked over to the jungle gym the ———s had given Dinah for her first birthday and straddled the iron two-way swing. He was drunk and the party was going on without either host or hostess. The swinging motion of the play equipment rocked his stomach with the passive nauseating roll of the boats Hulder took them on; in one minute he could throw up into the clover and sink his face into it and be done. He got up abruptly, shook his head to hammers hitting its sides, and walked around the east side of the house, heading for the patio.

There near the barn which used to stand on Eloise and Uncle Shorty's property but which had been sold and moved across the fence to the neighbor's—he also a horseman—was Eloise. Her back was turned to him and she was alone.

She didn't turn around as he walked up to her, although she must have heard because he stumbled over the uneven unlit ground with the clumsiness of a drunken husband.

"I hear they're having a party inside," he said.

Her hair covered the side of her bent face and her mouth was obscured by the process of chewing a long wand of grass. "You can't just stand out here and sulk, Eloise," she said.

"I didn't say that." He stepped closer to put his hand on her shoulder, stumbled; his hand hit her arm. "I'm sorry." He tried again for her shoulder and made it. "What's the matter? Is it Hulder?"

"No, it's not Hulder. It's Uncle Jesse. It's Hulder, too. It's everybody. All Uncle Jesse ever says to me is that I'm a good housekeeper. I have on a pretty dress and I'm a good house-keeper."

"Where'd he get that idea?"

"I won't be cheered up!" She turned suddenly toward him and put herself in his arms. The quick weight threw him off balance from his own drunkenness. He tried to hold her, stumbled, got them both upright again. She pulled away with a cry.

The voices next door—Maisie's, Ben's, all of them—had stopped in the sudden coolness of sundown. Gus's eyes from the window had all the back yards in sight to themselves. The houses were dirty and so were the trees, and the yards looked like toy boxes made of fences by children who could think in one shape only.

Downstairs, the front door opened. In a few minutes, he

heard the noises of Dinah playing hostess with fifteen-year-old social phrases; then all human voices disappeared beneath a tidal wave of Bobby Short.

The telephone rang. Just as he said hello, another hello came from downstairs, backed up by Bobby Short.

"I have it, honey," he said.

"Hello?" It was Maisie.

"Hello? Oh, Daddy, hi. Is it for me?"

"No."

"Gus?"

"Oh. Goodbye."

"Hello?"

"Maisie?"

"Yes? Yes. Gus, are you there?"

"I think so."

"The people have all gone and the children are in bed if you want me to come over now."

"I'm all right, Maisie. Bill's here," he lied.

"Oh. Well, in that case, maybe I won't come tonight. I'm glad Bill's there. You sounded so depressed earlier."

"No, darling. It's very kind of you, but I'm fine. Can I call you tomorrow?"

He had stayed by the fence after Eloise went back to the party, leaning over it until the tall weeds tickling his nose sent him over to a clearer patch of ground, where he lay down. His head was lined up with the bay mare's stall—old man Springer had just bought her two weeks ago and every night for two weeks she had spent the hour before midnight and an hour at dawn kicking the sides of her stall. So it was

eleven, he thought, as her kicks split his aching head and he
tried to catch a rhythm in the syncopated poundings of the
mare and the whisky drunk in heat. He slept.

In the higher moon his watch registered eleven-fifteen. The
kicking had stopped, both in the barn and in his head. His
step across the broken ground was back to normal. As he entered the circle of light thrown by the spots around the house,
he suddenly stopped. The rooms were lit in all the right
places, but there were no shadows, no voices, no cars. He
looked at his watch again. In electric light the hand which
had been on eleven was now on twelve. He had awakened at
five of three.

He opened the door in the panic of four lost hours and
hurried through the kitchen into the living room, the need to
know at once what had been lost pushing his body with the
rush of a tricked child.

"Boo!" Eloise jumped out from the side of the door and
covered his eyes.

Gus reached for the telephone and misdialed. He dialed
again.

"Maisie? Look. Could you come over and have a drink? I
need you."

"Boo," she had said, and as he reached back behind his
covered eyes to touch her he felt her naked skin. He wrested
her hands away and his head around to face her. She glowed
like a baby from a tender bath and she was completely bare

except for a single strand of beads which hung to her belly.

"Why did you leave? We missed you." Her arms reached out to circle his neck.

Over her shoulder he saw, bent into the corner of the sofa like a black stick man, a stranger staring at him, black eyes sunk and pulling in with them most of a thin face whose bottom was covered with a dark antiseptic beard. Dick lay on the patio just beyond the opened glass doors, sprawled lengthwise in unzipped pants, his bare chest and neck covered with casual flowers and hastily pulled stalks of greenery. An unlit candle stuck in his navel. The carpet was strewn with glasses and shoes and ashtrays and their contents, the furniture scattered and propped at odd angles. The record player was the only clear surface—the records and covers of an evening's noise were now stacked on the bench or the floor or dropping motionless between the two. He looked again at the stranger. The table by his end of the couch was clear, supporting only a brandy snifter with its brandy inside and an ashtray clean in which sat his pipe.

Hulder came toward him. "Maybe we should all have some coffee . . ." He stopped midway, and in an instant his face froze, thawed, and dropped into flaccid horror at what he saw in Gus's face opposite his.

Gus was standing by the door when Maisie opened it. He grabbed her as she stepped inside, pulled her to him. He felt her thin body stiffen under his arms and he massaged her back between the shoulder blades to soften her. "I need you, Maisie." She pulled away and he backed her against the wall, digging his nose into her hair. She smelled of garden soot and fine brown hair and something cosmetically sweet.

"Gus."

He threw his body into her again and again, creating only a local coursing of blood and desire. His skin, the rest of his body, in particular his brain remained untouched. She held him, passive, unresponding.

"Drink or coffee?"

"Either. Gus, what's the matter? You look terrible."

"Thanks. You, on the other hand, look fresh and alive and as if you'd just returned from public action. Look, don't sit in that chair."

"I'm supposed to ask why?"

He handed her a cup of coffee and put his on the floor as he sat down on the children's couch. "Because you won't be comfortable. That's a terrible chair. It grabs you. It's shaped so that your body has to go the way *it* decides. You can't move. Do you want a chair to be in charge of your body?"

"So you're depressed because you've been thinking about chairs all day?"

"Did I ever tell you about Eloise?"

"Pieces here and there." Maisie got up to get an ashtray off the piano, and sat back down in the same chair. "I have a picture."

"Listen. They were there, you see—in my house. Eloise and I were having a party. . ."

The noise of music upstairs had stopped a moment before and was now replaced by the noise of Dinah and her date descending the stairs.

"Oh, Daddy, do you all have to sit in here? Barry and I wanted to cook some eggs. Hi, Maisie. This is Barry."

"We're not sitting on the stove," Gus said. "In fact, as you may notice, we're not even sitting in the kitchen."

"But you're sitting *next* to the kitchen."

Gus reached in his pocket. "Here're two dollars. Why don't you go down to Riker's and get some eggs there? You'll get to see all the bums at this hour, and other things. You can have eggs with a slice of life on the side." He said to Barry, as they turned to leave, "She can't cook eggs anyway."

"She's beautiful tonight."

"She looks a lot like Eloise sometimes." Gus went into the kitchen and heard the children's voices as they passed down the sidewalk below the kitchen windows. He heard Dinah, but all he could pick up was "Daddy." What went before or after? Just like Daddy? Daddy always talks weird? Pay no attention to Daddy?

He came back to the couch with a glass in his hand. "I decided to have a drink. How about you?"

"I'm fine."

He looked away from the strained concern on her face—looked at his drink and stirred all three cubes by placing his finger on the top one and revolving it.

"Look, I just don't remember, and I've never been able to understand it. I walked into a room I had left four hours before. I'd been asleep. Drunk and asleep. Eloise was naked. Hulder and Dick were there, and some man I'd never seen before named . . . I can't remember his name. Sex was all over the room, thrown all over the place like it was something that had been used and discarded or half-used and discarded because there was plenty more. Lots more because it was Eloise. All of them, all three of those guys—her brother, her cousin, and a stranger—had had all kinds of sex possible with Eloise. I know because they had pictures. Pictures of Eloise . . . look, Maisie. I saw the pictures, and there were pictures of all four of them, the three guys and her . . ."

"Gus."

"It was the stranger's camera, and I thought he took the pictures, but there was one of him, too, and I asked Eloise who took that. You know what she said? She said, You did.

Like she was surprised I asked. She said I brought the
stranger there in the first place, with his camera, and that I
took the pictures. All of them. Then she showed me one of
all four of *them,* all four in one picture."

Gus got up abruptly and stood by the piano, sitting against
the keys around middle C for a musical instant. He placed
his hand flat on a dozen treble notes, then closed the piano
and sat on its stool, facing Maisie.

"Look, they went home, and I made some coffee and
Eloise and I sat on the patio until dawn. She insisted that I
had been there, that I'd left the party for less than an hour,
when I'd walked outside—I remember that—and then came
back and everyone had gone home except Hulder and Dick.
Listen, she told me the story so clearly that I can picture the
whole thing, and sometimes I even think maybe I remember
it. . . . But I don't. It just became visual and familiar.
There was a glittering over everything—the story glittered—
the scene . . . the four of us sat down in the kitchen . . .
we were talking about sex, and I was saying things like freedom and prudery and spontaneous expression. I was twenty-
eight and a prig.

"Maisie, *I* called the man with the camera. His name was
Larry. Larry Kimche. *I* encouraged Eloise to let go, that it
was all right, I was there with her. I wanted her to feel free,
sexually free, whether it was exhibitionism or incest, both; to
behave like a whore. I wanted her to trust me, to be absolutely sure I wouldn't try to pour her into any mold, restrict
her . . .

"Look. We were sitting on the patio facing the creek that
divided Eloise's part of the property, the end where the
horses used to be, from her mother's, where the big house
was. Now when we'd moved out there and built our house,
there was nothing on the horse end of the land but scraggly

prairie bushes and weeds and a fringe of trees by the creek. The ground around the house was shell and ironweed and crabgrass. Do you know how Eloise grew her lawn? She went over to her mother's side, dug up a square patch of St. Augustine grass, and planted it on our side. It sends out runners, you know. All the first summer she watered that patch and watched it spread, then the next summer she split it and made half a dozen patches, watered them and watched them spread. By the third summer she had a sizable area of lawn. She was immensely proud of it. But you know you can buy squares of St. Augustine for a quarter, and she refused to use even one single bought square for help. She did the same thing with the pine trees. She bought those, but the dollar ones, which are only a foot high and an inch thick, and scattered them over the land. She watered them, too—sometimes she stayed up all night long during a dry spell moving the sprinkler from tree to tree from midnight to dawn and measuring their height against her own. This summer they shot above her and she felt they were her sons on their way to the sky. The second summer we were there, because I thought she loved trees, I gave her a thirty-dollar pine with a three-year growth behind it. She gave it its share of water and feed, and planted it in sight to please me, but she was really watching for one of her own trees to overcome the handicap, catch up to and surpass the artificial head-starter. It was then that I thought that her greatest need was for me not to interfere, no matter how backward and inchmeal and painful her processes of growth were.

"But we were sitting out there on the patio, and her eyes had lost their glitter and were like lead. I knew only that I'd made a terrible mistake. It was as if we only had the night, the hour or two left of it, to correct in; once the sky became light and Dinah woke up to be fed and the day began we would have to go forward and bury the evening forever. You see, I was afraid—that something had happened that no one understood, something had been let loose. It was just a year since Eloise had tried to kill herself by cutting her wrists, and I asked her again. I said, 'Eloise, why did you want to kill yourself?' and she said, 'But I don't think I did, Gus, really. I only wanted to die.' And do you know what she said? She said that for a dozen years of her life she'd been left alone, to spread unnoticed over the land, as she put it. And then she became female and had to wear dresses. She said that dresses with shapes of their own surrounded her body and forbade it to wander off into indistinct outlines; dresses closeted her and confined her into the standard girl-mold and wouldn't let her go, held her there until she thought she would burst or rip them away. She said she sometimes did slip out and shift free, but that she was caught and reprimanded and poured back into her mold with such fierceness and loss of love that she often couldn't muster the energy to escape with.

"We were sitting there on the patio, absorbed in the gradual predawn lightening of the air, changes which are imperceptible and leave the eye suspended in a fluid of unreality. Invisible birds were singing—first one, then another, then a newcomer joined. The first thin line of pink cut the eastern edge of the sky. Eloise was looking at the trellis, to the west. On it grew wisteria vines, and the blue blossoms were tinted to purple of an unbelievable richness by the red sun. Between the wisteria were climbing roses, the common ordinary kind which grow wild in Texas. Most people espalier these vines —you know, cut off all the branches that grow fore and aft and leave only those in a single plane. Eloise let hers grow wild in all directions, and in another month the long branches would sweep up and out over the patio and the yard in a tangled mess. Eloise knew it was a mess. She said, 'But when the young trees reach, eager for the sun, they thrust their twigs up and out on all sides. They grow every which way and the result is a tree. But the wisteria and the roses are a mess. Why?'

"It wasn't a question, you know, but Dinah woke up then. We heard her talking in her crib, cooing, and it was day. It was a tired day. Sunday. Elly cleaned the house, and laughed at supper, and after we put Dinah to bed she said she wanted to get something at the drug store. After an hour I called the police. They were just getting ready to call me. She'd driven the car off the bridge into the San Jacinto River. She was dead."

Gus's thumbnail was marked by horizontal grooves of varying depth, recording moments of emotional crisis—a creeping ticker tape giving only hindsight information. Since the imprint occurred at the root of the nail, he did not see it until the growth cleared the flesh overlap, a delay the days of which he could never accurately measure because as everyone knows nails grow at their own caprice (not, although some *Vogue* scientists would have it so, merely fast in summer and slow, etc.). It did not matter; the groove was not caused by an event the inception of which it was important to date, but by a sudden emotional spasm of his physical system, an upheaving which he could sometimes feel even as it broke. To see it recorded on his nail ? number of days later gave him confirmatory satisfaction.

The record was brief: he kept his nail cut and thus could only refer to events of the past two months (more or less).

Nine nails were free from this Dorian notching; his left

thumbnail took the total of marks upon itself. According to this poll, his body showed a ten-per-cent connection with his emotional life.

The grooves varied in length, depth, and also in shape, and this fact fascinated him. Some were sharp and relatively deep, as if scratched with a sudden pin; others were wide and smooth although actually much deeper, like chasms worn down by implacable centuries of rivers (yet they had to be formed in something under two weeks). A methodical man would try to discover the matching quality in the recorded emotions.

Rebecca

The robust sanitation trucks were being boys outside his window, through which a slanted four-by-four of sunlight came. The sunlight was sprinkled with dust which was dancing because it was Saturday in July. The Greenwich Villagers on parole made arm-in-arm noises up and down the block.

All this mattered.

"Morning, Mr. Gus," said Hattie, bringing him a second pot of coffee. "It sure is a fine day for a walk."

"Good morning, Hattie. I took a walk once on a Saturday just like this one. Such a walk should have a name. The long walk, the last walk, the lost walk, least walk, lust walk, let's walk. Probably not list walk. I married Mrs. Ferrarri—the second Mrs. Ferrarri. The brilliant Rebecca." He reached for a box of kitchen matches on the table in front of him, chose one, split it with his thumbnail (the traumatically grooved one), and poked between two molars which touched each other at the top and stood primly apart at the bottom to form a daily cantaloupe trap. "My mother, the original Mrs. Ferrarri, used not to understand why people got married on Saturdays. It ruined her Saturday nights, because it put her in lines and made her mouth mouth phrases of the loveliness of the bride. At any other Saturday night she would accept the attention center for herself. But I married Rebecca on Saturday anyway. Like all rebellious, I hedged. We were married at five in the afternoon, and kissed, photographed, and dismissed by eight. I thought it was so that Dinah could be there."

"I remember her," said Dinah. "That was when the dog bit Alice."

"Bit me?" Alice stood up, rolling the kitten to the floor like a lapful of sand. She slithered in next to her father, her eyes shining with blue ice. "It was that bird dog next door. I remember. I was trying to kiss it and it bit me."

"That's why you have all those scars on your face," said Dinah, reaching in front of her sister for the jelly that stood by Gus's plate (it was grape).

Alice glanced at her sister on her right and then at the mirror on her left (on the wall), needing simultaneously to fly at both. The mirror won. She tilted her head back and sideways in a common mirror contortion and pulled at the skin on her lower cheek. "You can hardly see them," she said, and positively sat back down at the table. "Can you?"

"Oh, you can see them all right," said Dinah. "But you don't *notice* them."

"Hattie, can I have another piece of toast?"

"You've had three pieces already, and you haven't had an egg yet." Hattie leaned closer to the child and thrust her face into hers as face-thrusters do. It was Hattie's belief, from which she never budged, that the body could not stand too much toast without there being a stabilizing egg thrown in periodically. "I'll fix you an *egg* and another piece of toast, but you have to eat the egg first. How about you, Miss Dinah?" She gave her *Miss* the slightly swinging intonation servants use when the baby they have nursed passes into young ladyhood and just plain *Dinah* won't do. The lilt to the *Miss* announces that they remember, though; and are capable of reminding everybody.

"Tell me about my mother, Daddy," said Alice. "Did you call her Becky?"

"Rebecca Becky? I don't think so," said Gus. "Your mother was a very intelligent woman. Hattie, would you fix me an egg, too?"

Hattie turned briefly back. "You don't eat breakfast."

"You can have my egg, Daddy," said Alice.

"Aren't we being sweet today," said Dinah, grabbing the *Times* and turning noisily to the music page. "Hey . . ."

"I'm not being sweet; I *hate* eggs," Alice screamed. "And you shut up!"

Gus left the table and went upstairs to the living room.

She glowed, that's what she did. He lifted the lid from the mahogany box on the coffee table and took out a brown-wrapped Philippine cigarette. The hinge on the box was still broken, and its lid clattered to the table. He stuck it back with sticky fingers. In healthy homes, broken hinges grow back together, Rebecca said. But at Rice Institute even the ideas of the students have to be glued to something—(gether, perhaps)—before they'll stand up.

He crossed his feet on top of the coffee table, admiring the clean firm shape of them in shoes. Yet they stuck up very high. They didn't fall into any human position in shoes.

He was positive that there was sugar in the brown paper, a tiny bit, impossible for an adult tongue to taste but there, fleetingly, to his nose. The tobacco was violence to an un-breakfasted stomach unlikely to be. He took a deep pull on the long thin brown thing and shot to the surface of the morning with inside pain filling his chest.

Rebecca had breakfast in the morning, and put on her shoes, and was gone before he got up. She liked to be at the library at seven o'clock. It was the light, she said. The early-morning light affected even the flat adobe rectangles of the Rice campus and made it appear as if it were possible for minds actually to work there. Such illusions disappeared like dew (like everything but sweat) under the Texas noonday sun. He rolled out of bed as he heard her car drive off down the shell road and had long sloppy breakfasts with Alice, while Dinah sat politely at the end of the table and waited for Hattie to come and fix her an egg.

Gus put out the cigarette, reluctantly lowered his feet to the floor and out of sight (the movement too slow to be described as putting either one of them down) and returned to downstairs. To an egg, or a stubborn lone pot of coffee?

Dinah, who must have swallowed her egg whole like a snake, was leaning back in her chair reading the paper. Gus saw that the plate at his place supported exactly one egg, which scowled at him through one half-closed eye.

"Dinah, don't you lean back at the table."

"You do."

"That's different. I'm your father." She went on reading. "Dinah, sit down."

Her chair came down hard on the floor. "I don't see why I can't lean back at the table if you can. I'm not a child." She glared at him through two scowling eyes, the flesh of her face petulant.

"When you're the father of the family, you can lean back in your chair too."

Her eyes went round for an instant before their lids covered them, and a quiver began beneath the plastic skin. She got up and hurried from the room, clumsy.

"You're excused!" he cried. A swell filled his pit and then ebbed away, leaving its back-sucked ache. He left the egg where it lay (what? a chicken?) and climbed three flights to his room.

Hattie showed Josephine (whom she called Miss Jo as if it rimed with *gizmo*) up three flights to Gus's room, repeating all the way (breathlessly) how glad they were to see her.

"Liza!" Jo said.

Gus sat cross-legged on the floor, his feet down the slant; he looked like a country fisherman stuck to the bank of a river whose name mattered locally. He was in fact absorbed in the surface of his recent emotional activity as mirrored on his thumbnail, judging the meaning of a series of unremarkable ripples. He didn't look up.

Hattie whispered to Jo.

"Gus?" Jo said twice, first to Hattie to confirm that she had heard what she thought she had heard, and second to Gus himself, a question. Hattie left the two ex-roommates-at-college together, shutting the door with a firm confirmatory gesture of her own.

The room came between them immediately. It wasn't just that the two available seats were on opposite sides of the room, or even that the unsanded boards and unvacuumed surfaces made Gus suddenly aware that Jo's dress was clean and pressed and that he should keep his unkemptness at a distance, to avoid dirtying her, or, by flashing a comparison, exaggerating himself.

It was that she worked on a small political magazine with a neat, intelligent format, and he hewed boards to make a crude rectangle (with an inefficiently asymmetrical floor) of dust and splinters, both of which kept his hands unshakable.

They sat tentatively down.

It had been two years since they had seen each other, with only one letter from each exchanged in the interim (and that just after the seeing). Gus flipped through a mental deck of possible opening phrases, rejecting them all, and sat frozen, across the room's immeasurable distance from this unexpected friend.

She had come to see him: it was planned help, accidental help, Karma help; he had merited it or it was a free, predestined, or capricious gift; for or from whatever reason a friend had come and was holding out her hand to him, and that was a melting

"Excuse me," he said, and went into the stripped and gaping bathroom and washed his hands and face.

"Jo," he said

"Good heavens," he said

"It's you," he said

"You're really here," he said

"I can't believe it," he said

"Wait a minute," he said. He wanted her to tell him what had happened to her in the last two years. That first.

He sat still but barely listened, because he was watching Jo's face and body for landmarks, tiny forgotten expressions and expressionless gestures which would connect the stranger sitting here before him now (surprisingly aged) with the other people he had known over the past quarter-century who went by that name and face.

She was describing the present state of the magazine—of which both she and Sam were editors—when he caught the first: her diagonal nostril quiver, followed by a swift pursed-unpursed mouth. He moved from his chair to the floor beside her and asked an encouraging question.

She was in a surface summary of the children—the older boy now a freshman at Yale and the younger in love with his first girl—when her left hand (white, lotioned, soft) moved to her hair, removed a number of strands from the permanented cap, twisted them into a rope and left them there, sticking out of place, when she lowered her hand again. The rope as wound looked the same as that removed from long dirty strands at Vassar; the neat cap disappeared and he saw only the thin fingers and the chosen tress. He offered her coffee and got up to heat it.

"Jo," he said. It was his turn. That he was Gus, she knew

that. That he was building a room inside his room she could see. He couldn't begin, and they sat there, looking at each other.

Her eyes had a limited number of faces—three: one taking the lion's share of her feelings behind itself, the other two splitting the residue. The one was calm. (Calm is a noun.) Most of Jo's thoughts—minutely personal, complex, scrupulously analyzed, bare, quivering, fundamental—were sent out through the topaz glass of calm. The other two were anger and hurt bewilderment, but they were mixed with calm, too —were not pure intense glasses, as if they had been placed over calm without calm having first been removed, which business gave their colors a softer glow.

Pure calm looked at him now, and he wished he had something public to say.

"Since I saw you last I've thought of going back into the academic world," he said.

"Really, Li . . . Gus?" she said.

Ligus he liked. It had a Roman nobility.

"Not recently. Not any more." He looked around the lopsided solid that contained them, to indicate it. "As you see, I'm building this room." And he explained that he would live here until the space beneath the floorboards filled up with dirt—live (he called it that) with the molecules which were bound now in this human shape freed to disperse themselves over the inside of the room according to the natural laws governing particles, or gases, if that was what he became.

In a minute she spoke. "There has never been anyone in my life with whom I felt I could talk as freely as I can with you," Jo said. "I was thinking about that, as you talked, and something just occurred to me. That there are no barriers with you—of self-consciousness, fear of criticism, poses to be kept up, loyalties to be protected. And there's never been another person besides you with whom I could completely relax and say anything I wanted to from any area and know it would be welcome, feel it would be understood or could be explained. And you see, I'm sure it isn't just me who feels that about you; it's your quality—what we would call compassion if we used the word. And so now I wonder, Li–Gus, how you can be so open to other people's needs and so . . . closed, shut up . . . to letting someone help *you*." She paused to light a cigarette. "Do you see? In a sense you are the person I've loved most in my life—excepting the boys, of course, but that is a different kind of thing, and perhaps not excepting Sam, although that too is different. I mean, *I* know that you can trust me, although I don't now understand why you need to build this room, or what your reasons are for wanting to withdraw completely from yourself and everyone else. I wish you would feel that you can trust me, absolutely, to *try* with everything that's in me to understand, and let me help you if I can."

"Jo," he said. He was feeling something he hadn't felt for a long time—the thin beckon of temptation.

"Partly I don't understand it because you have always seemed to me to be such a strong person—you've had plenty to crack up about, more than most, and there are lots of people who break with much less, but I've always thought of you as fundamentally tough—I don't mean in the sense of impervious, far from it; I mean tough in the opposite sense —resilient—which is real toughness, I think, and the ability to grow through whatever happens to you, however painful. One of the things I've always envied about you was your good humor, the way you are always cheerful, laugh at things which would make the average person cry—not because you don't feel them, you obviously feel them very deeply, but out of some wonderful kind of vitality and—*intelligence,* real intelligence, which gives you the ability to stand off and look at the moment of pain with a suprahuman—or just utterly human, the essence of human—perspective. And I've thought too that it is part of your great kindness, involving both a refusal to inflict your suffering on others and a kind of attempt to help others—by example, you know—by showing them that you understand their problems and this is a way, a possible means, because it isn't the merely negative virtue of bearing but is a really courageous facing of things, and learning from them, and sharing them with others in a way which strengthens *them*. I can't tell you what an inspiration you've been to me, many times."

The beacon had peaked and departed. "I no longer care about others," he said.

"I don't believe that. You do care. You are hurt—I don't know how much or by whom or what altogether. . . . I don't know that one can ever know exactly what combination of things brings about a final crisis in someone else, no matter how hard one tries to understand, understanding must be in some sense incomplete—but I know you are very hurt, Li–Gus, and maybe what you need is someone you can trust and someone who can help you. You've helped others; now it's your turn, and I want to try to help you—I want you to try to let me help you, because it would mean a great deal to be able to do something for you."

Gus suggested fixing them both a drink. A glass of wine? Sherry? Jo didn't want anything. In this sense she was not willing to help him at all. He fixed himself a drink, heated the coffee for her.

"Look, Jo. I've had projects from time to time. You know that. Beginning, I suppose, with the Thomas Wolfe project when we were freshmen. I was determined to become a belching concordance of the indigestible Tarheel, as you must remember." (Beginning at birth, he thought; the project myself. How build a man not allowed to be a man?) "So how is Sam? You didn't tell me."

"Sam . . . well, I don't know . . . something happened, you see. A crisis, in a way. You know I have always respected Sam, his integrity, even when we didn't get along ourselves or agree about things concerning the boys, but last year Sam got involved in something to do with the magazine —something financial—that almost made me lose respect for him altogether. It *was* a crisis, really. His position was simply unethical; frankly, dishonest. It was a terrible shock to me because I could never have believed Sam would do such a thing, for money. But maybe I shouldn't tell you . . ."

"No, go ahead, Jo. I've always seen that weakness in Sam —greed, really—and wondered how you could . . ."

"You did?" Hurt bewilderment slipped its glass over calm. "I thought you liked Sam or I never would have begun the story." Hurt bewilderment was snatched away and the thin disk of anger covered calm. "Of course I can't tell you about it now."

She was going and Gus frantically grabbed for her to pull her back. "Jo, I didn't mean that. I do like Sam, and always have. There was just a strain—not a weakness, even, just an edge. . . . Please go on, Jo. It's just that it's hard to see you unhappy and resist the temptation sometimes to blame Sam. Greed was too strong. That slipped out. Somebody else said that; I didn't."

Calm said, "It doesn't matter. I'm not angry at you. But I'd rather not tell you right now; you can understand that. Besides, there are the boys, and I wouldn't want to do anything to change their picture of him." (There was a cigarette to be lit here.) "Are you . . . seeing anyone, in particular?"

"No."

"I'm sorry. I hoped . . . look, maybe I will have a drink, to celebrate our meeting again. Two years is a long time. Do you ever see Junius?"

"The children, the couple next door, occasionally Jamie —I don't think I knew Jamie when I last saw you. That's all." He began to feel the reproach of childhood, to be faced with neighborhood gangs and just-met or could-be-met or why-don't-you-go-meet children endless children, and he looked away. The map of the world was reflected on the shadings of her face. "Maybe I will have a party for you, though. A few friends." A half-dozen names or faces emerged as pins on the desert of his own face, pricking him. "Just people you would like. I hope. I will. Jo, I'll do that— for Saturday."

Gus was humming. Hattie noticed it first.

"I'll say one thing, when you do start having a party you sure become a party-giving Jessie."

"It isn't a party, Hattie. These are just my friends. Have you ever allowed yourself the exquisite luxury of inviting just those people you really love to come to dinner, whether they even know each other or not?"

"No sir. Most of the people I love are coupled with the people I don't, and they all know each other very well."

From the window on the north, Gus watched the people running to catch one of the New York Transit Authority's buses, standing at a bus stop on his side of the street but toward the end of the block. By looking to his left (this necessitated leaning out the window) toward the other end of the block from the bus, Gus could see the beginning of the protagonist's action—the decision, as he looked up and saw the bus waiting, whether to try to catch it before it departed. During the decision, the mind involved would have to weigh the chances of catching the bus and thus being sped toward his destination (the positive value of going on this bus instead of the following one) against the possibility that he would just miss the bus, even if he ran, or would miss it (it would pull off) somewhere between his present position and the end of the block. If it left almost immediately, only a few running steps would have been wasted; but suppose it waited until he was right up to the door (the negative value of anxiety, frustration, embarrassment, to be weighed—we are stuck with that word—against the forementioned positive one).

The present man, in the summer suit of a real estate broker, made a quick decision and ran. As he passed beneath Gus he quickened his running; as he entered the last third of the block he accelerated his pace again. He would make it. He had handled the entire situation with a smoothness that made Gus dislike him. The man's relief was superior as he boarded the bus, looking behind him to see if others, slower in deciding to run or less fleet of foot, would be left behind.

Gus turned his head back to the far left. (Actually, the whole process necessitated leaning out the window, except for the middle action which, since it took place directly beneath Gus's window, permitted a slight indrawing of the head, or, more than slight, sufficient even to enable one to say that one did not have to *lean* out the window—even so, the effort required to change one's position was not justified by the brevity of the time one was allowed to remain in the changed position.) A woman was standing there, in a dress and stockings. She was on the borderline between the age when one ran and the age when one did not run. She hesitated; perhaps she had forgotten which age she belonged to. She looked at the bus and then down at her person. She had on shoes, it is true, with a slight heel, but not really enough to impede running; she was carrying no parcels; she had a handbag which hung on a strap—the optimal handbag for running. She looked back at the bus, her face cleared, and she started into a kind of run—the female lope belonging to the borderline years. Just under Gus's window (a stroke of luck!) she dropped back to a walk, a rapid walk, still anxiously watching the bus. He looked down on her head, brown with some gray and handled by beauty shops. He had an impulse and threw a kiss down on its crown. Just beyond his window, she broke again into a lope; a little farther on, walked; and just before reaching the bus, her head up, she blew her reserves and moved her feet rapidly in short running steps at the same time raising a hand to the driver, who could perhaps see her through the open door, to wait for her, she was coming; she breathlessly boarded.

Gus turned his head back to the far left. This time an aging beatnik stood at the starting line. His face up, he saw the bus, made a quick bearded decision, and ran. He ran fast. He laughed all the way to the bus (with nonlaughing breaks to catch his breath). He waved and shouted. He made it easily. On the steps, still grinning, he looked back at the sidewalk audience, flooding them with his embarrassment. Perhaps he wondered if he had gotten it all across—the full meaning of the human being running to catch a bus. It was a Zen thing; only a few could understand. Reluctantly he disappeared inside.

Gus turned his head back to the far left. On its way, however, he felt the shadow of someone behind him, and instead of letting his gaze go in the path of the tennis ball he held it to the racket and turned his head around in the curve of the follow-through.

"Jo." He stood up and came inside. "I was just watching people running to catch the bus. The bus never goes anywhere, you see." Jo's eyes were yellow this morning, matching a yellow cotton suit with a lively white collar.

"What bus?"

Gus led with his body and pointed with his arm to persuade her to the window. The yellow was too crisp to touch. "See? It's a New York Transit Authority bus, and it has a number, but it just stands there. People get on it, people see it standing there and think it's just leaving and run to catch it (and they all make it) but it never goes. You'll see, it'll be there this afternoon. And tomorrow."

Jo looked with her own eyes, not trusting him. She turned her head to the left and saw a mother with two shaggy-haired boys running for the corner. She took in the situation in a few seconds, and pulled her face away in a refusal to watch. To Gus she wanted to say, "You're crazy," and couldn't. "It's crazy," she said. "You mean it really just stands there? Why?"

"I don't know why."

"But what do the people do, the ones who sit there waiting for the bus to go?"

"They get off, sooner or later. They all get off after different intervals, and say different things about it. Some ask each other what's happening. No one knows. They slip off or stamp off or hump off, by the front door or the back. You can sometimes tell how they'll get off by watching the way they get on. It's not a bad game. They get off, others get on." Gus too turned away from the window, although one of his favorites had appeared at the corner and looked at the bus: a twelve-year-old girl, chewing gum, with her money in her hand. He wanted to bet that she would walk the length of the block at a rebelliously natural pace.

"You didn't have this painting the last time I saw you, did you?" Jo stood with her hands clasped behind her back the better to view a painting. "Look." She sat down. "I want to call Bitsy while I'm here. If she can, why don't we all go out to lunch?"

"Go out?" Gus sat down on the other end of the couch, facing her, returning her calm yellow look briefly, then meeting it with a questioning one of his own. "What do you mean, go out?"

Jo's face bent toward the ashtray where a long white fore-finger repeatedly tapped her cigarette, gracelessly as a young girl awkwardly learning to smoke. Her mouth pursed, un-pursed. She frowned. "I just don't see the point of it, Li–Gus. It's almost as if you've made a pact with yourself and now you won't break it no matter what. Do you remember when I first met you, the pledge I'd made—to a Catholic God—not to drink until I was twenty-one? And then I no longer be-lieved in God, but since I had taken the pledge when I *did*—in faith—I felt it was somehow still binding? Do you remem-ber that?" A long drag from the cigarette here, thin fingers held whitely stiff, unstained, still unaccustomed.

He reached across to touch her hand. "Jo, do you know that you still smoke like you'd just learned how? Do you know that?" He laughed. An instant touch again before he withdrew his hand. "I'd forgotten that." The smile slowly contracted back. "Of course I remember. Maybe I was wrong to laugh at your logic then. Maybe the vow was still binding. I knew a lot."

"You *weren't* wrong! Don't you see? I was tied up by *words* I had said to *myself* and you were looking at what *was*. There is no reason for you not to go out of the house at twelve, and come back into the house at three. Come back and stay in, for that matter."

He got up and walked over to the bus-focused window and dropped the blind, shutting out half the room's day. "The light hurts my eyes, Jo." He turned back and faced her. In the half-light her round white face regained its seventeen-year-old prettiness, dark blonde hair curling around it in soft secure waves. "The sun in my eyes makes me sneeze. Did I ever tell you that? It always has. If I open my eyes and the sun is shining, I start sneezing. I keep on sneezing—in series of threes, of course. There is another thing that makes me sneeze: looking at myself naked and even thinking about myself naked. I've been outside, and sneezed, and looked in mirrors and sneezed, and thought and sneezed. Now I don't do any of the three. I no longer sneeze. Put it that way."

Jo sighed and crushed out the cigarette, every last spark of it. "You make it sound like I don't respect your feelings, —Gus. I always have."

"Now, Jo, of course I know you respect my feelings." Gus pulled up a smile of charm from an earlier era. "You know I know that." He turned to face the painting, his arms hanging straight down. Black water streaked with off-black green swirling beneath a black bridge. There were streaks of yellow intermerged but he kept all light away from the painting so the yellow winked in vain like freckles on an African nose. Rain-ready sky or soot-blackened land stretched beyond the bridge. "Do you like the painting?"

"Well, I don't know. I can certainly understand the mood you were in when you bought it," she laughed.

He turned to look at her. A streak of sun from the un-blinded window caught the yellow of her dress and the tip of one back curl. Twenty-five years ago he had briefly held her, awkwardly conscious of two female softnesses coming to-gether. She had been deeply shaken by something too horri-ble to speak, and could only sob that she was hideously tainted inside and ought to kill herself. He had comforted her then and felt strange, and guessed the obvious possibilities. To these she shook her head, and could not tell him.

"Jo, do you remember that day when you came into the room at Vassar and said you were too evil to live? You never told me; could you now? What was bothering you?"

"Oh, that. Yes. Well, it doesn't seem quite so traumatic any more; as you can see, I'm still alive." She opened her purse and closed it again. "Look, I'll tell you someday. Not right now." She held two white gloves in an awkward hand and disparaged them with a kind of smile. "White gloves," she said ruefully, and meant that she never thought she would be bowing to *that* nice New Jersey girl convention.

He leaned out the uncovered window and watched her walk away, into a lunch with Bitsy. He followed her loose, swinging figure down the block (she took a direction which led her away from the still-stopped bus), seeing it blend and weave through other swings of red or white or aquamarine, capable, at any moment, of stopping and exchanging hellos if an unexpected acquaintance was threaded this way. Hellos and goodbyes.

It was after eleven when Gus came downstairs to coffee more bitter than early medicine. A scant cup was left in the pot. It rose in a boil before he turned it off; abruptly it descended, leaving its scum in a ring two inches above coffee level. The acrid smell flared his nostrils; the first swallow drew his mouth, flailed his stomach. He drank all of it.

Since he had the kitchen to himself, he made another pot of coffee and ate a piece of last night's pie. Lemon meringue —sharp, tangy, excessive sweetness. He ate another smaller slice, leaving the last piece. As in the past, he thought, the last piece will stay in the icebox until someone throws it out, finally, spoiled; because he would not eat it, thinking Dinah might want it, and she would not eat it in order to save it for Hattie. And Hattie would think of Alice's midnight sweet tooth and desist herself. Although from day to day one of them would pare away a small slice to taste, so that by the time the week was out and the spoiling complete there would not be the same portion-sized piece left at all but merely a fraction of it; nevertheless there had to be something to throw out. As an offering to prove that they loved each other, were not gluttons, could sacrifice?

He reopened the icebox and took out the plate with its last piece of pie. Deliberately he placed his fork squarely across the point, cut through, put the bite in his mouth. It was too sweet now and he did not want it. He took another bite, then another, eating quickly so as not to feel the discomfort of his already full stomach until he was through. He scraped up the last remaining filling and flakes with his fork, licked them off, and put the plate into the sink.

The party. He found a cookbook and sat back down, turning its pages, scanning its enthusiastic recipes hoping for an inspiration as to what to have to eat. Dishes from past parties marched across his mind like Macbeth's kings: baked ham & potato salad (16), beef & kidney stew (19), chicken curry (22), oyster stew (25), steak packed in salt (29), beef Stroganoff (33), shrimp in beer (37), hash & grits (39). Since then nothing.

Tonight? Beef Bourguignonne? Chicken breasts & apples?

He thought of all the women in New York who loved to do this sort of thing, and all the men who had them as wives. Then he thought of all the men in New York who loved to do this sort of thing.

"Hi, Daddy." Alice came through the door with a thin eel-like girl whose name he thought was Sandra. "Daddy, you know Sharon." Alice opened the icebox door, scrutinized its interior. "Who ate the last piece of pie?"

"Of course, hello, Sharon. I did."

"You did? Daddy, how could you?"

"I'm sorry, honey. Did you want it?"

"No, of course not, but I wanted to save it for *you.* Do you mind if we make a cake?"

He left the kitchen to them, and the cookbook.

Back in his room, he was made aware again of the curious thing that had happened within him since Jo's visit. He had conversations with her—usually himself in front of a mirror, but sometimes sitting in a chair, and for at least an hour after he was in bed at night. He talked to her, talking for her when it was required that she say something. Out loud? He was talking out loud now, he noticed, although not loud. He was whispering. He watched himself and saw that the whisper remained, even when it sank so close to the threshold of silence that no ear could hear it. A sharp-eared brother in a bed a foot away couldn't have heard it, but it was still a whisper, or at least his lips moved and his tongue and helpers formed the actual words.

He was trying to explain to Jo that he really didn't care. "Because I know you think," he whispered, "that I won't hold out my arms for help—whether from pride or fear of dependence or what. But the fact is that I don't want help. I don't want to come back to life, but to get farther away from it. The motive power is lacking. I don't bring you my problems for us to talk out together, hoping to get some relief from the discomfort they cause me——because I don't want to solve my problems . . ."

"You have children," Jo whispered.

Of course you have to say that, Gus thought in silence. Everybody does. Do they really mean anything by the phrase, or is it just evoked as a formula because they feel a duty to save me; despair at finding a real reason throws them back on fundamentals. "Hoping to strike a childhood chord?" he whispered back. "I am aware that I have children, and also aware that they thrive under qualified professional care—*thrive*, I mean; grow in a way that they can't, hampered by me. I don't give them up only because I am too selfish; I could not bear the shame of being an unnatural parent in public, so I hide and keep up externals and hope that later physiological discoveries will allow that emotional disturbances can be caused by structural or chemical or electrical aberrations so that, when my children display their neuroses, the public will be sufficiently confused as to be unable directly to lay the blame here. Thus I save my pride. And who can disprove me? Who can re-raise them and do better?"

"You sound like you hate them very much," Jo whispered with a compassion and accuracy that startled him.

Hate them? It does sound so. Perhaps I do—hate all children who are talked to, all people who are free, productive, interinvolved. Otherwise I would let them go. Wouldn't I.

Rebecca looked terrible. Not the day Gus married her, or even the next day, but Monday. She got up that morning and washed her face by throwing water over it with her hands, letting what hair would, get wet. Then she sat back down on her bed beside the table which room service had left a few minutes before. He had not waked her until the table arrived, so she had just gotten up and washed her face and sat back down—that was all she had done so far this morning. She looked terrible.

"How do you feel?" he asked.

"Why? Do I look terrible?"

"Your hair looks like it's been pretty thoroughly slept in."

"Why do you think terrible-looking people look better with their hair combed than with their hair uncombed?" She reached across the table, her half-filled coffee cup in her hand, and emptied its (cold) contents into his cup. It *could* be cold already, for her, so he did not make that remark, and he waited for her remark that *he* liked it cold. She had said that the first time she emptied her second half of a cup of coffee into his cup because it was cold, and she had not said it since. It was the kind of phrase people repeat, usually a number of times, because it helps them establish you as an identity. (Of course they know it irritates you—so slightly that you would consider yourself childish to take note of it, so you say nothing and are left with the slight irritation itself to get rid of somehow.) She didn't say it this time either, and he sat holding the irritation he had prepared in advance to meet the phrase that didn't come.

"For Christ's sake, I didn't say you looked terrible."

"I'm sorry, Gus." Her sardonic look disappeared and she leaned across the multiple coffee equipment to touch his hand. "I'm projecting again. *I* think I look terrible so I imagine that's what you're thinking, even though you didn't say it. And I suppose I'm so used to Mother saying it that I *expect* you to say it so strongly that I am left with the same irritability that I would have if you *had* said it, and react with the same defenses. I am a mess." She squeezed his hand to underline mess. "Help me *stop* projecting."

"Rebecca, you look *terrible*," Mrs. ———— said, often enough, this time at five o'clock of the afternoon they returned from the three-day honeymoon neither of them had wanted. They were putting things away in ninety-five-degree heat. "Why don't you go get cleaned up and I'll get some ice and Gus can fix us a drink?" (It *was* cocktail time.)

"Rebecca, you look *terrible*," Mrs. ———— said. Rebecca was seven months pregnant and it was hot *again*. "I certainly will be glad to see you in something besides those revolting pants, won't you, Gus?"

"She looks just fine to me."

"Oh, *she's* pretty all right—as pretty as she can be because she's Rebecca, but *pregnancy* isn't attractive on *any*body, I don't care what they say."

"Rebecca, you look *marvelous*!" Mrs. ———— said. "Doesn't she look *pretty*, Gus? Isn't it marvelous to have our girl back again?"

Rebecca smiled (he saw her). Alice had been born three

days before. This morning she and their daughter had been brought back from the hospital. Now, at five-thirty (it was cocktail time) she was dressed in pink linen—bursting through pink linen with milk-full breasts and girdle-flattened stomach, her legs slender as a princess from three days in bed and her eyes and skin rich with gloss from internal chemistry.

"Did the doctor say you were supposed to be up on heels and martinis the third day after birth?"

Rebecca had no use for what doctors say—no real use for doctors, because they were men and by profession timid. They were in favor of the *status quo*—one's health yesterday was what they wanted to preserve. She thought and felt that she was hostess to a new health today. Today's health. Exhibiting the height of civilized female on her slender high-heeled legs, she would exhibit also the black-earth health of having dropped her foal and gained strength thereby.

"Fuck me, Gus. Please. You must."

"Rebecca, I know the doctor said . . ."

"Fuck the doctor."

"No."

"*Do.*"

"Does it hurt?"

"Yes. Oh yes. *Darling.*"

Rebecca's depression was extreme. Post partum, the doctor called it. After a month? Over a month? They were in Havana, having cocktails before a sheer glass wall looking over a secret city below. "Cuba is too American on the surface for one to have any clue as to what is going on underneath," she said. "American?" he asked. "Yes." Rebecca ordered a martini this time, because the daiquiri had pulled the inside of her mouth into elasticized felt. "Yes, American. There is neon and chrome and materialism everywhere.

Cokes. Money. Clothes. Blank faces of people who think only about raising their standard of living. Days marked off on calendars to clock improvements, like kids at boarding school crossing off the days before Christmas, or women on diets counting days by pounds lost. Americans mark off days on calendars. No other peoples do, except prisoners. Maybe prisoners of all nationalities do that. But it's only done when one can't live in the present, and it's always done for material things. Americans see time as the building up of a bird's nest, day by day—six months, ah! we've paid so much on the car; two years, at a raise of $12.50 a year, in three more we'll have. . . . Cuba is like that—all we're allowed to see of it. What's going on underneath? Oh, Gus, I feel like crying."

She pulled her hand away and excused herself. The ladies' room, the waiter pointed, was at the far end of the room, just beyond the huge curved stairway which cut its arc out of the belly of the floor. She started past the stairs and stopped a few feet from the banister. Both hands reached out to grasp the banister as she moved in on it and held. The position? He could not tell whether she was pushing herself away from the rail or pulling herself toward it; the tension in her body caught him first and as he stared it seemed that both forces were exerting all their strength and her static body was the result of the pulls in each direction being identical. For a few minutes. He rose and reached her just as a second of fear washed over her face and she let go the railing and fell (or seemed to drop herself) to the floor on her knees. He took her past the stairs to the ladies'-room door, waited for her, and with his arm around her led her past the gutted floor back to their table.

When Alice was six months old, Rebecca arranged to enter Rice Institute (it was then) in the fall for an advanced degree in English.

In April she took the graduate record exam. The night be-
for this exam Gus did not come home or call. She went to
bed early, at ten, hoping to get a good night's sleep (she was
afraid her IQ was shockingly low, around 110 or even 120;
this would have been a blow she could not endure. From her
mother's health prescriptions she respected the value of food
and sleep for higher IQ scores). She lay awake wondering
whether Gus was out with a woman; was drunk and just now
having a serious automobile accident (she listened to every
siren that screamed down Post Oak—a siren-full roadway—
imagining it an ambulance carrying her husband's maimed
body, unfortunately not killed outright), until well past midnight. By one-thirty fear turned to rage. He was deliberately
ruining her IQ score.

The Graduate Record Examination, as it was officially
called, was being given at the University of Houston at ten
o'clock in Room 000 of ——— Hall. Rebecca drove fast because she was late—from a prolonged dressing. Tossing her
hair (clean and bouncing) as she turned away from a bright
asking of directions, she switched down the hall with an
equivalent bounce in her walk and smiled charmingly at the
boy behind the desk.

He began explaining the directions to her, pausing to smile
the first two times she interrupted with a subtle joke, pausing
to look bewildered the third time. Rebecca caught the impli-
cation, and became serious.

"I think I understand," she said. "It seems clear and simple enough. Shall I begin?" She took the booklet and pencil
he handed her. "Who takes these exams?" she asked. "I
mean besides people. . . ." She wondered who the others
were who would score below her, because she had heard that
no one scored below 85 per cent.

Seated in a row by herself, legs crossed and tummy pulled
in flat, she began breezing through page 1.

At noon the boy monitor called time. Quickly she marked one final answer and closed her book. She had finished very little of the math part.

Outside, the sun was hot and colorless, and the heat got between her clothes and skin and antagonized them. A forelock of clean hair fell limp and flat into her face; once it began that it would keep doing it for the rest of the day. He was just a kid, no more than seventeen or eighteen, and I was flirting with him!

He had suggested the Student Union building for lunch but she couldn't find it. That way—straight through those buildings and around to your left. You can't miss it. She walked up the walk of a building through the windows of which she could see tables that looked like someone could eat at them. At the door, after half a dozen boys had turned to look at her (she was a runaway crocodile), she realized this must be a boys' dormitory or fraternity house: there wasn't another female within thirty feet. She backtracked, saying, "I'm sorry you have the wrong house you're sorry—" a sentence the absurdity of which made no difference to anyone but herself since it was said in a mouthed silence only and only to the air.

Back at the main sidewalk, she headed farther into the campus in the presumed direction of the Student Union building. Around a bend she saw another candidate. This time she walked up to a window on the side and peered in. Students milled over the floor, some eating coffee and sandwiches between books. She turned away in tears, imaginary bread clogging her throat. She cried out (silently) in sobs against the choking assault of a sandwich. There were people everywhere, and nowhere she could go to be alone. A passing male voice called, "Cheer up, baby!" She screamed silently back: Leave me alone! I'm twenty-eight and have a baby! Her own skin through tears swam uncertainly, like soft bread in the doughy sunlight. There were a thousand student looks defending the path over which she'd come. She lowered her head and began running until she reached the parking lot and found her car and locked herself inside its airless pocket and wept, safe for an hour from the world persecuting and mocking her because she was ugly.

Rebecca took to Rice like a duck takes to ducking. She was thin, stylish, electric. She wore rectangular glasses with gold wire frames. Her hair was short (cut for the Institute). Gus's brother Eric commented hugely, "You really look great, baby."

Rebecca nodded. "It's the clothes. They're expensive. None of them are made in America, you see. Not *is*. Purists are as far out of fashion as Puritans. So far out they're in again. Have some gin."

"So what goes on out at Big R these days?"

"A boy held the door open for me, and when I thanked him, he said, 'You're welcome, ma'am.' "

"They're afraid of you."

"Not yet!"

"What have you done there so far?"

"I wrote a paper and it was brilliant. None of them can write; graduate students can't. They told me it was so well written it could be published. I said that I was opposed to commas and personally hoped they disappeared from literature, and they looked at me as if it were important."

Rebecca was charming, although it doesn't sound so. The things she said were really insufferably rude, conceited, callous, and oblivious of or deliberately wounding to other people's feelings. How then could she get away with it? These things were preceded by a smile, an expression that denied the sentiment to come, and followed by a face that said, oh what a terrible thing that is to say; if the smile of denial didn't work, the apology could. Usually neither worked in the sense that anyone believed one or the other, but both together worked in a different way: their direct contradiction of each other amusing the listener, and most listeners forgave for that.

Everyone was amused by Rebecca, but—Eric was right— they were also afraid of her, so they stood apart and watched. She had an enormous circle of friends, but they were formed in a semicircle around her performance (or, to keep the word *circle,* make her theater in the round). This too kept her sometimes cruel wit from cutting. It was said she could charm the eyelashes off a gnat at twenty feet. Few gnats came closer.

Except Eric. His brown physical stringiness wrapped itself around whatever part of her he could entrap, and consistently insisted that she was really a woman.

"Let your stomach stick out, baby. You've had a baby. Advertise that softness. Have you ever cried?"

Rebecca laughed and put her other leg up on the table, crossing it over the one already there. "I cry when I play Medea."

"Who's Medea?" asked Betty, Eric's pretty wife.

"The goal of all women, darling. She was a barbarian and a sorceress and she had magic, and when Jason left her because she grew ugly she killed his children. A brilliant revenge, considering the circumstances under which children are conceived. When she was beautiful he desired her; now that he no longer desired her she was no longer beautiful. She would destroy the products of that desire. It is unbearable to see reminders of one's beautiful era walking about calling 'Mother' as if to mock. It is shame, because he did not now desire her. No woman can bear to be ugly, don't you agree? Think now, Betty—isn't that feeling at the root of all your depressions?" She turned to Eric. "Medea couldn't cry."

"How do you know that, Rebecca?" When she was serious, Betty seemed a child. When she was laughing, or commenting on the fate of being married into the ———— family (blessed are they who expect nothing, for they shall not be disappointed), she sprayed the wisdom of an old Irishwoman, but when she really wanted to know something, she let everyone see how little she did know and how hard it was for her to think in grown-up probity. "You're not ugly."

Rebecca stood up and delivered her speech from the sink, turning to minister to her drink when she needed a punctuating action. "You're right, Betty! Of course! That's the whole point. If I were ugly, I would have accepted it by now; or if I were beautiful. It's just this middle ground, this being slightly homely, plain, uninteresting-looking—just this just-missing being pretty—that causes all the trouble. Because then you see I hope, and I try—I take tweezers and pull out hundreds of hairs to change my hairline because I've decided, ah, there's the trouble; you'd be pretty, Rebecca, if you just didn't have such a low forehead, and it works. For a day or so (hour or so) I'm pretty. Then I think, no, it isn't the forehead really, it's your mouth. It's too thin. As a child I remember during the long automobile trips we used to take, I discovered that the little vent window in the front seat became a mirror when the sun shone at a certain angle—an odd triangular mirror in which I could see the lower part of my face, mouth and chin. I looked there and practiced holding my upper lip up, spreading it upward until my mouth took on the contours of the most voluptuous mouth on any Hollywood face. I was wildly pleased at such easy success, and thought, There! Now I'm pretty. It was the mouth that was wrong." Rebecca laughed. "Then that fall we had our annual pictures taken, and of course I wore my new mouth. I hadn't considered that the vent window was a small mirror, good for detail only. I could see my mouth, but not the rest of my face. The spread lips were there in the photograph, all

right, but they caused a queer contortion of my nose—drew
it up like this, spreading the nostrils as if I were smelling an
extraordinarily repulsive smell. I was mortified when I saw
the proofs. Everyone else jeered. 'Where'd you get that *face?*'
they laughed. But that's the trouble. One has to be just near
enough to being pretty to long to be, and to believe a man
when he says 'You're beautiful,' but far enough to know, always, underneath, that it's a lie." Rebecca hit two ice cubes
hard against the sink to separate them and fixed a brutal
drink. "Christ, I feel like crying. *Now.*" She turned and sat
back down. "There you are, Eric. A near tear."

Tuesday Rebecca read her paper to the seminar. It was
morning when she got up that day, early morning. Through
multiple glass she described the air outside, soft, hazy, the
tiny leaves of the water oak threading through it, whispering,
birds calling clear notes through a day still unbegun, yet beginning to be begun; she could hear other noises of trucks on
the highway and someone feeding the horses next door; abstract morning dwarfing the day's activities in advance with
its overcloak of air and trees and birds. She felt she had
never seen beauty but this.

Her paper was subtle, of course. The question: was one to
take Sidney's *Defense of Poetry* seriously (i.e., as his literal
belief). Granting him wit—soldier, poet, scholar, lover, darling of Elizabethan courtiers—could one compare the situation there, then, with the position in which a similar man
found himself during the McCarthy Red-baiting trials. Rebecca herself never insisted upon meaning what she said; it
was natural that she should pull Sidney over to her corner.
The heavy hand of sincerity had shouted at her from American classrooms all her life. You mean it, you care, you are
expressing what *you* really see (in your own words); it was
a merit badge and it proved that you could *feel*.

In Sidney's sixteenth century, thick clumsy tongues were

accusing poetry of being a painted fantasy sent to delude men into chasing evil (although extraordinarily beautiful) chimeras and thus departing the paths of virtue. What is virtue? Then it was easy to define; you could tell it anywhere by its dress. Whatever was brown, thick, stiff, heavy, covering, and similar was good. Heaven was presented in increasingly strident colors as the shadow of the medieval church retreated and the sunlight shone in ever larger patches on the world itself. (These tints here, we see them for the first time, are alive with brilliance!) *No.* If anyone thinks the color he sees in the early haze of morning is extraordinary, it is only a shadow of the beauty it reflects, eternal beauty. (Fantastic shadow!) *No.* Look away. Turn your eyes up, up, up. (How can we tell the road to heaven?) You can't miss it: wherever you see people with burdens of flesh bending their backs, with breath pulled in through wads of cotton, with scratched and groundward eyes—that's the way.

Sidney said: I have seen beauty tame more often than curses. As wise mothers slip a taste of sugar into the bitter stuff they give their children to make them well, so poets know that virtue painted in pleasing colors will tempt those to listen (unaware) and drink in the healthful moral tale and be healed before they are aware of what is happening and have time to stick out their tongues and refuse. If one adds up the score he will find that many more have been persuaded in this slippery way to look on virtue and learn than have been frightened into it by bitter words and threats of stumbling rocks.

Sidney said this, and Rebecca could not believe that he was serious. Her mother had often claimed that happy people are better people. Happiness therefore is something one should strive for in order to be virtuous. As beauty in its own right? Shhh. Let beauty come in through whatever trickery it can. As the Catholic Church had learned long ago, go with the rules of whatever game is being played, and slip your inestimable treasure in through any available door. Beauty is important; defend it by whatever lies are necessary. If they are in love with moral precepts, make a case for beauty's power to seduce to virtue. If later they fall in love with money, tell them that a man who comes home to a beautiful painting restores himself and is stronger to make more money the next day. If with science, show them that the conscious mind with its pencil and paper figuring comes to a quicker and truer result when it does not suppress the thirst for beauty pressing tirelessly from underneath.

Sidney, a clever man, knew that his client's life was all that mattered; he would defend her on whatever terms would be accepted. See his tongue in cheek! ". . . . . ." How could one help but see that he was laughing at them all.

Rebecca's face began to crack and she could see herself from the position of that student at the far corner: white morning light turning orange the blush foundation which had covered her mottling skin according to golden bathroom bulbs; black mascara standing harsh and glossless over blood-streaked eyes. She pulled in her eyes. But my eyes used to be beautiful. Used to be, used to be; used now and dead. You are old. Beauty, her voice rasped. Sidney knew that it must be preserved at all costs, by any necessary lies. But clever lies. Her voice became sharp and firm with conviction: examples abounded from the dead advocate's silver writing. A man who (a later paper will demonstrate) knew Greek and probably read Aristotle in the original (see reference) did not know what he was doing when he wrote this line? Its double meaning slaps you in the face.

Her double meaning. My duplicity. I have become Sidney and will only let him out through the cramped glass of myself. I ingest him and shine him out to you through what looks like flawless plate; look at this glass in a careful light, though, and see the imperfections swarming like bacteria on a slide.

A black high-necked jersey blouse through which breasts pulled too high butted like jacked-up tires giving the illusion of solidness. Soft squishy breasts pushed into the shape of a youthful bra (of necessarily heavy cotton) standing rocklike, unnatural shelf. Sidney had grace. *I* am ugly.

Beauty. She spit him out all at once and got inside of him. Her mind whirred on dexedrine. See what he means, this paragon. At least poetically in love with another man's wife, and writing sonnets to *her* beauty—does anyone believe these were written to win men to virtue? *Yes. This* is virtue, being in love with a physical woman. But Sidney, in talking to the poetasters, need not add that when he uses the word *virtue* he may mean a different thing from what they mean. Let those who choose take it in the old heavy sense; they will lose and deserve it. None can accuse him of lying. But Sidney knew from looking around the world that what passes by common consent as the way things are isn't enough for the lover of beauty. He turned to the world to find a structure to hang his poetry on, then wrote the line: Fool, said my muse to me/ Look in thy heart, and write.

Rebecca's own heart was huge as a seed caught between the teeth. She felt it there, stuck between the ribs of her chest cavity, a petrified lump which a little probing could dislodge and flick out. Dry, dry; the blood had gone to her brain and she was strong. She was within Sidney now, and safe. She was in fact so safe that she could let herself go soft inside; there were no holes in this dead giant through which sticks could poke and tease. She thought of sending a measure of blood back down, to float the pebble free and soak it full again. Her eyes, behind Sidney's eyes, turned then and looked back at her own face: flat, bulbous, frowning. All their poems were in praise of women's beauty; I am ugly. I hide here inside Sidney so that he can't see that. Be smart, then! Don't worry, pet, my father used to say; beauty is only skin deep. But ugliness drives through to the heart and freezes from the center outward.

"Your voice, Rebecca!" Wayne said. "You must know how beautiful it is. The paper was brilliant, but we all expected that. But it wouldn't have mattered if it hadn't been; I could have listened to your voice forever."

"Really?" She didn't know that. "I thought I talked too softly, mumbled; that I was hard to understand. Gus complains."

"I heard every word. It is deep, your voice, with body, and a strange mixture of accents—no one stands out, but they all play against each other and mingle and smooth each other. I've never heard a voice like it."

Wayne was beautiful, with his sandy raw Texas thinness and his eyes faded to white-blue as if parched by the flat prairie endlessly reflecting sun. "Do you have time for coffee?"

"You are going on, aren't you? I mean, to get your doctorate." Wayne drank coffee with extra milk and it was the color of mud in the Mississippi and curiously blended with his beige skin. He was no taller than she, but his knees in khaki pants stood bony, not covered with fat. She pulled down the too-tight skirt.

"Should I?"

"Should you!" He laughed at her laugh. "You know you should. You have to." His hand reached to pat her knee, pulled back. "Sidney needs you," he laughed again.

Coffee black in a paper cup with wax floating across its instant surface. "Couldn't they use hot-drink cups? For a dime, you would think. This coffee couldn't possibly cost them more than a couple of cents. In fact I bet they get it free. They powder coffee grounds they salvage from old garbage cans."

"Look, I remember when there was no coffee here at all. Just a basement."

"I think I would rather go somewhere else besides Rice," she said. "You know, being a woman. Something happens to women who go through a men's school—on the graduate level, anyway. They begin to wonder whether they're really women at all. You know, they are competing with men and working with them and as a result they begin to take on masculine traits. To maintain the dress and trappings of women confuses them when, in a seminar, they speak angrily to a sexless academic point. So the ones I've seen drop that and become gray. You've seen them."

"I don't think *you* need to worry about that."

Rebecca froze like an African cat. "What is the thing—you know, it isn't conventional—that you find in certain people that makes you suddenly make contact with them? It's usually sexual, but it doesn't have to be, I don't think. But you must have felt it—a quickening in your pit, a stab of another person getting through, and from that moment you turn on when this person is around. From what particular thing do you usually receive it?"

"I know what you mean. The most beautiful woman in the world may not have it, and you look at her face and agree that she is beautiful and then you turn away because her beauty doesn't matter. Then suddenly someone you hadn't noticed before, or thought much of, does something . . . yes, I know what you mean. But I have to like the person, I think. It follows, with me, something that the person does which is special, a smile which brings back the tenderness a child feels when his mother kisses him goodnight, and then that person is utterly desirable."

"So was your mother." Rebecca's eyes sparkled.

"I didn't mean that."

"Yes you did." She laughed and they became glinting silver. They shone through him. "It's the eyes with me," she said. "A look in the eyes, of fire, excitement—a look that penetrates into me and makes me burn. The person can be ugly as virtue itself, but if he has these eyes . . ."

His face drew back. He stared. He turned to drain the last mud from his cup and looked at the clock. "Almost five. I must be getting home."

"Look," she reached for him. "You don't have to go yet. Let's go somewhere and have a beer. I'm sick of this coffee. I need a beer. Can't you call Louise and tell her you'll be a little late?"

Wayne picked up his books and got up. "No, I have to go. I'm grocery shopping on the way home. Have you read this yet?" He held out Tillyard's *The Elizabethan World Picture*. "I've only read a few pages. It's brilliant."

"Tillyard's an ass." She got up too.

"Oh, do you think so? He beats his own drum, of course, and sometimes too loudly, but he knows an enormous amount. Which way are you going? I'll walk you to your car. All of them do that, I think. It's an occupational hazard that comes from concentrating so much on one small area of scholarship. I know what you think"—he held the door open for her and she stepped into the friendless five-o'clock dusk. "You want more comparative literature courses. Stratify graduate schools horizontally, not vertically."

"It's the way the world was, at least in the sixteenth century . . ." her voice faded thin into the heavy smoked air. "Goodbye, Wayne. See you tomorrow."

Like a blunt mole she crept along the smoothly oiled freeway slipping home in the homebound stream. The air itself was so choked with gray moisture that her tears stood over her eyes, filling them with a magnifying and wavering drop of liquid. Five o'clock was the hour she could not bear. Lights were turned on in living rooms and she looked through their windows and saw a red overstuffed chair waiting, a table set, stoves merrily bubbling and a pretty wife in a pretty dress patting a dog and hugging little children and waiting with tenderness on her lips for a rougher tenderness who would be here any minute, who would fill the house. . . . She laughed and blinked and heard Gus say, The houses look like that from the road, but if you were inside them you would be looking out at you and all these cross ugly cars and how would that be? To be inside me looking out is to spare me the pity of being outside me looking here. That is the consolation of five o'clock. To be with the worms on the road is not to be in the houses looking out at them. My mother drew the curtains, Gus. We lived on a street with trees and looked across into other windows, but even so she drew the red brocade draperies across our living room and shut all that warmth inside. He came home, then. He went upstairs and went to bed and shouted for quiet from an upstairs window.

He was a sick man.

But that's not why I killed him. I killed him because he never kissed me.

Insatiable female child, glutting yourself on fantasies no amount of stuffing could sate. Dainty southern ladies, comparing the size of the white stick with the black one by measuring them into yourself like the thrust of the oil gauge discovers the depth of that black liquid. Wipe it off, then *in,* pull out, wipe off, the other *in,* pull out wipe off, *in* out, *in* out, *in* out. *Stop.*

But that is brilliant, she said. That is a brilliant image.

Cruel, competitive, crude.

Brilliant. And *I* dare say it!

Her own driveway, freckled with white shell, curved

through scrubby pines another woman had miserably tended.
Inside lights glowed through the lattice of the window; blue
and yellow and orange smeared a clean boxlike room. Dinah
was there, and Alice laughing in her high chair. "Where's
Gus?" she said.

"Daddy's not home, Mommy. *Look* at what I . . ."

She fixed them frozen fish sticks and canned peas, and a
halved slice of bread full of preservatives and air, spread with
oily margarine. Milk in silver cups, each child her own, given
just after birth and still waiting to be taken to be engraved.
She gave Dinah a bath and ached at the time it took and its
wetness. She put Alice and a plastic bottle (cold now that she
was older) into the crib whose ribs Dinah had smeared with
her poohpooh every afternoon at nap time, on a contour
sheet tearing at the foot end of the mattress where it didn't
matter because Alice's feet didn't get that far. She read
Dinah a story from an A & P Treasure Book she had reached
for and been given during this morning's shopping—a story
of See, Jane plays with her doll on the front porch and combs
her hair to get her ready for Daddy when he comes home.
Look, Johnny in his red wagon stands at the edge of the front
walk and watches for Daddy. Blackie watches too, and wags
his tail. There, a bus stops at the corner, and Daddy gets off.
Johnny and Blackie run to meet him. He picks up Johnny but
he does not pick up Blackie. He puts Johnny down and goes
up the front steps. Jane holds her doll out to be kissed, then
drops the doll and holds out her own arms. Mother is fixing
dinner inside. Daddy is hungry because he has worked very
hard today. Mother sees that Johnny and Jane wash their
hands, and then dinner is ready. See, they are sitting at the
table. Their faces are serious and turned slightly down, so
you can see them as bowing their heads and saying grace if
that is the kind of home you have, or as just appreciating the
warmth of food and being together if it isn't. If you have any

other kind of home, read another kind of book. After dinner, Daddy kisses Mother to thank her and goes out to the garage to get his tools and fix Johnny's wagon. The wheel is loose. Jane helps Mother with the dishes. . . . *Stop.*

Rebecca went back to the kitchen and got out ice and fixed herself a drink. It was eight o'clock. She went into the bathroom and looked in the wall-hung mirror stretching the length of the double basins set in white formica. Pretty, pretty, pretty, you're pretty, it said. She turned sideways and stood on tiptoes. Slender waist and lovely hips and breasts high and girlish. She looked more closely and saw her skin drying from all-day makeup. She took a bath—hurry, hurry, he will be home any minute—a quick bath, a total bath. Rubbed with blue lotion and glowing with rouge and moisturized foundation and exotic now in the nighttime mascara, she dressed in pink wool pants and a matching pink silk shirt. Very expensive. You can't wear pink unless it's very expensive. Thin. You're too thin, the mirror complained. She looked at her small round buttocks curved like a child's just the right size to be cupped by matching hands. Not too thin, she said. She put on a wide black elastic belt with a mockantique silver buckle. It looked cheap and she wouldn't wear it outside the house, but it drew her waist in to where it was before the baby had spread it, and she no longer looked too thin at all.

" She fixed another drink and sipped it. Any minute. The great chain of being, indeed. She could flatten Tillyard in a paragraph. He didn't know how to use language. He had no sense of when the phrase he chose was ludicrous. He was an easy target, holding his own bull's-eye right up to the point of her tongue.

She fixed another drink and felt the glow leave her face and its skin slow down and pull at her flesh, irritating it.

Her face was cracked and dry and the pink pants wrinkled

and her stomach rolled out softly beneath the cinching elastic belt, not in one round curve but in tiny rolls like snakes children make from clay. She went into her study and began writing about Tillyard, and Sidney.

Tires mashed shell and a car door slammed shut. Then another car door.

"Hi, darling."

"No, come on in, Eric," Gus said. "Rebecca's not mad. Are you mad, honey?" He kissed her clumsily. Fumes of whisky blew out of him as from a giant bellows. "We've had a couple of drinks and I'm sorry I'm late. I'm sorry, sorry, sorry. Always a bastard."

"Better to be than father. Eric, let me fix you a drink."

Eric put the two arms of his bellows around her. "He's a son of a bitch, to keep a wife like you waiting. A real tool. Ummmmmmh." He cupped her cuppable buttocks. "Betty'd sulk all evening."

Gus lumbered over to the sink and mixed two elephantine drinks and set them on the table and himself at it. "Yep, I'll say that for my old sweetheart, she doesn't nag."

"It's because I'm afraid to." She stood at the open door of the refrigerator, peering inside. "My image of myself is at stake. Here, you boys need something to eat, if I have to talk to you." She put a tray of Camembert and crackers and Velveta for Gus on the table. "We also have a superb dinner of beef Stroganoff. You have to eat it."

Booming male voices filled the room and Rebecca was happy. *This* was noise. Not the tinsel sounds of graduate students or the tissue-paper talk of the men she had something in common with, but this crude drumbeat of drunks whose combined flesh quadrupled her own. She had a quicker, stronger drink and glowed.

Elliot and his newest wife (she was Mexican and had a name that was spelled like Alicia but pronounced in some

other way) dropped in between parties. They stayed just long
enough to have a drink and do the *bomba* (their variation
of). Eric kissed Alicia goodbye, his hands reaching back in
an effort to cup her uncuppable buttocks. He cupped her
breasts instead (almost as far from being cups as the buttocks). He howled. She squealed and laughed.

Alicia said, "Where is that marvelous baby, Rebecca?
God, she's so beautiful! I could hold her for*ever*."

"Do you like babies, Alicia?"

"I *love* babies." She made a pucker face. "But I can't have
babies."

"Why can't you have babies?"

"It's because you wiggle."

"Eric!" She squealed again.

They left.

Rebecca put the beef Stroganoff and candles on the table,
and they ate.

"And she can cook!" Eric flicked her with his eyes. "A re-
markable girl. A real pepper."

"You can say that again. She's my pepper shaker." Gus
grinned, becoming all teeth and grooves and neckless. "Shake
it up but don't break it, wrap it up and I'll take it!"

It was Thursday night. They didn't usually have sex on
Thursdays, because Friday was a night when Rebecca
wanted Gus to come home.

Sex with Gus. It was a subject that overwhelmed Rebecca
in its imperviousness to analysis. If any examination had
been given her including the question: describe your sex life
with your husband (fifty points), she would flunk the course.
She had no idea. You mean really *no* idea? Well, so many
conflicting ideas that their sum amounted to a confused zero.
They seemed to play a thousand different roles. Each. You
mean there is no discernible pattern at all? Well, yes, we have
sex on Mondays and Fridays—and drunken Saturdays if you

count that. Tuesday night Gus doesn't come home (unless I point out to him that he doesn't come home on Tuesdays, after which he *does* come home on Tuesday night and postpones his not coming home the night after sex until Wednesday that week). Friday is different, of course: (a) we usually see Betty and Eric on Friday nights, and we always have sex after being with them; and (b) the next night in this case is Saturday, and Gus is too much of an American not to come home on Saturday night no matter *when* we had sex. The only pattern you can isolate then is calendarical (It was half question, half statement. There is no such punctuation mark that I know of. Unless: ./? ? Or, perhaps, $\dot{?}$. But no typesetter can get that; I can hardly type it.)

Tonight, however, Rebecca brought the subject up (i.e., she sent out sex thought waves because that was where her sex was, in her head). Gus got them because he had never bothered to acquire resistors—his entire flesh acted as a primitive conductor for just such waves. Then Gus lay there drowsily but Rebecca was not satisfied. She went into the dressing room-bathroom and returned after a bit dressed in a long chiffon scarf which began as red at one end and decreased to pink at the other. It was fastened like a diaper in her diaper region and draped like a cowl across her breasts (it was a very long scarf, and quite wide, of a kind only briefly in fashion). She danced, enticed, bit him and darted away, and asked him if he was sleepy. "I was but I'm not now," he said, grabbing her at every pink and accessible place. It took a long time to get Gus ready (he had had a lot to drink) but finally they had another sex of a sort and after this time Rebecca cried.

"Don't cry, pet."

"I can't bear it. I'm always so frustrated."

He stroked her hair. "It's my fault."

"How could it be your fault? No, it's my fault. It's me."

"No, look, maybe you were mad at me. If I'd gotten all dressed up and gone to as much trouble as you did to look pretty—sexy—for a husband then had to sit there and wait hours for him and when he does come home he's half drunk and brings his drunken brother with him—if I was a woman I'd be pretty mad at him, all right. I don't blame you."

Her spine had stiffened under his fingers halfway through sentence number two (if it is possible to divide such sloppy syntax into sentences at all). She was off the bed and standing up when he got to "all right," her face red as the scarf's red end with anger although he couldn't see it in the dark. Her slap landed just as he said, "blame you," distorting them beyond recognition if they had not been words that are universally recognizable through any amount of disturbance.

"Goddam you. I didn't get all dressed up for *you,* sit around waiting for *you,* big strong you, to come home to pitiful little me, and please pretty please give me some of that you have that feels so good can't you squeeze me in *some*-where in your busy busy day. . . ." She had her bathrobe on now. "You conceited . . . *mother!*" She had reached the door. "I was *writing.*" She shut the door behind her and then opened it again. *"Were."* She yanked the door closed.

Rebecca left the house fifteen minutes earlier than usual the next morning. The sun was low and blazing, the windshield grimy, and there were reflecting particles of dust filling the air—which is why she ran into the back of the truck. She saw him stop at the stop sign; she knew the moment he should start up again (there were no cars coming the across way). She had turned to look at a flock of azalea bushes in full bloom. She got out, furious. The car, her car, her yellow MG, was crumpled like a bulldog's nose, both lights smashed. The truck was an old pickup truck with its rear flap hanging down—luckily; she would have gone under the trailer otherwise, cramming the windshield and the truck's tail into her face. The truck was unhurt. The driver, an old illiterate man from some nearby country farm, seemed to think she owed him something. My car is hurt, not yours, she explained. See? The only damage is to my car. You're not even scratched. The MG looked pitiful, ugly, destroyed; her head ached viciously where it had knocked the windshield top bar.

She drove on to Rice, ignoring along the way the shocked, reproachful looks of men who loved cars, and parked behind the library. She let herself in by the side door to which graduate students had keys, climbed the dark back stairs to her cubicle. She sat down and got immediately up again, and went into the disinfected ladies' room and wept.

She did less than thirty minutes' work during the next two hours. Gloom settled over her brain like black smoke from an oilfield burning waste. Leftover sadism and guilt from infancy—hogging the whole sky!

Noon was time to go to lunch. Rebecca turned the top sheet of the papers on which she'd been making notes over and placed a book over that. Scrambled eggs might produce a change in her metabolism which would beneficially affect her brain chemistry. The movements required to get these eggs might speed up her circulation and send more energetic blood to her head. A shocking piece of news along the way might rechannel her electric current, which was now stuck before the nonconducting casing of her unconscious. She might even break a leg—perhaps someone else's.

She crept down the back stairs, ultimately aiming for a non-campus chrome joint a few back-alley blocks away.

At the landing of the second stair she was about to slip past the door to the stacks and dash down the last remaining flight to baked asphalt and her own patient, encapsulating, crumpled white charger when the door slowly opened. She stepped politely back, and with her free hand pushed each corner of her mouth into its adjacent cheek. A slanted face, tiny puppy's eyes looking up through the shaggy overhang of brow, a soldier's triangular grin for her—it was Dr. Thom coming up to her shoulder. She laughed and simpered and probably danced a bit during the gentle exchange of pleasantries, and clapped when he said that no one wants a really new book but something just new enough for them to recognize. She held the door because she was on her way into the stacks he was just quitting. "All work and no lunch makes Rebecca a hungry girl," he twinkled. The last dregs of laughter in her came out as hysterical tin. "Just one thing, I want to look up just one thing before lunch, and then I'm going to lunch, you're right, yes, really, of course! Lunch is all!" She slipped into Biblical Criticism like a Jew.

But now it was too late. Noon was everywhere. All around her there were graduate students and professors turning papers upside down and putting books over them. Their individual sighs combined into the library's decorous answer to the noon whistle. The ladies' room would be crowded with girls. There was no escaping lunch, a word whose hunched ugliness offended her eyes as it swam across them in roadside letters.

"Rebecca!" It was Ben Parsons, last apple-cheeked choice of Dr. Thom's pre-retirement. He was clean and scented and fresh from a month-old bride. He was on his way to the Faculty Club (of course). Of course she would join him. Of course she was hungry. Of course it was lunch time. Of course she would be happy to have anyone who joined them along the way join them. All the cockleburrs their combined skirts could collect.

Still inside the library, Mack (rubberized at birth) hurried up to them and held open the door. "Hullo, Rebecca, I didn't know you were out here today. I mean there's no reason why you shouldn't be, I just hadn't seen you. But I guess you can't work at home, can you, with the baby there?"

Since Ben was on her left, he took his place on her right like a gentleman, to enclose her. It would be Mack who stepped back when oncoming hordes or narrow doors demanded that one of them step back. If she closed her eyes away from Rice it was always Mack in his stepped-back position that she pictured—occasionally hopping alertly forward into the front line, but usually back, leaning his round shape forward, legs tripping to balance, his downy voice just behind your ear, feathery, tickling; Mack eagerly making his words express all the cheer and good will of his sibilant nature, cut off from help from his behind-the-line-of-vision face, words tumbling over each other as they had to come out faster & faster—so much amiability and all of it to be carried by just a voice.

Ben, on the other hand (!), walked through the population of Rice like Jesus through Galilee, bestowing his smile on all. She had watched him surge down corridors and across campus walks, brightening the people as he passed like a trail of phosphorus in his wake. She looked to find a trace of the professional in his charm. In vain. A timid man, Dr. Thom liked to laugh. He chose his faculty members accordingly.

They went down the front steps. By the time they had reached the entrance foyer, Rebecca had worked her mind around to right side up and facing frontwards; the smile came and went without the need for manual manipulation. (Surely an insane redundancy.) (By itself.) As Ben stopped to chat with two or three in the crammed outward-flowing twenty feet, Mack hanging over his shoulder, she tried welcoming the coming group lunch. There were sure to be several more at their table; the polite size of Rice let even the shy run as extroverts.

They had reached the door and were ready now to join the cross-campus two-way stream. (Not two equal ways; the current moving in the direction of the faculty club was a skinny thread next to the channel-sized student mass going toward their lunch place.) Mack was back on her back about babies as if nothing had intervened. "Maureen is expecting next month, you know," he fluttered. "We hope it will be a boy" (how could it be?); "we're going to name it after Dr. Thom. Clarence." He rolled the *r* and let the sibilants float out into the oven heat. "A venerable name, Clarence."

"Certainly venerable," she agreed.

"Like the Bede."

"Concede."

"Indeed?"

Mack's eager laughter drowned out the rest of their poem. When he finished wiping his eyes and calling them cards (once, twice, three times: a whole deck), he returned to Dr. Thom. Mack had heard him talking about *Catcher in the Rye* this morning and was determined that they share his amazement that the oldest man in the department (seventy-four next February 28) was also the most avant-garde. None of the other faculty members had read it. Of course they were all going to. "By Salinger," Mack explained.

They entered the faculty club with Polly Price and René LeClerc forming the bottom spots of their five card. They saw two friends (Philosophy and History) sitting at a large table at the far end of the room. In between were Engineering, Chemistry, Mathematics, Biology, etc. Self-consciously Liberal Arts, they grew at once quiet; heads turned down and shoulders stooped, they eased through the tables crowded with science. Rebecca recognized an old boy friend (Physics) and smiled meekly. His returning smile allowed that she might have done better to have captured him. (He had married a debutante.)

At their table, Rebecca sat down in the seat held for her. Immediately she got up. The seat was wet. Her hand reached back to brush her skirt and felt something sticky and slightly gritty and liquid. The napkin came back from its wipe red with the tiny grains characteristic of tomato juice over it. "Christ, somebody spilled tomato juice in the chair," she said. Mack touched her hand as an about-to-be father who cherished women, looking delicately away. She saw the small juice glass where it had rolled to the edge of the tablecloth. She looked at her beige cotton skirt. The grains were gone, but the stain remained.

"Excuse me," she said, as she slipped around the table behind Ben.

"Where're you going? Oh."

It was going to be a long walk through science. She should have left the grains there. Ex-boy friend was going to look up; she could tell from the corner of her eye. A wild thought flipped up: I'll go back and get them!

"Gee, that's a shame!" The girl was younger than she, with glasses and a slide rule and an open Texas face. "At least the skirt's washable; that's something. Hey, don't use hot water! It'll never come out."

The cotton acted like a blotter. In spite of Rebecca's efforts to wash just the juiced area, by the time she finished the whole back half of the skirt was wet. She pulled out paper towels as if she were dealing a deck of cards. *They* didn't seem to act like blotters at all.

"Here, you sit down and rest; I'll do that for you. My name's Penny."

"Hi. I'm Rebecca. Thanks, but I'm all right. No, look . . . it's very kind of you, but . . ." Four hands patting paper towels on one skirt was a child's version of Bedlam. Rebecca turned to sit down.

"There's some on your slip, too. Don't you want to wash that?"

She felt. "No, it's dry."

"Gee, you've got circles under your eyes, just like me. I always get them. I had this happen to me, too, once—I was in high school in a white dress, and I got up to sharpen a pencil and the girl behind me leaped up and tackled me and sat me down on the floor." Penny laughed and her eyes glistened like a grandmother recalling her girlhood. "Was I surprised! Plop! She sat me smack down on the floor. She was a real friend. Now I get horribly depressed just before it, though. Do you? I don't know why. I never did until I read in a magazine about pre-menstrual tension."

Rebecca laughed. "I was depressed as hell this morning, yes." She laughed again. She kept on laughing. She had the giggles. So that's what it was from! "Are you a graduate student, Penny?"

"Assistant. In Physics. Do you know Dr. Leroy? I help with his freshman classes. Smilin' Jack, we call him. He knows we do, and he doesn't mind. Gee, he's a *brilliant* man." She looked up and the light from the window reflected the awe on her open face.

"I used to, yes." Rebecca had the skirt back on, still damp. "Thanks an awful lot, Penny. You've been wonderful, really; a real friend. I hope we meet again around campus."

Smilin' Jack. She bet he wouldn't on the way back.

She began the walk back through science tables to her own. Each pair of pinning eyes hit her like twin electrodes, grabbing her flesh at points an inch apart and pulling in opposite circular directions. Her muscles were twitching like those of the pithed frog at Vassar, when, for sport, six girls had simultaneously applied their electrodes to its paralyzed body—six progressive-school graduates who knew self-expression and individually tried to make the frog a belly dancer, a prize fighter, a kicking baby, an epileptic—and two more. Damp, with microscopic Mexican jumping burrs swarming over her skin's inner lining, she reached the safety of her table and sat down before the plate someone had ordered for her.

"Rebecca!" Ben turned a whole face in her direction. "What do you think about the Mountain Critics? Do you think a poem is or means?"

(Rebecca! What do you think about the Mountain Critics? Do you think a poem is or means?) The words knocked across the surface of her mind like balls bounced against a children's song. (Rebecca! What do you think about the Critics' Mountain? Do you think a poem means or is? Is or means?) She tried to force them through, into the brain itself. A violent ringing whirred in her ears.

"Is or means?" She reached out and took a swallow of water. The ringing diminished to background sound. She spoke again. "Is or means. Yes." She shoved hard and they went in, poised briefly, and darted to the outer surface again. "You're talking about Kradnow?" *That* was familiar. What else? "He believes that one has to dissect the poem, thoroughly, but that the major value comes after the putting of it back together?"

Ben, puzzled: "Of course. You know, you were telling me about the article you read in *Rime,* where he took exception to Smith. You remember."

You remember. She reached for a cigarette and tapped it. She started to light it and glanced around the group. Everyone was eating, but had put his fork down now waiting for her words. No one wanted her to light a cigarette in the middle of lunch and blow smoke all over the circle. They glared at her.

"Yes. Kradnow. He says that the first step, but the first step only, is to dissect the poem. You have to remove the meat—very carefully, without messing up the skin." The circle stared, slowly concentricizing itself into a huger one and pointing its ring of eyes at her. "Then you disjoint the carcass and see exactly how it *was* put together, and then you're ready for the real operation, which is putting it back. Including fitting it back into the skin, I think. *Then* you know what the poem is *and* means, and neither matters at all because you've gotten beyond such words—the poem belongs to you as if you'd whelped it yourself."

She took two rapid sips of water and sped up her voice. "The article was called 'Approaching the Poem in the Classroom.' It tells you exactly how to go about the whole process, beginning with preparing the bait and setting the trap. It even includes a kit of hand cleanser and paper towels for when you're through."

"Yes. Well, Ben" (Mack tried to clear his throat. You could hear the feathers brushing against each other, then settling back) "I think the Mountain Critics are out on a limb—ha ha—when they claim that the New Critics are old hat, though. There's going to be a meeting at Mountainside next summer, a symposium, you know, and Tracey Roderick will be moderator . . ." Mack's voice drifted off into its own downy cloud and Rebecca heard her chewing played against its muffled noise and a distant faraway ringing very faintly in the background. She glanced quickly up and saw that they were all looking at Ben now, with fleeting darts of gratitude at Mack. She shot him a crooked one herself.

The waitress came up then, leaving Mack with the thin thread of his sentence half in and half out of his still open mouth, like a string attached to a child's expectant tooth. Waitresses never came up when Ben Parsons was in the middle of a sentence; as if they waited (knowing how) until the Macks of the world were in the middle of their sentences— not because waitresses bore Mack any ill will; on the contrary; it was as if Mack's sentences beckoned the alert corners of their eyes. Mack knew there was no tooth there, and was grateful.

Lunch could not last forever.

Hattie was waiting to be paid; Dinah ran screaming toward her; the furious sun threw a haze of hate over them all. Rebecca tried not to scream herself when Dinah's sticky hands hit her skirt; tried to disengage them gently and postpone them for just a few seconds; wished the child were taller so she could lay an arm across unemotional shoulders. She put her hand on the back of Dinah's head and scooped her inside, saying "Hi," "All right," and "All right" in a mechanical voice.

She wrote out a heavy check for Hattie, resenting every inch of ink. She had overpaid her; Hattie said so in a wondering tone (wondering whether to mention it all, seeing the mood she was in, for fear she'd take it as criticism). Rebecca told her to take it anyway and they would settle it next week.

She left the room, and Hattie to hold Dinah back even if it meant she herself were late getting off. In the bathroom she mentally filled the tub with water and sunk into it, submerged, and quietly drowned. She put her head in her arms over the basin and hid there, breathing cold tile, until her associations led to adolescent whisky vomiting and she raised her head. I can't bear it, she said. What? she asked. I'm stupid, and I can't bear it. Why not? There's nothing else. When I was twenty, I would be an artist. And if I couldn't, I would be a teacher. And if I failed there, I would be a mother. Now that I fail there . . .

She went into the bedroom and lay down on the bed and imagined that she was dead—floating on a cloud that sometimes settled on the sea and tilted foot up and down across the waves and rode gently out toward the horizon and it was dusk. Dinah is blonde and beautiful and faces outward and Mrs. —— prefers her because *she* never was. Alice is dark and twilike and mine. I could make Mrs. —— prefer *her*.

Couldn't I? I could, beginning now, insinuate the younger
. . . and when Alice grows up, and squirms inside, not
knowing why, and demurs, I could say, Trust me. I am the
mother.

She jumped the raft closer to shore and got off. The children's dinner.

"What do you think you're doing?" Dinah's suspicious
gray eyes followed her from the red chair.

"I am taking things out of the pantry, everything we have
in the goodie category. We're going to have a picnic. I'm
going to be a mother. We'll have dinner on the terrace, all
goodies. Would you like that?"

"Yes." Dinah's eyes looked only slightly less watchful.
"You are a mother, aren't you?"

"Quién sabe?" She spun a can of olives through the can
opener. The lid held at the magnet for an instant and then
clattered to the floor. "That means 'of course.' The surface
tension of the brine olives are packed in is too strong for the
pull of Lazy Lulu wall can openers."

"Hey, I'll make Kool-Aid!"

Flat on her back, not a single tree stood in her circle of
sight. The old trees by the creek were too far away and instantly began to run downhill; the pines around the house,
Eloise's trees, were still too short. There was a North Carolina pine in her mind which shot up seemingly from one's ear
and bolted into the blue. Green freedom in the sky, the other
end firmly based in the ground.

But I panic. She looked down at her feet; imagined her
feet looking back at her head. Lying prone, neither end was
base. I panic and behave like a rubber ball attached to a pad-
dle by a piece of elastic. Such balls shoot crazily out over
chasms and up into air and wildly at any angle, snapping
back in between for the next spank. Fun. Not free. Don't you
want to grow?

Last week there was a tiny sprig sticking out of the ground within the circle of the cedar's shade, and she had bent down and seen that it was attached to the ground, apparently by roots. She called Francis to come and look. It means the old tree's getting ready to die, Francis told her. When they start sending out babies like that, it means they're going to die. They put the little one right next to them, you see—not two feet from their trunk. There's not room for both of them to grow there. The little one is going to replace the old one, that's what.

Francis called the cedar *they,* and she liked that. She couldn't bear men who went around calling inanimate objects *she.* The word *she,* it was suddenly clear to her, had a disgusting sound. She. She said it out loud, and Dinah looked up with a question. "She," she said again. "Nothing, honey." *She.* If the tree is identified with the mother in primitive religious worship, it is also identified with the father. In the Bible, it holds knowledge. Adam and Eve ate from there, and then had to be male and female. If one could get back to the tree, like Daphne, who turned into a tree to escape Apollo . . . You're too proud to be a woman. I'm too proud to be a man either. A pox on both your sexes. (That usually happens.) Babies can't stand to be held down. Have you ever tried to hold a baby's hands and feet, and seen how it squirms and becomes frantic with anger? Rebecca had; although it would be going too far to say that she enjoyed it, she had done it and been fascinated watching the child struggle to free itself. That was you, Alice. You couldn't bear to be caught. And the race? Caught by the strings of someone's arms and legs because they are your opposite? The whole of one which doesn't need a complement tied for life by this part which does? Men worshiped trees because that's what they wanted to be, male-female together. The Tiresias complex.

"Androgynous," she said aloud. Dinah looked up in a question. Rebecca turned her head. "Do you want some more Kool-Aid?" Alice had seized upon the bright red-and-white package of cigarettes and tobacco dripped in strings from her mouth. "Give Alice some."

"She doesn't like the taste," Dinah said.

"The weeping willow was the despised tree of all us children when I was your age," Rebecca said. "Because it dripped. But then I was a crybaby. Did you know that? Can you say *androgynous?*"

"Androgynous."

Alice sat staring off at the corner of the patio. Suddenly she dropped the cigarette package and lit off in a plump diapered crawl toward another interest. Dinah turned her head the other way to watch. A second's stiffening of Alice's back, an uncharacteristic pause before grabbing—Rebecca held her awkwardly aloft and looked at the small colorful snake which looked uncertainly back from its own confusion.

"Ugh," Dinah said from behind her mother. "Was she going to put *that* in her mouth?"

"It's a coral snake, Alice. It's deadly poisonous." Rebecca was soaked with adrenalin. Limp. "It's beautiful, though. Isn't it beautiful?" Dinah was inside the house. "If the red bands are separated from the black bands by yellow, it's a coral snake." Rebecca was talking to a squirming Alice.

"Kill it!" Dinah screamed from behind the door.

"Or is it the other way around?"

She put Alice indoors beside her sister, and went to get the hoe. She was not Rebecca now. Puffed up and directed with simplicity, her walk was a march and her arms' muscles bent in the efficient way to hold hoes. Her mind was a kaleidoscope suddenly stopped at one distinctly outlined picture. "Stay back," she commanded in the voice of grandfathers. She stepped to within three feet of the tiny menace; paused.

The snake lay obligingly on the stone chopping block of the patio's floor, his head at a convenient angle. In spite of the lethal nature of its poison, the mouth of the coral snake is so small that an adult would have to put his little finger inside the snake's mouth to get bitten. She had on shoes. Even so, she was terrified of it lying there and of herself opposite it with raised hoe; only the audience at her back and the traditional role she was playing allowed her to act (forced her to). She brought the hoe down with a clatter that sent sparks up from the concrete blocks. The blow released a flood of hate and she was on fire. She hit it again and again until it was quite severed in two. She put the hoe down and held herself stiff until the trembles subsided. "It's a beautiful thing," she said to Dinah. "Come out and look." Dinah wouldn't come. She picked Alice up, knelt with her on her knee, and gave her bits of the pidgin-English admonition of parents trying to convey the idea of a simple danger. With this half-hearted sop to books, she was silent. She knelt there, watching the snake, an occasional after-death spasm bringing a return of terror. She touched its tail segment. The colors were hard and glaring, undiluted no-nonsense colors of snakes. It went vividly with the flower colors of the bed bordering the patio, and with the sunset background. The ants were already arriving. Did they run in pairs? She lifted it up with the hoe and carried it to the hedge, tossing it over into the field beyond.

The children had run to greet Daddy—she heard them— but she stayed absorbed in the snake a few more minutes. She heard his *Hi,* she heard her name called, but still she remained with the snake. Her experience. Crushed under foot by Genesis, re-erected by Freud, this tiny deadly snake no thicker than a finger could have killed her child, was killed by her, was beautiful.

She said so later with Betty and Eric. "It's that sentence in

Genesis that causes all the trouble. You know: male and female created He them. He didn't do that; we all started off ambiguous in the slime. Why does he want to make us feel guilty now about feeling ambiguous sometimes still?"

"I pass," Gus said.

"What on earth are you talking about?" Eric asked.

Betty laughed. "Hush, Eric. I love to listen to Rebecca talk, even though I never understand her. She talks marvelously."

"You wouldn't think so if you did listen," Rebecca shot back. "It's *your* Bible I'm after. Look." She addressed the men again. "The man who wrote that was scared—that it wasn't so. This is the oldest hang-up in the world. He was confused, so he made a god who would simplify: me male, you female."

"Simplify?" Gus snorted.

"Well, it's a hell of a lot simpler than having people who switch back and forth from male to female all the time and you never know which they are."

Betty was angry. "God made us; we didn't make God."

"Shut up," Eric said. "So what are you talking about?"

"Just that—what Betty said. I saw a title in a drugstore today, a How to Win Friends kind of book, entitled *How to Make People Like You.* But I read it as if it were a manual giving directions for constructing a people-making machine: how to make people like *you.* Which is what we all want to do, right? That's the basic wish of mankind, and that's why it created a god who has this as *his* basic wish. Religion is a simple case of projection. We make gods like us who in turn make people like them. Why do you think women get pregnant all the time, and why do you think men resent it so? Do you ever read population statistics? By 1970 Russia will have surged ahead of America in population, and this fact caused

Dr. Jonas' voice to break when he stated it. We're *eager* to de-seminate birth-control techniques to other nations."

Gus roared. "That's my girl. She can get from Genesis to geopolitics before I can finish a drink."

"*I* think it's very interesting," Betty said, "although I don't believe it."

"Look, let's get back to nature, then," Rebecca said. "Big systems spring from individual wishes, like social groups from self-preservation instincts. But we also have an instinct of freedom, as you can see if you try to hold a baby's arms and legs so he can't move." (She repeated her words of the afternoon, feeling unreal.) "We want to be both protected (alive) and free (alive). It's the effort to juggle these two sometimes conflicting drives that has written history. We really want to be trees, because they're both. That's why people worshiped trees in the beginning, and why different power groups fought over them—the early matriarchal tribal groups claimed them as fertility gods, and with the later patriarchal overthrow they became phallic. When we lived in trees we identified with them and felt them as part of our own bodies, and we've been trying to get back ever since."

"Is that what that wonderful poem means—only God can make a tree?" Betty asked dreamily.

"Only God would *want* to," Gus felt sure.

"Yeah, sure," Eric said. "Man made God so God could make trees because man really wants to make trees. It's his idealized image of himself."

"The weeping willow was the despised tree of all us children when I was a kid," Rebecca said. "Because it dripped. But then I was a crybaby." A slight tingle encased her brain for several seconds, floating her in its current.

"What are we?" Betty cried delightedly. "What tree am I, Eric?"

"Birch," Eric said, cuffing her head.

"Dogwood," said Rebecca.

"Horseshit," said Gus. "Who's ready for a drink?"

"And Gus is a surly oak," she laughed.

"What's going on here?" Mrs. ——— stepped into the room with a drink in her hand and pale-blue silk swirling around her legs. "Everybody talking? Having fun? Hello, Betty! Eric."

Eric, caught by the swirling blue silk around slender legs (Betty was pregnant *again*), leaped to his feet and kissed her. Mrs. ——— suffered it with a straightened back. "Is everybody having fun?" she said.

"Mmmmmm," Eric continued the kiss after she sat down. "You have the most beautiful legs of any woman I ever saw." He tilted back his chair for a better view.

"Thank you Eric." Mrs. ——— turned to Betty. "It's wonderful to see you, Betty! How pretty you look!"

"Doesn't she have fantastic legs?" Eric asked.

"So what's going on?" Mrs. ——— asked.

"Rebecca was telling us about trees," Betty said. "How everyone wants to be a tree."

"A tree?" She put her drink decisively on the table. "Now don't pay any attention to Rebecca. Sweetest child in the world but you can't listen to a *thing* she says. I love her dearly" (she blew a kiss to her daughter) "but she's nutty like a fruitcake. Now don't you pay any attention to Rebecca, Betty. She's just like her father—talk, talk, talk. You're much too pretty to talk, baby." Her voice became high and mimicking. "Just look pretty, baby."

Rebecca excused herself. Betty found her in the bathroom, crying, which was why Betty liked Rebecca.

Rebecca had had two hours' sleep each for the past two nights, and was feeling the drag of sandy irritability that Sunday morning. Since time was slowed down, things got through that under time's ordinary speed wouldn't have had time to, and everything scratched. Her thesis was due Monday morning at eight o'clock, and she hadn't finished writing it, let alone typing it. (Let Betty type it.)

The coffee scoured her stomach like yellow acid burning off another layer of lining. She sat at the typewriter and added hours. There were twenty-one left. If Betty could type seven pages an hour. . . . She was back in ninth-grade anxiety. Betty couldn't type seven pages an hour; Betty would need breaks for something and explanations about footnotes and she herself would have to scribe in the Greek. She started reading the last page to see where she was.

"Hi." Gus stood in a shaft of sunlight, looking clean and sharp. "Listen, I don't want to break up your work, but this land deal I told you about—I told Harry I'd let him know something tonight. Will you go on the note for ten thousand? What's the matter? You look like you think I'm trying to shaft you."

"Would you mind moving out of the sunlight? It's gritty staring at you there."

He moved a hard chair up on the other side. "So look, Rebecca. You know I'm broke, and this is a chance to make a small killing. I'll lay you ten to one that you get your ten thousand back double." His voice became sharp and incisive. "There're more mullets in this town than you can shake a stick at."

"Gus, I wouldn't see the money if you made fifty to one."

"That's just the point. You'll get it this time—that's a promise."

She rubbed her eyes. "You know I'm not going to lend you any more money. There's no point in bringing it up."

"This isn't a loan. It's a steal. Don't you get the point?"

"No, I don't get the point."

"Do you want me to be blunt?"

"And cut off your point?"

"You act like I'm trying to bleed you."

"I feel bled."

He got up. "All right. Goodbye. You can forget about my taking the children off your hands this afternoon."

Automatic tears whipped her eyes as he slammed the door. He opened it again. "And don't think I don't know where you were last night, and why you wanted me to take care of the children today! I know you've been screwing that professor—what's his name? Ben Parsons?" He slammed the door a second time.

She took a pen and went through the pages looking for spaces awaiting Greek inserts. Everywhere the text called for a Greek word she scribed in *shit* (σκωρ) or *fuck* (φυτευω).

For the first fifteen minutes of her thesis oral Rebecca answered mechanical questions in a surly voice. She heard the sound of her words ring back on her as if she were in an empty gasoline drum. The voice of her thesis advisor became soft and coaxing. She felt she was letting him down. What was the matter? She knew her subject; it was only an M.A. exam and a formality.

"So you feel that Sidney is setting up a straw man?" the gentle question came.

"What?" A distant ringing sounded in her ears; the beginning of an electric tingle coursed beneath her scalp. They were sitting in a circle whose diameter was less than six feet; how could she not have heard?

"You feel that Sidney is setting up a straw man?" There was slight bewilderment in the repetition.

"A straw man?"

"Yes." The voice of Ben Parsons became parentally encouraging. "A straw man."

"What's a straw man?"

"I mean, you think he is putting up a false image, a hollow concept, only in order to reveal it as false." Ben was puzzled. "I am just rephrasing what you said, Rebecca."

"Oh, of course," she said quickly, irritably. "He's setting up a straw man." She lit a cigarette and blew smoke over them all. "That's *obvious*." She looked defiantly out for the next question. The ringing grew louder. *What* is the matter? some sane part asked the rest of her. Four faculty members she knew well sat facing her, friendly and unthreatening. She tried to turn them into vultures. She answered the next question in a short angry voice. She picked an insane argument.

"Would you like a ten-minute break?" Ben asked.

"Of course not," she snapped. "Let's get this over with."

It was Mack's turn. He talked for a minute or two, then paused, having placed a question mark at the end of his last sentence. He was merely repeating what the thesis said, and everything he asked was prefaced by his statement that he was just seeking clarification. For five minutes she was required only to nod or say, that's right. He went on for five more, as insurance. Was she all right? his solicitous eyes infuriatingly asked.

She began talking, repeating what the thesis said but replacing the careful literate argument of its pages with extravagant language and exaggerated claims. She listened to herself become more and more demagogic. She slipped back into the clichés of childhood arguments. You're nuts if you think he didn't mean that (she actually said that). Sentences began Any fool can see . . . and What gets me is that these guys (other scholars) treat Sidney like he was an idiot. She said *shit* once. She shoved a cigarette into her mouth because through the louder ringing she heard herself getting ready to say, so do you want to make something of it?

Hal McGregor's turn came. He asked her a rapid series of

questions, all to be answered by the name of a poet. At question eleven, she broke into a sweat. There was only one answer. The poet called for had the first name of Richard. He was available to be met, and several of the people she talked poetry to knew him. They called him Dick. She looked at Mr. McGregor's obscene eyes fired at her. She looked straight back into them until black speckled smears obscured her vision. In the middle of the swarming black a huge black stick formed, penis-shaped. Through the louder ringing in her ears the word *dick* shouted, alternating with *prick*. She was icy cold. If she said anything, she would say fuck. She would scream. She hated them all. "I don't know," she cried. Mack objected: "Yes, you do, Rebecca. You were quoting him just yesterday." "I don't know!" "Try to think, Rebecca," Mr. McGregor's voice leered. "I don't know! I never heard of him!" "Rebecca, are you all right?" Ben asked anxiously.

Rebecca slept, with waking periods of no consequence, until noon on Friday, when she went to the beauty parlor. She returned in time for Betty and Eric's evening visit.

"You look great, baby!" Eric said, hugging her hugely. "What happened?"

"I love your hair that way," Betty said.

"I look like a *madonna*," Rebecca answered. "I like it too. Meanest woman you've ever known, Betty—I think it's delightful that I look just like a madonna."

"You're not mean," Betty said. "I think you're sweet."

Rebecca fixed them all expansive drinks. "Not mean to *you*. Just to men. Men I hate. I'm not fighting it any more. There'll be no more smiles and sidles. No more please." She stood back to the sink, straight gin in her glass. "I castrate," she said. "I love men if they have penes. I collect these. All sizes and flavors. I yank them off, cut them off, sometimes just pull and they separate themselves from the major body as if they had already been perforated. You'd be surprised how many have. Just tear along the dotted line. What do I want with them? Nothing. That's the beauty of it. I just toss them all in a barrel on the back porch, like pickles. Theoretically, anybody who wants his back can come get it, like a grab bag. Or try another one. That I have nothing to do with. Everyone'll have to find his own Wendy to get it sewn back on."

Or use a sewing machine, for it was just after this that Rebecca entered her machine period. Gus became impotent, and they separated after one of their arguments. Divorce was imminent. Rebecca looked at herself in the mirror the next day, and signed up for a course at a reducing parlor.

The first three days she was sore, and then, with Epsom-salt baths and return bouts, her muscles threw themselves into the machinery like virgins of three days ago into bedtime exercise. The revolving steel dug into her flesh and her flesh dug back.

To firm the fat on the inner thighs, one straddled the machine. Quite by accident one day Rebecca made an erotic discovery. Astride the rolling metal, her arms holding on to the end bar, she lowered herself an inch. Flashing silver like a thousand minnows swirled beneath, saliva formed in an aching fury in her mouth, her hands gripped the bar, her teeth each other, explosive sex swelled to unendurable violence and she felt she could not stay there, *would* draw back, had to move, could not bear it one more second—when the pop came. She heard it. Go pop. She was shattered, and clung to the revolving steel as if she wanted to remove every centimeter of flesh—clung there after the timer began dinging. The head of the reducing parlor looked at her curiously. Limply, she picked up the timer and reset it for five, and turned to do her buttocks.

She drove the car to a shady spot by the side of the road and lit a cigarette. To think. An intellectual child, Rebecca had never had an orgasm in her life, until today. She thought her sex was in her head (it was there she got electric currents which tingled and shut out the world, and were her only experience with the quality of ecstasy other people talked about when they poetically described sex). She had believed that she couldn't feel it elsewhere; today canceled this error. It wasn't her body which couldn't respond, it was the means she elected to cause the response which were inadequate. I.e., men.

The next day she bought one of the machines and had it delivered to her study. She unenrolled herself for the fall semester at Rice. Ph.D.'s seemed hopelessly out of date—why sublimate? She bought a large drawing pad and several mathematics texts.

The point, she thought, is that everyone should be free from the sloppy mixture which is now a human being. For sexual needs to carry as their price a lifetime of relating to someone else in the most difficult situation imaginable (marriage) is out of date. We don't spend our lives growing crops and tending animals just in order to eat any more; if factories can deliver us ready-to-go food we thank them for the time saved.

Why haven't people thought of machines for sex before? Of course they have. The trouble with fucking machines, and factory food, is that it's apt to be dull. Homogenized and sameness. Tasteless and bland. So unsurprising that soon it no longer satisfies any but the most rudimentary appetite.

She made careful notes from the later chapters of her mathematics texts. A machine built like a human being with an electronic brain inside. A machine that can learn. The customer orders a basic kind (male or female to start) which has been taught in the factory to perform simple operations.

Then, included in the order is a training period. We show the customer how to teach the machine to adapt itself to the individual needs of the owner: how to reward it when it bites the ear and spank it when it bites the nose, for example. There is no reason to suppose that the machine would perform any less subtly and with any less variety than an actual human being (there was ample evidence that machines did this in other fields); in fact, given the imaginative limitations of the average human being, the machine should be a vast improvement.

There would be a problem of marketing. Properly to build and distribute these machines would set their cost at about that of a home swimming pool. That didn't seem prohibitive, considering the year-round recreational possibilities of the product. Of course, lower- or middle-income groups would have to pool their resources and buy a club machine (perhaps two), and obviously a machine used by a number of people would not have as fine a sense of discrimination as an individually owned one. This problem was no different from that horseback riders face. There seemed no way to avoid the truth that the middle and lower classes get a watered-down version of everything.

Would it be a threat to marriage? Not necessarily. Sexual happiness however gained would increase dinner-table harmony, and the children would benefit from a home of decreased constipation. But it would certainly free those people who didn't want children or whose children were grown from the saddle of marriage. That was progress. Biblical criticism had cried before: let fact be fact and God be what it can; Rebecca was ready to face its modern corollary. Let sex be sex and marriage what it can.

High on her own brilliance, she stayed in her study until dawn, experimenting with the reducing machine and making notes. She didn't always pop, she discovered. Usually there

was a slowly building, warm welling, culminating in an explosion of warmth radiating outward from her. Once, almost
at the end of the buildup, she heard a sharp crack coming as
if from the door. There was no one, but she had wheeled
around and the whole process abruptly froze, everything
gone; she wrote: users will have to be careful of infantile
guilt feelings, and machines will have to be kept in rooms
with absolute security from instrusions. Once she imagined
that she was hurting herself, and looked in the mirror, and
fancied that grotesque distortions had taken place on herself,
and she panicked. She made a note: beginners will have to be
assured that absolutely no physical injury can result from this
machine. Obviously, there was no danger of pregnancy or of
other involvements.

So it looked that dawn, but the next morning (late) she
woke depressed. It was too antiseptic, much too isolated. She
forced herself to bathe and dress, and went out to Rice, repeating all the way that people need the real world of human
contacts.

She went out to Rice and walked through the heavy air of
May's end up to the English Department offices. Ben Parsons
was out. She went back downstairs and walked over to the
library and up to its second floor. Halfway through the first
page of an article on somebody's symbolism, she saw Wayne
come into the stacks with a bearded graduate student she
recognized but could not name. She sank down and sideways
into the inadequate pamphlet.

"Hi!"

His name was Lou. He picked up her article and glanced
at it. "Oh, my God!" he shouted into the sacrosanct quiet.
"So that's what they're going to do to Japanese literature.
They're going to *discover* it. Oh, my God. Discover it. What
next?"

She felt like biting him.

"Wayne"—she was going to say, Go away, get the hell away, however she could phrase it, when she saw his face: crinkled, blotched, hungover eyes and the smell of sour whiskyed no-sleep. "What happened?"

"Hi," Wayne said again. "Can you come down for coffee? I wanted to talk to you."

"I don't know," she said. "I have to read this. What's the matter?"

"Rebecca, please. I need you."

Lou smirked at the table's corner. Wayne thrust his face into her eyes. Seductress! she cried. Unfair!

"Wayne . . ."

Lou said, "Let's go, Wayne."

Rebecca said, "Wayne—I can later. Could you make it in about an hour? I . . ."

She went downstairs an hour later but there was no trace of either of them. She left the library to try the English Department again.

At the top of the outside steps she saw, emerging exactly opposite her position on a diagonal, Dr. Thom stepping onto the top step leaving Anderson Hall. He grinned a huge Rice grin as they poised there, facing each other. She grinned back and stepped onto the second step; he stepped onto his second step. Three; three. Four; four. Her face ached. Down! She turned to walk along the cement path; it led to the end of the library and then turned at an exactly right angle to lead an equal distance into Anderson Hall. The walk was covered with a portico supported by arched columns. She took three steps and moved herself to a position behind the first column. Dr. Thom had done likewise, and although she couldn't see him now she knew that in two more steps he would emerge through his arch just as she appeared in hers. They did, and there was the second grin. She stepped behind the second column, just as he did, and anticipated the second arch and its grin. There it was! There were seven columns and six arches on each of their walks before the two walks met at the right angle. Each of them (she and Dr. Thom) would obligingly take the role of grinning dots being moved from point $a_6 \ldots a_0$, their grin lines forming the bases of successive isosceles triangles. At the third arch they grinned again, and the cotton air surrounding her scalp whirred like drunken bees. She would not. . . . At arch 4 she grinned again. They would meet at zero and isoscelate the triangle to death. At arch 5 she grinned again and moved to column 6. Quickly she stepped back and cloistered herself behind it, huddling under arch 5 like a criminal. He found her there, having occupied arch 6 in solitary, and laughed hugely.

"Can I give you a ride to your car?" he said.

"No, thanks. I think I'll walk."

"Be glad to give you a lift."

"Thanks anyway. I really like to walk." Hop, run, skip, pirouette—she would never walk again. "Goodbye. Marvelous to have seen you!"

She shut the door of her room behind her and turned on the roller machine without bothering to put on tights, and straddled there. Tears flowed but not saliva. She moved forward a bit to a different conformation, then back again—she was moving too much. Relax. She hung there ten more minutes. Nothing. She moved lower, then lower still, until her pelvic bone itself was hitting the metal. She cried and pushed down against it, and cried again at the pain. The changeless cycle of the roller pounded against her flesh and bone, bumped, thudded, bruised her, pounding in its own steady implacable rhythm, and she clung there, digging her thighs and genitals into the rolling steel, holding on as to the back of a runaway horse who is digging you through forests and scraping you through bushes and you have given up hope and cling there, knowing death will come if not this minute then the next. An hour she rode until she fell to the floor, numb, exhausted, the machine still turning.

Divorce papers were filed and the waiting period almost over when Gus heard of this. He ran immediately to see Rebecca. Through her laughter he shouted, he shook her. "I can't let you destroy yourself," he cried. "You're a woman!"

He practically had to rape her to make her accept the point.

A month later Rebecca discovered that she was pregnant. When a week passed and she could no longer deny to herself that the next eight months *were* going to follow, when she heard in advance the words of her mother: Rebecca, you look terrible!—when she heard the word *mother* hammering into her ears with each heartbeat of her own heart and of the baby's, like the deafening shouts of an obscene train— mother MOTHER mother MOTHER mother MOTHER mother MOTHER mother MOTHER—she planned her suicide.

The moon, not full, was yet a full half, and the path it made from foam to rim was ample for one.

Rebecca took off her clothes in the dune brush and stood naked, suddenly apprehensive. The beach was bare at the dead turning point of night. But in the darkness existed men from every newspaper or past incident in kind which hinted these; forms moved and suggestions whispered through the wind; obscenity and invasion always impossible to misunderstand, whether one knew the words or even heard them clearly—as a child struggling to rime beauty is suddenly stripped with Do you want to pee?, Rebecca stood now helplessly enveloped in the fact of her own sex. A sudden brutal crack in the shadow behind her made her swing in panic, and brought the impulse to make a dash for the sea and swim away from shore as if that were the danger. She forced herself to stare at the shadow until there was nothing there, and then sat down, trembling, on the sand. To be cheated of feeling to the full one's own chosen death by being reduced by fear to cunt and that is all—a surge of tears gathered in her chest and threatened against her eyes.

You will have to wait. Sit here until you go blank and then begin again. She remembered a time when she had been strong, and had announced to a group that she was going on the beach now whether time was up or not. An uncle (she thought) had grabbed her and turned her across his lap; he pulled up her dress and left her there while he laughed, his hand in position above her pants, before he spanked her. I'll teach you to sass your mother. Her mother laughed. Next time I'll pull down your pants. Her father laughed. Rebecca lay her head down on the gritty softness of the sand beneath the dune, drew her knees up and wrapped them with her arms, and huddled there. She longed to cover herself with a blanket, a dozen blankets and quilts and comforts, bury herself deep in the still center of a lost bed. Lost? The sand under her face smelled of sea and nothing human. They snatched it away. Be angry then.

She stood up, and thrust her head into the sky until no one on earth existed beneath that vast dome and this endless beach except herself. The path of the moon reflected stretched smooth and pure. She would slide across it with the grace of a geometric line for an endless hour, and then, somewhere near its end, slip easily down and sink into its huge water. I choose, she said. Her brain was on fire. It's mine! She ran toward the ocean.

Running, her breasts swung distractingly, so in less than a minute she slowed to a walk. The air blew naked across her genitals and she wanted to touch them with her hand. The playful waves on her ankles made her shiver and brought goosepimples over her skin and she hugged herself and felt her own softness.

She dove forward into the cold sea. Once the swim begins my body will blend into the water and change substance and desire. She had plunged too quickly and her hands hit sand on their downstroke and the small shore waves broke awkwardly in her face. She put her knees down and sat on her heels, closing her eyes as foam splashed noisily over her face; water changed depth according to its own notions of rhythm, covering and uncovering her body without design.

She stayed there until she was made numb by the monotonous jumbled roaring of the waves against the beach and had sobbed her consciousness into exhaustion—how many tears she could not tell because each efficient rise of wave washed across her face, taking the salt water from her eyes into itself. Then she got up and pushed with her head turned sideways and her eyes half closed, past the breakers and into the deeper water. She began swimming, a slow limp crawl, barely kicking, barely raising her arms above water. The moonlight path was off to one side; around her the water was black, with churns and jagged edges instead of ripples. She closed her eyes and swam slowly, her body rolling from side to side, knees bending sloppily, arms unevenly splashing the water. Far out, she stopped and turned to look toward shore. She was a long way out, but the water stretched endlessly the other way to a blurred horizon, endless boring water and she was suddenly sick of it. Look at it! Looking, the jagged points of the black waves turned into sharks' fins and terror jarred her body with an unbearable current of panic. She kicked frantically and swept the water outward with her arms in a child-learned swim used to clear her path of jellyfish; the sudden exertion took the last coughing spurt of her energy and she closed her eyes and let her body become marshmallow and sink downward into the water. The thought that she was sweeping sharks aside like jellyfish made her laugh, and she kicked back to the surface and flopped over on her back and laughed. An instant blinding crack of pain ripped through her from her hip and all her blood and insides gushed out into the sea. A second shark took her arm as she tried to shield her face and scream. She had begun menstruating.

Lila

It was always a bright and sunny day when Mrs. Ferrarri came to dinner, no matter what the condition of the skies in the morning or the weatherman's prediction. Somehow, between the time she began dressing to leave and the time she arrived at her son's, the heavens had been let know what was expected of them. Gus gave Dinah a ten-dollar bill and sent her to the delicatessen.

"What shall I get?"

"Get lots of extras, ten dollars' worth of extras. Things people nibble on or look at and don't eat. Grandmother isn't happy unless there is food all over the place. A table set only with necessary food is her idea of starvation. I remember during the Depression we had our guests on the day she did the week's grocery shopping. Every bit of food we were going to eat for seven days was spread out on the table. Mother beamed like Times Square, urging the cousins and aunts and uncles to eat hearty, insisting there was always plenty of food whatever else might be short, like money, and by God they did. I sat there and watched while Sunday's supper and Monday's lunch disappeared. Sometimes I had to leave the table, on the days when they got all the way through to Wednesday. I left the table and went outside and cried while Mother kept on telling them to eat hearty. Then when the locusts left she took the food they hadn't eaten, divided it into six equal portions, and spread it out over the rest of the week."

"Dinah's gone, Daddy," said Alice.

Her surface was as shimmering and fluid as a secret childhood pool which one knows would respond to the most delicate touch and which, for that reason, one does not dare touch—Alice's face seemed the thinnest shield between her inner tender core and the windy world that it was possible for a human being to have.

"Then I will talk to you."

"Yes, Daddy." She balanced in flight at the slightest sign that attention was to be directed toward her. How long would she wait there? Forever? A creature so totally responsive that she could originate nothing, a tentative filly dependent upon the expert hands of her rider. A risky way to enter the game under the present rules, and with such a father. He had been unable to give her even an inch of hide. She belonged to another era, like meringues and handmade lace and magic flutes.

"Alice, one could no more live with you than with a poem."

"A poem?"

"The reason the dawn is so brief and fleeting, so tenuous that it disappears before your eyes as you look at it, is that man is such a clumsy piece of work that the mounting excitement of looking at that intense a concentration of beauty would crack his rough-hinged slats and burst him."

He laid his hands around her head, feeling her thin hair like spider's silk beneath his scaled palms. "Do you know that you are as brief as a drop of dew on the topmost lily-of-the-valley bell at the edge of the woods at the moment the sun's first finger stretches toward it?"

"Am I a fairy, Daddy?"

"You're my fairy, yes." He took his hands away before the impulse came to crush her head beneath them. "Your grandmother is like the largest float in Macy's Thanksgiving Day parade. Had you ever thought of that?" He had lit a cigarette and was looking out the dining-room window onto the scraggly back garden, not looking at her now. Freed from his eyes, she could have moved, but she changed position only slightly.

"Because she is puffed out and covered with paper feathers like Donald Duck?"

"Exactly. She is an enormous inflated bosom which pushes the air before her aside and clears her path right through nature itself. Grandmother operates at an altitude of about twenty feet, above the heads of everyone else, where the air is absolutely her own. That's why she's like the largest float in the Macy's parade. She's very impressive, and everyone has to crane his neck to see her, or climb up on something to gape down at her. She fills up her airspace in a full-blown colorful way, and that carries a lot more weight than there is actual matter to respond to a gravitational pull."

"Hello, Miss Hannah! Why, if you're not a sight for sore eyes! You come in here looking like the sunshine itself," Hattie said, her hands weaving as if she wanted to smooth and rearrange the air for the welcome guest. "You sure are looking fine and this house sure can use some brightening up, I say."

"Hello, Mother. Hattie's right, you look as pretty as a Christmas tree. I think you add a string of beads every time I see you."

"One a year, that's all. When a woman gets old, she might as well cover up as much of herself as she can with something pretty. I don't hold with modern ideas of skimpy jewelry. There's enough of me to carry it, so I add a piece of jewelry a year. Add a little extra gin to the martini, too." She laughed. "I'll stay younger than you ever were."

Gus took his mother's coat, for which a thousand minks had given their lives, and tried to take her arm. "Don't hang onto *me*," she said, wresting it away. "You'll have to get upstairs on your own."

Hannah Durach ———— so disliked the combination of names Hannah ———— that she had hesitated long and thoughtfully before marrying Gus' father, had, during this marriage, continued to be known as Hannah Durach (a doublet easily acceptable to a South weaned on Mary Louise and Fanny Mae). After her first husband took his life, she felt more Hannah Durach than ever, and when, some years later, she remarried a man named William, she was grateful to have preserved the Hannah Durach and to be required merely to attach a second ————. She privately congratulated herself for thus having preserved this continuity of herself, and when subsequently William himself died, so that now she was left alone, she could at least feel that she was in touch with her origins, the blanks could blur into one another and confuse no one, and Hannah Durach endured.

That this need for constancy was important to his mother astonished Gus, for she was, to him, a person one always looked at as if one had never seen her before. Even when he was living in her house, each morning at breakfast the first sight of his mother was startling, and he had to look again. Her particular quality of vibrancy was such that she looked as if she had just been created, or had created herself anew in some way overnight: impossible that so much protoplasm and vivid life-color could remain in any one state for long, and so it must have just changed itself into what it now was.

Today, in a dark red wool suit trimmed in black fox, over

which she wore her countless strings of beads like the giant redwood wears its rings, her thick hair swirled like a mound of Dutch-chocolate frosting, she looked more than usually dynamically unstable.

"Dinah, if you had a little color in your cheeks, you'd be a beauty today." She had given Dinah a kiss that left a red smear catty-cornered across the girl's pale mouth; now, with spit and the corner of her handkerchief, she was wiping it off and examining Dinah. "Look at the strong bones in that child's face, will you?" she said to Gus. "She didn't get that from you."

"You should have them, Mother. They go with your personality."

"They won't do Dinah any harm either; it won't matter whether she's graceful or not with a face like that." Dinah, whose innate gaucheness always increased as she attempted grace for her grandmother, stumbled as she turned to sit back down in her chair, and hit its seat like one who had misjudged the height by half a foot. "You won't have to please, honey. You can command."

"Here's your martini, Mother. I'd drink to your health except that you obviously don't need it. Alice, come on down. Grandmother's here."

Alice, poised on the bottom step waiting for her moment to enter, slid lightly over to her grandmother and kissed her slowly on the cheek, as if she were carefully smelling that smooth aged soft flesh for scents that had been added since last time. "Hello, Grandmother. I have a kitten."

"You are a kitten, pet. And someone should buy you a decent dress. You look like a gypsy stray in that get-up . . ."

"Mother."

"I tried to tell her that this morning, Grandmother," Dinah said. "She looks common in that thing, but she likes to swirl the skirts in front of the mirror . . ."

"Dinah, that's enough." Gus moved nearer to Alice and reached for her hand, but she held it away from him. "Alice looks like a gypsy because she is a gypsy girl—anyone can tell that by looking at the sparkle in her eyes and watching her feet dance when she thinks she's standing still, but mainly because she has a magic charm in her fingertips which makes people invisible when they start criticizing her . . ."

Everyone has a flaw by which I love him, a crack at which I look and see a crack but through which I glimpse the quivering cherry jam from Switzerland in a gourmet's house, unstable on a plate. Where then did Mother split, rend, tear, gape—at the sides? Under the thick aggressive hair? between the toes? around the nails? Where did a thread tear and seam pull apart and let the soft marble of flesh pulse through?

Gus sat down. "So, Grandmother, tell us a story about Granddaddy."

Hannah Durach pulled the corners of her mouth down and turned her eyes in a diagonal that ended at about knee height—knee height to Gus—which pose, because her head was slightly aslant and tilted back, was intended to and succeeded in conveying the distinct impression that she felt she was being made fun of and didn't like it. She never conveyed an indistinct impression, nor did she do else with impressions but convey them. Then she laughed, keeping her eyes on the diagonal but the force of the laugh closed them a bit more —a laugh which came from the covered wagons and Bessie rifles of the childhood she wished she had had. The children listened while she laughed, and Gus heard it again from his dark room upstairs, heard it swelling the living room and bringing into sharper focus the guests below, heard it warm and captivate and pour over everything: a thick, dark-brown gravy of a laugh.

"So I will tell the same story I told last time and the time before," she said, "and I may not even tell it quite the same.

It's about your great-uncle Jesse—Alice, you don't remember him but Dinah might; he used to have a huge rifle he carried with him all the time, called Old Bessie, and you used to play with it when you were a little bit of a thing, honey. The first time your mother saw you crawling around on the floor in your little lace dress and bloomers and that big wicked-looking black thing lying on the floor like a crocodile . . ." Hannah Durach stopped talking and burst out with the *hah* she used to announce that a laugh was coming. " 'She wanted to play with Tom's rattlesnake and this was the only thing that would quiet her,' Jesse told your mother."

"Men were men in your time, weren't they, Mother?"

"Some of them were and that's for sure. But Jesse had his faults, too, just like everybody else."

"Wasn't it against the law to kill people in those days?" Dinah asked.

"Sure it was against the law, honey, but it was more against the law for some than for others. But I was going to tell you about the time Jesse went to see Mr. Gaiter. Mr. Gaiter had married your great-aunt Henrietta, who was a beauty in those days even though she weighed 200 pounds. Mr. Gaiter was a slick oily sort from Baltimore, and he gambled. He didn't gamble like a Texan at all, but like an easterner—he took Sis's money and tried to make more money from it. By the time she told Jesse about it, he'd already lost Mother's garnet ring, diamond brooch, and 200 shares of stock in a land company which Daddy had given Sis. Now Jesse was not a big man—he was about five seven is all—and already a little bald, but he had a big head and a kind of quiet powerful voice that put the fear of God in people, and he had Old Bessie. So he went to see Mr. Gaiter—they were living in a suite at the best hotel in Austin then—and he knocked on the door and Mr. Gaiter opened it and Jesse stood there, his hat in one hand and Old Bessie in the other,

and he said, 'Mr. Gaiter, I've come to have a talk with you.'
Mr. Gaiter said, 'I'm pleased to see you, Jesse. Come in. And
you can call me Henry.' Jessie said, 'I'll call you Mr. Gaiter,
and you'll call me Mr. Durach, because what I have to say
won't take long and after I'm through there won't be any
need for us to be friends.' 'I don't think I understand you,
Jesse,' Mr. Gaiter said. 'Course we'll be friends. Now come
on in and have a seat.' Mr. Gaiter was getting a little nerv-
ous, but he was smiling and acting like he didn't see Old Bessie at all. 'Mr. Durach, Mr. Gaiter,' Jesse said. 'Now Jess—'
Mr. Gaiter began, then he tried to laugh, then he said, 'Mr.
Durach. Of course it'll be Mr. Durach, if that's your pleasure. But seeing as how we're in the same family . . .' 'Mr.
Gaiter,' Jesse said. 'I don't imagine your life's worth five
hundred dollars to anybody but you, but I'm bound to offer
you a choice. You write your name on the back of this check
and ain't nobody gonna bother you. Now you'll notice I've
got written on it, For Mr. Gaiter's disappearance. As soon as
this check's cleared, you've signed yourself a contract, Mr.
Gaiter, and I know you'll keep it because it'll be a damn sight
easier on you to disappear your way than for me to have to
do it mine.' "

Gus stopped listening and watched his children's faces:
Dinah, composed, wondering if she would get the moral
point of the story, trying to translate her grandmother's char-
acters into hip values (in which case Uncle Jesse was the
hero, but wasn't he an arbitrary reactionary bully whom she
should oppose?); Alice, intent, picturing a scene in her imagination and letting herself float in the robust color of her
grandmother's tale—float a little apart because she was
frightened of the physical vigor of such a world. Gus looked
at his mother. She would never need to build a room. She
would grow cataracts if necessary and print her world on
their inner side.

At dinner he said, "Mother, because you have given the children such a glamorous picture of Old Bessie that I'm afraid they will want to marry a man who owns one, I'm going to remind everyone that my father and brother and your husband and son took Old Bessie and shot themselves."

"You don't need to make it sound like it was four people when it was only two." Hannah Durach raised her ringed and attenuated hand ready for underlining. "And I've had enough of this foolish idea of yours that Dick committed suicide. He was three thousand miles from Old Bessie and was shot by a Communist."

"He stood up and took that bullet and the gun that shot him was Old Bessie and you know it." Anger burst blood under his skin and he felt his face tighten and grow ugly. "You give a little boy a name like Dick on purpose . . ."

Hannah Durach blazed back and her voice dominated. "I won't have you talking like that, I simply won't have it. Stop it this instant or leave the table."

For the next few minutes they each talked simultaneously, Gus raised out of his chair and leaning across his plate, Hannah Durach's hand flashing.

"You think you're clever and modern and *psychological* with all your talk about sex and how horrible parents are —everything is your mother's fault, mothers are to blame for their sons' weaknesses and it doesn't matter whether the mother loves the son or hates him she's wrong either way, and if you ask me the

"You forget, Mother, that this is *my* table and with all due respect the time has passed when you can order me to leave any table. Someday you're going to listen to what I say, and you're going to *hear* it. You called that child Dick and gave him a big black legend of a gun for a father because you *wanted*

whole psychological thing is just another way for a lazy generation of half-men to get out of doing any work or trying to be men. You can't take it, none of your generation can take it, and you don't even try, you just lie down on some couch and whine about Oedipus complexes and mothers and fathers and I for one am sick of hearing about it, I'm just *sick*—you make me *sick,*—it just sickens me to hear you talk like that."

him to make that black-and-white comparison, and you never did anything except hold Old Bessie up to him. Oedipus complex? No, Mother, you're way ahead of the Oedipus complex; you're out in front of Freud; you eliminated the middle-man completely and gave my brother Old Bessie itself for a father."

"Oh, does our family *always* have to *scream?*" Dinah demanded as she stood up, knocking over her chair, and marched from the room.

"Come back here and pick up your chair," said Hannah Durach.

"Mother," said Gus. "Dinah, come back and ask to be excused."

"No."

"Daddy, please let her go," begged Alice, in tears. She jumped up and picked up her sister's chair.

"Put that chair back on the floor where it was, Alice," said Hannah Durach. "Dinah's going to pick it up herself."

"Mother, I cannot have you ordering my children around."

"Somebody has to order them. The way you let them live there's complete chaos around here."

"Please, Dinah, come back and pick up the chair," said Alice.

"I *hate* this family," said Dinah. She stomped back to the table, picked up the chair which was still upright and slammed it, legs against the floor, said "May I be excused?" through her teeth, and left the room for the second time, without waiting for an answer.

Hannah Durach began laughing, and Alice's tears disappeared as she turned to watch her grandmother, astonished, listening to the brown swelling laughter that suddenly flooded the room. "Well, I declare," she said as she caught her breath. "There's spirit in your children, at least. Dinah's all right, and I'm glad to see that. Yes, there's spirit in your children; some of the Durach fire slipped through you into them, I'm glad to see. Or at least slipped through to one of them." She covered Alice's hand briefly with her own. "You could do worse than take a page from your sister's book, little one."

The knock was so faint he wasn't sure he heard it the first time, and he said, "Yes?" in a tentative voice, feeling a midnight foolishness.

"Daddy?"

"Yes? Who is it? Come in."

Alice slipped around the barely opened door like a fragile blue shadow and stood just inside, her eyes shining as she took in the room her father built. "Daddy, you slanted the floor!"

"Yes. Do you like it?"

She tiptoed across the room, and then danced on tiptoes back, and sat cross-legged at her father's feet. "You slanted it so people would have to walk on their toes, and I like that. But it's hard to sit on. This way, your feet keep slipping down." She turned around. "This way, your bottom slips down."

"Try the chair."

"It's wonderful for dancing, though," she said, and sat in the chair opposite her father. "Daddy, I wanted to talk to you. Why does everybody in our family die?"

"Everybody in all families dies sometimes."

"But we die sooner. Is there something wrong with our family?"

"Like a curse?"

"That's what I meant, but you smile like you're making fun of me. *Is* there a curse on our family? I think something horrible will happen to me, and you'll say I killed myself." She shuddered and cried out with fright, hugging herself and shivering. "I don't want to die yet, Daddy."

"Alice, do you want me to tell you why I think your Uncle Dick killed himself?"

"Can I sit over there by you?"

He put his arm around her fluid shoulders, shivering himself as his hand felt the frail birdlike bones of her through the slippery nightgown, felt the plump golden skin covering them, felt her spider's head nestle into his chest.

"I saw your Uncle Dick just before he shipped out, talked to him for an afternoon and a night, until dawn, in San Francisco, and would have talked to him for forty more except that dawn was his sailing hour. He was always sad, Alice— even his infrequent hours of joyfulness had an underlying sadness to them. But I've never seen such a total sadness as that which filled and overflowed him that night in San Francisco. 'I'm going to die,' he said, and he was announcing not his fate but his purpose. Everybody says that sometime or other, Alice, and people like your grandmother think they're cowards and people like your future friends who dig psychiatry think they're bidding for the title of most sick. He said, I

am going to die, and I was sure he meant it. His life so far
had been aimed at just that target, like the monster gun itself
which mocked him."

His daughter was asleep. It was past midnight, and the city
was silent. No, the city was private. The hours from midnight
to dawn, when the clocks aren't working and there is no danger of people intrusions, were his.

Gently, with a gingerly tenderness, he held Alice's head up
and slipped his body away from under her. Alice moaned in
her sleep, rearranged herself on the new and lowered surface
of the couch and, still surrounded by sleep, smiled as the position fit.

*

I have explained the room to you a hundred times, if you
had listened. It is a concept which makes clarity and perfect
sense; how could you not understand? It is simply a matter of
choosing what you can't avoid in any case. I have been out in
the world, and my brain is as good as yours, my heart perhaps less so but adequate, adequate—at least to begin with. I
have tried to get through in as many ways as I can think up.
What happens I don't know. There's a two-year-old child on
the beach out the window, racing for the surf. The waves
knock him down once; he gets up, retreats, and sits on the
sand to think it over. A mother figure brings him something
—a pail and shovel? Yes, a pail and shovel because the
beach is made of sand. His mother's education was cutting
out and pasting into scrapbooks colored advertisements from
magazines (because *her* mother knew how to handle children: give them something to do). So this child does not
keep on racing for the surf and being knocked down by the
waves, retreating, racing for the surf, being knocked down,

retreating, racing. . . . He will play in the sand instead, which is better.

"The trouble is," said Maisie, "you try to relate to people intellectually. You should relate to them emotionally instead, like I do."

Gus whirled around from the window through which he was imagining lay a beach, child, and mother, and scissored across the back of the near armchair to sit cross-legged in it facing an abacked Maisie. "Do you want me to tell you about the time I was in love? Do you want me to? I *was*, Maisie. I did relate emotionally. He had green eyes. I have no idea what color his brain was."

She laughed, and her ash face grew suddenly peach. "You're wonderful. You know that?" She got up. "I'll get us some coffee."

"Get us some *drink*," he lilted after her voice.

"I'll get us some drink," she lilted back. "Then you'll tell me about the time you were in love."

"He had green eyes and a face of shifting flesh, and a name something like Charlie."

"Barley?" Maisie giggled. "I love champagne. It makes me so drunk!"

"Maybe Barley. I'm sure it wasn't Billy or Fred. The rest of his face was unremarkable when it was in its resting street position—in fact, if you ran into him on the street he looked like a fresh American boy—but when he talked, and sometimes when he listened, it moved. It moved almost as dramatically as his feet."

"Which way?" Maisie curled her own dainty penis-substitutes under her wraparound skirt and took a slow sip so the bubbles could spray the inch of air beneath her nose.

"Spirally. When the spin was counterclockwise his face went in, and most of it disappeared into a lean rabbinical furrow; when it was clockwise it went out and burst into the space between you plumped out like a freshly heated oyster."

"It sounds like a very complicated face," Maisie said through sip four. "I like complicated faces."

"It was. But his feet were simple. They jerked. That's all. Like legs in knee reflex tests. He used them for punctuation, like you do your *hmmm?*. He would say, 'How do you feel about wanting me to make love to you?'—*jerk*."

Maisie sat up like a sudden unscrewed screw, spilling sips five through eight. "He would say *what?*"

"That's what he would say. And then . . ."

"No man says that."

"Well, he did. 'How do you feel about wanting me to make love to you?'—and jerk goes the foot."

"Gus." Her face laughed. Ash to rose this time. "He was your *doctor*."

Gus closed his mouth firmly and stepped defiantly back over the chair back. Facing out the window, his back toward Maisie, he withdrew into a common stone form of silence.

"All right. I still loved him."

"Gus." She was still laughing. "It's just that I can't imagine falling in love with someone when there's absolutely *no* chance that he will love you. He *can't* anyway."

"Of course. That was the point."

Because she was twirlable and could cry in a way that did not upset people but actually made them feel closer to her, she could let her feelings bobble around the surface of her in a never-quite-disappearing way like the cork on a fishing line. No strong pulls from below bit them under.

While he, on the other hand—let Maisie say it. "People *do* like you, Gus, and everybody would like you, if you'd just give them a chance." (I'm a raffle prize.) "Actually, I think you're afraid of people. No, I mean that; I think you're really afraid of something—you want to be close to people but you can't trust them."

Maisie was high: her hands were intoxicated, waving through sun-shafts like babbling truths. Gus refilled their glasses. She giggled and said she loved him nevertheless. He said (because he was still absorbed in piscian imagery), "I am a dark unrecorded fish inhabiting the bottom ten feet of the ocean, that's what I am, baby. Sometimes I swim closer to shore where I can see shrimp fluttering and behaving in an altogether tasty fashion, but I can't tell those which conceal hooks from those which don't. Neither can you, but you're lucky, or too small for a meal, or inedible. Or you don't really want to be caught. I do. I lust to swallow a terrible hook and be ripped and gutted and finished. If you're overwhelmingly murderous you don't carry knives. And besides there's all that noise."

"I understand," she said. "I really do. Ben's self-destructive, too. This is marvelous champagne, and I'm going to drink to you because you're marvelous too, Gus, you really are."

"Maisie, did I ever tell you why I wanted to build the room? I mean the real reason?" He lit again on the chair facing her and held her pale childhood face with his eyes. "Because I wanted to burst out. I was sick of being confined in this brace, always having it push me in, never letting anything out—it's not secretiveness, really, it's an iron surface which something put around my outside and now it doesn't matter whether I trust someone or not—because I trust you —I can't break it or crack it or pierce it with even a needle of I love you. Because part of it was sexual, of course, and I was forty-two and that was past."

"What do you mean, past? Ben was forty this year, and I refuse to—look, do you really mean that? Is it really past?"

"Not for you. For me. I mean if you haven't made it by

forty-two . . . I just found that I'd begun begging, lowering standards, meeting impotence and less than desire. *I* did. I mean I couldn't use the sex avenue out any more. But it doesn't matter why; the point is that within this room I could be utterly free, and that seemed a nobler death than gradually to fade out while walking around the world in a prison. A man can go outward until beaten, but then, instead of seeing himself becoming shreds, he can choose instead to go inward with the same gusto. Meet defeat by choosing it. Out in the world, the shell was merely thickening."

Maisie laughed. "How can you be an iron cast and shreds at the same time? Gus, you're marvelous!"

He drank the last half of his glass. He laughed too. "I don't know. But it's right. One is outside, the other inside. Open the cast and see all the shreds. Anyway, that's how I figure it. Inside the room I can burst, and that's a better way to die."

"Hello." Ben came into the room, dark, a dancer. He slid across the floor and into their circle like a wire shadow. "It's because you're dying and you know you're dying. Maisie doesn't understand that; she's a child. You are, you know"—he turned to her—"you accept the world because it's here and you can explore it. You two are playmates. But Gus, he wants to take it apart and see what makes it whirr. He throws himself away. That's good, but it's not you. He was alive, and now he's dying and he knows it."

"What'd you do with the kids?" Maisie giggled. "I'm drunk."

Ben switched into his charming face—little-boy, devilish, grinning. So openly façaded, both of them. Gus felt like the Salvation Army. "I left them playing a game," Ben said, and to Gus: "Now listen to this; it's marvelous. They were playing a game"—Ben's hands moved like a Calder mobile blowing— "and they asked me if I wanted to play. 'You can play, Daddy,' Ralphie said. 'You can be the last loser.' Did you hear that? The last loser. Isn't that——? Yes, it is. Isn't it? Ralphie said that. The last loser." He laughed and got up. "I'll have a Scotch."

"That's marvelous!" Maisie laughed. "That's great, Ben. Isn't Ralph brilliant—just like me! No, you!"

Gus couldn't compete with her enthusiasm, but tried to express his appreciation. It came out pale. He tried again, by telling a story of his own.

"Yesterday," he said, "Alice came home from school and told me that they had a new rule—at lunch everyone has to eat at least one of everything. Well, they served peas, and she was sitting next to Sally. They both said 'No, thank you.' The teacher reminded them of the new rule. Sally leaned over to Alice, and said, 'I'll split one with you.' "

Maisie laughed and repeated the punch line for Ben, who used it to carry into a new subject. Gus barely listened. A silly story, not his; Dinah had told it to one of her friends and they had both enjoyed it as a demonstration of Alice's delicate put-ons. It belonged to children. He retreated, as Ben talked and Maisie listened—this time into a silence of cotton. Stupid.

Champagne was churning his stomach into bubbling syrup and he went downstairs to fix himself a cup of coffee. The first floor was quiet and dark. Waiting for the electric stove, he ate several handfuls of cold peas from the icebox, and a cold Brussel sprout. There was time only for instant coffee, which he hated; it was never hot, and not-hot it tasted nauseatingly instant because he made it triple strength.

He took it up to his room, passing Maisie and Ben on the second floor and briefly excusing himself.

I tried when I was Lila, he said to the slanted boards. Lila: thereby hangs a tale. Lila had the world by the tail.

When I was Lila the world's tail and mine were twisted into a symbiotic rope. We wagged each other.

Really?

She belonged in hammocks. It was there that she felt most open to the world, there that she held out, not just her arms, but her whole self, to air-breathing; phallic sunshine/prahna /pollen; to whatever bits of desultory fallout might be floating there. Gus watched her swing, and sighed. After round and sensual Eloise and wiry Rebecca, she settled over his life like dough. She was boneless. The children absolutely adored her.

"Are you going to be our mother?" Dinah said. There was only one thin string of skepticism holding her back.

"I *am* your mother."

"I told you!" Alice said, plunging into the hammock and nestling into a soft dent.

Dinah broke free and jumped in on the other side, scooping out a corresponding hollow for herself. "Swing us, Daddy!" she said. And he did; the hammock a bulging oval lump the shape of nothing, groaning but still clearing the ground by better than a foot.

Lila seemed soft, even shapeless on the outside, but inside she felt her own direction. "The flesh goes there," she said, pointing to her upper arm whose fat spread and dipped over the iron bar of an outside chair, "because that's the natural place for it to go at the moment. It's not shapeless at all; it's fluid. It is unnatural to want autonomous flesh, flesh that sticks tight to your own bones and pushes against the world. You have to give with whatever other thing is out there, and then you melt into the world. It's the only way to keep from being bruised, and once you start getting bruised you also start holding back, tiptoeing, feeling your way with your hands, and even wearing shinguards and shields."

"Some people wear spikes," Gus said. "Do you melt into those too?"

"Yes," she said, and climbed back into the hammock, closing her eyes.

She carried her water-principle into the house, too. Anything that exists for no other purpose than to be looked at, should go, she thought. "If we got rid of things that no one uses, things that are merely cosmetic, then the house would grow its own decorations according to whatever project was in progress at the moment: a book being read, bills hoping for payment, a doll dress half-made, somebody's recorder—do you see? We don't need a coffee table except when we're drinking coffee, do we?"

"No, but do we have to move it away, and then bring it back every time we do want coffee?"

She sighed and got up, touching his arm gently in forgiveness. "We don't drink *that* much coffee, do we, Gus?"

There was, however, something extraordinarily pleasant about the house after she had had her way with it for several weeks. It felt like the house Gus now imagined had been his when he was a child—if not during dutiful winters, at least for three truant summer months. Such a house his mother had not wasted her efforts on, since it was merely borrowed (albeit for money) and, no matter how tasteful or timely her decorative ideas were, would revert in September to salt air and dust covers and, the next summer, to people very likely of no taste at all. During these summers (or so his fantasy went) a house became a prop, a background landscape, a barely noticed floor and walls and windows with furniture which moved easily according to where the light was lying. Rooms were not militantly *for* something: beds were on the porch where the family sat in the afternoons, the dining-room table was either in the kitchen or the living room, clothes were in a box in the hall, and Gus's bedroom (assigned to him the first day and then the question of its ownership forgotten) was often for shells and sometimes for nothing.

Since Gus left this present house every morning for an architectural office which had always grown its own decorations, it was the activities of Lila and the girls that strewed the place with meaning. And, since during those first weeks the girls hovered around and behind Lila like a chorus, the projects of the three of them formed a unit. Each project was consistent, intense, and, because an hour has a very long timespan when one is young, rapidly changing. The house had rhythm. For a week there was sewing, through and over the living room. Lila worked at the machine on first a dress for Alice and Dinah each, then nightgowns, and Dinah sewed meticulous and lopsided shirts for her dolls while Alice cut and pinned and ran needles in and out of bits of cloth and stuffed animals. The room was a family being clothed: every anthropomorphically shaped toy in the house was somewhere in that room waiting to be dressed.

The following week they cooked, and the wall between the living room and the kitchen was only in the way. It had always been in the way: Lila had come out firmly against that wall since the day they were married, but Gus was not persuaded to remove it. The kitchen equipment backed up to it, for one thing, and it was the only unwindowed or undoored wall in the room.

"Look," he explained. "If we took that wall away, we'd have to move the stove and things to an outside wall and shut out the yard."

She considered that. "We could put a window between the sink and the cabinets and only shut out part of the yard."

"But we're only shutting out part of the living room.

There's already an oversized double door connecting the kitchen and living room, and you can leave it open." She did anyway.

"But it's a so much bigger part of the living room than it would be of the yard!" she said.

Nevertheless, they cooked that week with the wall where it was, and managed to include the living room in the kitchen by letting the kitchen activity spill over—just to the area directly in front of the double door at first, and then, as the week progressed, the living room took on more and more the aspect of a caterer's shop. Soon every table had received its portion of food or food product and even the farthest corner got its crumb. The two rooms were a cornucopia, and toys were eating everywhere. The goodies varied: Alice worked with dough and rocks, Dinah with batter. Gus ate exotically.

"Lila," he said one night, stroking the dark silk of her hair. "I love you."

She nestled against him. They were together in the hammock. All happiness in the world was inside her, and she could hold no more. "I'm full," she said.

"I don't wonder," he said.

The third week Gus came home to nothing. All traces of cooking and sewing were removed, and the living room was empty. He walked quickly through the house, alarmed. He called her. The sight of nothing having been done in those rooms that day filled him with panic. Every table was empty, every toy removed. There wasn't even a chewing-gum wrapper in an ashtray. After two weeks of activity, the emptiness made him dizzy. Sick. "Lila!" he called. "Lila! Lila!"

Then she came through the kitchen door with Dinah and Alice. He hugged her and didn't let her go. "We went to the zoo," she explained.

"But then there's nothing *here*," he said.

The knowledge that a house decorated with activity could

be so abruptly stripped when the people went elsewhere for a day occupied his working thoughts for a week. It seemed to him that insecurity had been irrevocably defined. "You are here and it is alive; you leave, if only for the day, and it is dead. Totally dead. As if it had never even been." He tried to explain this to Lila.

"We've got to have some sort of bridges," he insisted. "Couldn't you leave a cake from last week on a table somewhere, or plan a coming project and at least put out the nails and catalogues? This way you have to start every day new, like there had been no yesterday."

"What's wrong with that?"

"It's very frightening. Darling, I love you, and when you don't leave yourself around or something behind when you go out, I feel that you just disappear."

"Yes. We came back, though, as you see."

During the next few days, his fear changed to irritation. She was being un-American for one thing, he told her. Every house in this country was part of a plan, was a report card, even, and every husband knew what he'd done that year by looking around it. There was the chair he'd bought his wife for Christmas from money saved up. He was standing on the rug which celebrated his raise in the spring; 1952—that was the year they'd had the kitchen done over instead of taking a summer trip. 1953: a terrace. 1954: a hi-fi set. Last month he'd made a wooden house to hold the garbage cans. And he was planning . . .

"People need possessions," he said. "To know where they are. A house is supposed to look a little bit better each year. *Your* house won't look better each year. In fact, it'll look worse. There'll be no progress at all."

"I measure progress by rings around the bathtub. If there are four rings around the bathtub in one week, then I know that I've taken four baths that week. Or somebody has."

"And then you wash out the bathtub?"

"Yes."

There was an overwhelming dome of stars encircling the hammock, and this seemed the one big fact in the Texas night. Everyone has such moments. Lila thought of galaxies. That galaxy is careening away from our galaxy (she smiled at the possessive) at so many thousands of miles per second. She sat up on one elbow and explained to Gus that compassion was the only thing that mattered. "Nancy was telling me a story about a psychiatrist in a mental hospital today. Listen. There was a girl, a patient, who was completely withdrawn, couldn't talk, was in a state of total isolation and suffering—she couldn't say a word but there were tears streaming down her face. One of the doctors went up to her and put his arm around her and said, 'Whatever you are feeling I am feeling too.' That was a wonderful thing to do."

Gus said, "It was dishonest. He *doesn't* feel what she's feeling. He can't."

"It made her feel that he understood. That was her greatest need."

"She could have sensed that he was lying, and felt despised. He could have said, 'I *don't* know what you are feeling but I wish I could share it with you.'"

Lila stood up. "That's *cautious*. Don't you see? It's only feeling that is limitless. It's only through feeling that we can experience eternity, in a *galaxic* sense. Feeling is all that *matters*."

Lila became pregnant. She was the only one of his wives who actually did look prettier when she was pregnant. Her already marelike eyes became a softer brown, her movements were heavy with a most delicious languidity. Her entire open accepting life had been directed to just this fulfillment, and it showed in her face. It was fuzzy with passivity.

She wore her child proud and high, and read every book she could find on motherhood. The house was happy and self-contained. She made every conceivable plan and preparation. Nevertheless, something was wrong. She was three months pregnant and had not been to the doctor.

She was afraid.

"Of what?" Gus kept asking.

"I don't *know* him," she said, again and again.

She was afraid he would criticize her. At last, sitting in the waiting room in a modern professional building, she wanted to make a speech. She hid her face behind *Baby Care*. She wanted to tell everybody that she did not think she was all that attractive; she just happened to be pregnant. She peeked over the top of the magazine. The girl across the room smiled at her. She was a young girl, no more than twenty-two, and her blue overblouse was bulging. Lila smiled back weakly. Lila was thirty-three. She felt like an exhibitionist.

She climbed up onto the examining table. She had taken off everything except her slip, which was much too short. "Oh, no; leave your shoes on," the nurse said in horror. Lila climbed back down and put on her shoes—high-heeled black pumps on winter-white legs—and climbed up again.

The table was not a whole table. Its lower end was an ill-disguised extension that slid back into the table body, leaving air where her legs now were. "Put your feet into these stir-rups," the nurse said, fixing her heels into metal brackets out to each side of her body. "Now move down." She moved down a number of inches. "Move down farther." She moved down several more inches. Her knees jutted into the air far above her like awkward skyscrapers on the Texas plains; her buttocks must be at the very edge of the extension. Slam! into the table went the extension, and she balanced on the edge of that cliff, her underside lit by the cold sunlight from the window.

Sex is a beautiful thing, she had heard from an embarrassed generation. They meant that unless you were beautiful you could not have sex. She was fat now, stretched out on this table like a virgin sacrifice, and the slip was gracelessly short. The examiner for the god would reject her summarily. She must be here for some other reason.

It was unnatural to have the stirrup pressing into the arch of her foot like this. For ten years of childhood she had carried her weight on the ball of her foot in a stirrup. It was the first rule of horseback riding. The metal circling her arch now and hitting her ankle felt so awkward that she moved her feet so that the ball was resting on the metal. This thrust her knees up still farther and pointed her toes in their high heels and bare legs above in what she suddenly visualized as a provocative pose. She closed her eyes, flattened her feet and pushed them as far through the stirrup as she could, bringing her knees as close together as possible.

The picture remained, though, graphic on her eyelids, and her entire consciousness was irretrievably focused on that part of herself which she had kept covered for a lifetime. She felt like sobbing. How did she smell, open to the air like that? The juices which kept her warm and moist the rest of the time were dried up now and she longed to wet herself. She was cold. She contracted the muscles of her vagina and tried to close herself up. She wanted to hold herself with her hands, but she was afraid the nurse would pop in at just that moment. She had known nothing but tender protectiveness toward this most babied part of her body; why did they leave her spread-eagled here on this machine like Prometheus . . . the thought of an eagle circling now preparing to dive and peck away at her grew larger and larger and she screamed.

"How can anyone feel natural and open about her body

when they make you go through things like that?" she said later, crying slightly into Gus's shoulder.

"You have to cut off your feelings, baby. Everyone does in gynecological examinations. Detach yourself from your body, refuse to feel, make it cold as ice. Identify with the doctor, or something. Imagine how that poor bastard would feel if he let himself feel."

"Cut off your *feelings?*"

In time Lila's natural curiosity overcame her natural shame during these examinations, and she began looking forward to her visits to the doctor. She began identifying—not exactly with him, but with his finger; as it stuck itself up her anus to touch the nearest membrane to *her* baby she found herself excitedly asking each time, "How big is it now? Has it moved? Look; it kicked! Because you touched it! Did it turn around? Is it still upside down?" And she would leave the examining room reluctantly but with a new overlaid feeling of fullness. Through a digital anal transference she had made contact with the baby.

She shared this contact with the other mothers in the waiting room. She included them in the arc of her self-contentment, smiled over them and expanded with them into a soft community of importance. She wanted to tell them how glorious it was to be female. She felt that only in this room could everything be shared: beauty and fruitfulness and the future, varicose veins and stretch marks, laundry and pain.

In pink calico and glistening eyes, it was after one of these visits to the doctor that Lila came home disturbed. She was fixing dinner in ten-minute standing spurts alternating with five-minute sitdowns because she could not stand up for longer than ten minutes at a time, her culminating insides pushed so fiercely toward the ground.

"I was reading an article today, Gus," she said. He listened patiently. It was her daily tell-article hour. "The writer was talking about how to love babies—you know, saying that you can't love them too much as long as your love isn't of that horrible seductive kind. They make it sound so awful—you know, because they just refer to it, without really describing it." She sat down. "I don't really know what they mean, so I was trying to picture something . . . and I thought of Dorothy suddenly. She was a waitress with me at Tosca's, about thirty-five then but she seemed so old. She worked to support her child, and she couldn't love—for whatever reasons, her own fault or not, it doesn't matter. Anyway, she was shut off, and all day she worked in that metallic world where the faces of the people looked like plates and they shoved each other for nickels and there was nothing but clicking and cracking and grabbing, all day long. And then she came home each night to her son, two or three years old, and he ran to her and laughed and threw his arms around her, and she fixed his supper and they ate together and she played a game with him going upstairs, and *bathed* him—Gus, imagine this incredibly soft beautiful child glowing from the bathtub, and you wrap him in a towel and put on him fresh pajamas and tuck him in his bed and read him a story, and this woman with her whole frustrated need for love and tenderness inside her, and he puts his arms around her neck and kisses her and his breath is like sweet warm magic, and she's not supposed to *love* him?" Lila got up and entered on to another ten-minute period of dinner. Alice came in in the middle of Worcestershiring the hamburgers and Lila hugged her for so long of the ten minutes that dinner advanced only slightly. "I have you, Gus, don't you see? Who did Dorothy have? But they say, 'As long as your love isn't of that horrible seductive kind.' Who says that? Cherished wives and professional men. People who live in habitable worlds. And who do they say it to, Gus? Who to?" She sat down again. "I don't know why I'm getting so upset about it, though. I just don't know what they *expect,* that's all. What do they think having a baby is all about? Who else can she love, for Christ's sake?" She was crying and he tried to comfort her. "What does natural mean, Gus? What does it mean?"

Gus ceased being in awe of Lila (for he was in awe of her, even when he disagreed with her or found her excessive) gradually during the course of this pregnancy. As the pregnancy progressed, Lila turned more and more inward; she was not soft and amorphous now, but defined; she had grown a shell very much like an egg does to protect her growing yolk, and this shell (however thin it was) had shape and substance. It was her incomprehensibility before which puzzled him, her constantly changing form which left him as if always faced with a stranger, her total responsiveness which made him feel that she didn't exist.

She was fixed, inside the tightly stretched skin which shielded her future child, and her thoughts, her identity even, was focused also here on this growing child as if it were a growth, an offshoot of herself, the central tenderest core of herself wherein all she was was concentrated. She sent out no more feelers to the outside world, no more softnesses to melt around external people or things. She did not hold out her arms to anything now, but kept them cupped around her belly.

In this condition Gus found her as easy to deal with as if she had been one-dimensional. She was deaf to all things that did not concern motherhood. She had only one wavelength, and simply did not hear sounds of other things. Thus her former hypersensitivity disappeared, in effect. Her feelings were never hurt; they were in her belly. She never felt rejected; she never left her shell. She no longer cared whether she was misunderstood; all understanding was centered in her own pit.

Gus rejoiced in his newfound rest. It was a relief to leave for work in the mornings and know that when he returned she would be in the same place. It was a relief to feel that what he said did not matter; in her self-preoccupation she would not hear him anyway. It was a relief to be separate and distinct from her. She no longer encircled him or folded over him with doughy demands. She remained in her eggshell. He remained outside. He worked better; slept better. He enjoyed a new sense of identity himself, a new peace.

At first.

Then gradually he noticed small irritations. She heard nothing—not only things which might previously have caused tears and left him feeling brutal, but *bons mots* as well. She adjudicated response—to questions he needed help on along with daily remarks she was wont to hear as critical. He was rested but bored also. He was independent and alone. He was left unencircled and ignored. He began to think of her as an Arp sculpture, not a natural egg. He began to fantasy that if she were in fact an egg, he would stick holes in her with a pin until she leaked and grew sticky.

He told her that he was worried about her—that it was not natural for someone who had always been so open to enclose herself so suddenly and firmly in a shell. He said that he was afraid that when the baby was born she would collapse. He feared for her stability. Dramatic extremes of behavior were dangerous. One cannot reverse oneself suddenly in mid-life without stripping gears. He suggested that she try to achieve a balance. He meant that she should come out to him when he felt accepting, retire when she was tired.

She smiled and said she would try. He felt much better, and went to work the next day convinced that he could cope with life and all its problems. Balance was what was needed.

For several days they met in the center. Gus held happiness in his hand. They each stepped forward from their corner, bowed and curtsied to each other, circled to the right and then to the left, and then gracefully stepped back.

Then suddenly one day they were out of phase. She retired when he felt accepting, came out to him when he was tired. The dance was over. She stepped hopefully into the center as he was tripping back to his corner; withdrew to her own by the time he had reversed himself and come out to meet her. They each occupied the middle in solitary panic. Each day Gus tried to readjust his own conflicting mechanisms. Each day Lila did the same. Each night they met each other out of phase but reversed. They chose the same days to do nothing and let the other reverse; the same days to change their minds at the very last instant. They each grew tense and anxious and the baby developed hiccups.

Lila suggested he take a short trip, maybe to a different time zone.

"That has nothing to do with it," he said. He was convinced her labor would start the minute he got on the airplane.

Lila had been unpregnant for a year. She had come out of her shell and grown soft and responsive again, but only to nature, not to people or other sharp objects. She smiled when the sun shone, and her tears mingled her body's waters with the heavens' when it rained.

"Why do you simply reinforce nature?" Gus asked her. "I mean, if there is already rain, your tears are not really needed; you could save them for dry spells. In addition, it is on gloomy gray days that we could really use your smiles, not when the sun is itself making cheerfulness."

"I don't know," Lila replied. (It was her most characteristic answer.) "I can't help it, I guess." (Her second.)

Their sex life was like that, too. When the sky was passive, they rolled with the undulant slowness and monotony of its swells and subsides; they became rough and choppy when the wind changed, brooding and incomplete in the tense expectant air before a storm.

The child had been born in June, and Lila had insisted upon naming him Junius. She called him Juni, over Gus's objections. He had round huge black eyes peering out of a thin face, and hair so fair it was indistinguishable from white.

"He doesn't look like you or me," Gus said.

"No. He is night and day," Lila said.

"Oh, Christ!" Gus said.

Lila adored him. "He is my nature," she began, hoping Gus would listen, but expecting him not to she pretended to be talking only to the baby. "When a female mother brings forth a male baby there is a completeness so utterly complete that there is no place to go from there. Then this child sucks my breast just as I suck your phallus—within this circle you see flow all the juices of eternity, life, everything. It's more than symbolic, it is. Don't you see?"

"Usually called a circus," he offered.

"With only one ring? I don't see that," she said doubtfully.

"Look. I could suck your breast while you suck his whatchamacallit. That's two rings."

"Why do you think everything I am serious about is funny?"

"Because so much nature doesn't have the ring of truth, that's why." Gus hardly dared hope she would laugh. It was overcast. "Look, Lila." He tried to match his voice to the day's gloom in an attempt to reach her. "You don't realize how difficult it is for an ordinary man (me) to live with someone like you. I don't mean that *you* are difficult; on the contrary. You are so undifficult that it is impossible to deal with you at all. *You* simply are. I mean, put yourself in my position. You are blonde in the daytime and brunette at night. It's always that way, except when it's cloudy like today and then your hair is gray, but even though it is always like that, or just because there is this inevitability to you, this changeless changing, I simply don't know how to deal with you. I mean, the absolutely only thing anyone can do with you is accept you. Can you possibly imagine how impossible that is?"

She frowned. "It isn't exactly clear," she said. Her face was clouded.

He saw his mistake, sighed, and walked over to kiss her. "We'll wait until tomorrow and discuss it then." Her kiss was damp with humidity.

"All right." She sighed too. "I really feel pretty low today."

"It's the ceiling," he agreed.

The first singing of birds had awakened Lila ten minutes or so before; now she sat in the open door to the terrace drinking tea with honey. Her head was light and trouble-free, but inside her blood was pushing and she needed Gus.

On the west she saw a mother skunk emerge from the plumbago by the fence and head out onto the lawn, steady, followed by two baby skunks. The mother watched all sides in front of her at once, her black rodent head held up and her tail curled high as if she were a creature of dignity; the babies followed thoughtlessly in an Army-straight line. They marched directly down the center of the lawn and disappeared into the shrubs on the eastern edge of the property. The skunks had passed so close to the house that she could see the blank baby faces on the little ones—simple unmolded shapes of faces, without alertness, following the parent until they grew to be a parent, and yet they were alive. This fact amazed her. That a baby skunk should be alive.

She took the children to the zoo that afternoon. It was spring at the zoo, too, and the animals had babies.

Now it was night, and Dinah and Alice were quiet in bed,

Juni asleep. Lila lay on the grass, her flesh like paste spreading over the firm St. Augustine blades. She itched everywhere at once, because there had been bugs in the past. A mosquito bit. She slapped at him, and waited. None bit again, or buzzed. Nothing. She turned over and stared into the freckled sky. "The sky is the inside of a beach ball," she had once said to Gus. "Like the kind you used to cut open when you were a child to see what produced its bounce. Remember how disappointing it was to find nothing? There was no bouncer; it bounced *because* there was nothing inside. *Nothing* made it bounce. It didn't make sense." Gus had been irritated. "It's just semantic, Lila. Isn't it?" His voice was impatient. "You know all these things depend upon our trying to make language fit natural phenomena."

He was short with her as he often was when he thought she was being childish, but the emptiness *was* there, between her and the top of the sky. There was nothing between her eye and the star dome.

She rolled over on the grass and let her head lie face-down on her arms just above the clipped stubby blades. Every day she gave Dinah and Alice and Juni (separately according to their individual needs)—love. Every day she reached, smoothed, opened, added a grain of strength to their store. And at the end of every day she felt the coming on of panic: she was dispensing grains from a stockpile that didn't exist; she was giving love from the red side of the book, she was robbing emptiness by closing her eyes and pretending there were grains, hoping that somehow they would become grains, that the air held in her closed fist would in passage granulize itself into a single tiny grain just once more. It had so far. But every night, in payment for getting her wish, she had to feel the full force of her own emptiness plus the minus emptiness from all her back borrowings. This of course increased (at the rate of two grains daily).

People err in thinking that nausea derives from something one eats. Lila's sickness came not from a stomach twice as full as it would like to be, but from one twice (at rough estimate) as empty.

Double hollow. She would step outside and look at the trees against the sky, hoping to gain a piece of eternity through traditional channels. But often she would cry instead, cutting off a possible grain source by blurring the receptors, and depleting yet further her own contents. (Yes, tears are contents when that degree of emptiness exists.)

It was only the arrival of Gus—at five-thirty or six or seven-fifteen or eight-whatever—that removed the hollow; filled it, not by filling it with content, but with hope of being filled. Gus, bursting through the door like a blood-plump plum, sending waves of possibility into every hitherto collapsed hole of air, Gus plumping up the feathers of her world like an energetic maid—it was the physical presence of Gus which made each day begin again.

She wanted him to hold her.

There was a cold strip across her shoulders which had been there since she was thirteen which nothing but his arm could warm; it demanded attention with such fierceness sometimes that she would cry out and rub and pound both shoulders with her hands to obliterate its need.

She wanted him to lie on top of her.

The hollow inside yawned with such a gaping hunger that she would press both fists into her belly, pull a heavy belt tight around her waist, wrap a sheet around her body as tightly as a child winds its finger in a rubber band. It was the minute after intercourse when he lay heavily on top of her, still inside her, two hundred pounds of him pressing her into the mattress, that she cherished most.

She wanted him to be on all sides of her at once and squeeze out the inside air which threatened to gnaw her mad.

Under the stress of this need she would do anything to please him.

He wanted her not to need him so much.

She got up and went into the house and stood over Juni's crib. Moonlight exaggerated the room. In the wide light his face was drawn in intersecting circles. Soft invisible lines defined his skull, symmetry of eyes, cheeks, the dent of a perfect mouth. The tiny pure grain of his skin swelled in curves and a rush of shadow. The inside of her own body became pulp and she shuddered. She enclosed him, her body melting over him in his mold, leaving a centimeter of air everywhere between them to protect his sleep. She reached out for his hand, underside up in a fist on the sheet beside his head. She pushed her finger into its grip; its fingers tightened and held her own. With her other hand she opened the sleeping fist— three soft, delicately drawn fingers side by side with a fourth, the little one, rounded in a stub at the second knuckle, foreshortened without a nail. He had been born this way, a perfect child missing only a quarter-inch of flesh and bone and nail on the little finger of his left hand. She ran her finger over the smooth unprinted stub. Her cheek brushed his cheek, his mouth fluttered in a rapid smile-unsmile on its touched side. The muscles in his eyelids twitched and she kissed them. Her hand cupped his head and her other arm reached under his body and she bent her own body to the surface of his and raised him with her, holding his head in the hollow of her neck. She bent her mouth to his, sucking deep of his incredible breath until her own eyes closed in a surfeit of joy.

He opened his eyes then and looked up at her and she lay him on the pillow on the bed. His eyes were round and black, and glinted like a forest animal's. She began to sing to him, and stroke the white down on his head. She sang to him and he smiled and gripped her finger. Love for him flooded her and she quickened the tune. Joy threatened to burst her and she picked him up; her muscles seized his body as if her arms were steel and she would crush him and press him back inside her skin. His cry broke their grip and she lay him back down on the pillow and put her head in the hollow of his neck and opened her mouth to his skin. He cried again and she got up and left the room.

Outside in the hall she stood with her back to the wall and listened to him cry. The rhythm of his cries rose and fell in peaks of anger alternating with soft pleas of need. Small seconds of silence split anger when he refilled his lungs with breath; long stretches of silence lay where she knew he must be sucking his thumb—this was not real silence and she could imagine and then hear the wet sucking noises coming from his mouth as it tugged and closed around the thumb. She closed her eyes and leaned her head back against the wall, the sounds of his small sucking mouth purring through her brain and floating her into dream. Abruptly he cried again, a furious wail of anger; his cry cut her dream and she cursed him. "Shut up!" she shouted. His cry increased, furious and demanding, faster and louder. "Shut up!" she shouted louder and louder, intermittently silencing him by her shout, hearing his in the silence of her drawing breath. The shouts played out their dance, her shout, his cry, an occasional split of silence when both drew breath at once. Her fists closed and gripped themselves against the wall.

There was a thud, followed by a high odd cry, and she ran to him and picked him up from the floor and cuddled him and stroked him and walked up and down the room soothing him and whispering him back into comfort and kissing him and feeling him soften in her arms and relax into contentment again. She carried him into the kitchen, cradled in her left arm while her right lit a burner, put a pan and water on it, took a bottle from the refrigerator and set it on the counter. She balanced his buttocks on the counter to use her left hand too to turn the nipple around; before he could cry from precariousness she gave him back that hand, put the bottle in the pan, and walked him until it was warm.

She held him in the red chair by the window while he sucked and watched her with black eyes fixed on her face. For the first half of the bottle his eyes remained fixed on her own, she stared back at him and laughed and said, "You're not sure you can trust me, are you? That's it, isn't it?" After she patted his back and laughed again at the force of air which jarred his small body and left his face surprised and bubbles of milk around his mouth, he closed his eyes and finished the bottle in sleep.

She sat there with him for more than an hour while he slept, until the ache of emptiness grew to a giant in her pit. His sleep contained its own dreams, his body relaxed and did not hold her, his warmed full belly and soothed brain shut her out in a total way, and an occasional digestive spasm pulled his mouth into a smile which flicked the hollow of her and mocked. She reached for his hand and pulled it to her mouth, inserting the three-quarter little finger between her lips. The arm pulled back and tried to return itself to where it had lain on Juni's chest. She lowered her head to his chest and held the finger from there, cradled on her tongue. She sucked it gently, drawing her upper lip across her teeth to keep her mouth soft. It was no bigger than a straw. It lay on a small portion of the top surface of her tongue, barely reaching the roof of her mouth. She caressed it and tried to concentrate on it, but it lay like a straw in the front of her mouth, sensitizing the back surrounding emptiness.

She pulled the finger out and looked at it, a hideous nub of deformed unnatural flesh. The skin was smooth and shiny but not printed. It was naked, raw. It was blue, not pink, and white like gristle.

She dropped it and got up, letting his body fall to the chair seat and resettle itself. Thunder cracked the silence of the sky and she stood before the refrigerator, holding its door open, reaching into cups of leftovers and putting handfuls of cold peas, beans, bits of hamburger, salad, into her mouth with her fingers. Lightning flashed and she ran into the bathroom.

She looked into the mirror. A face whose beauty she had accepted since Juni's birth looked back at her, a beauty she so took for granted after six months of it that sometimes she barely glanced at the mirror, sometimes passed without looking, often let her attention wander even while facing a mirror, so thoroughly had she learned in the past six months that she was beautiful. She looked into the mirror and beauty looked back. As she stared the mirror shook as if jarred, each of its molecules infinitesimally rearranged. It fell back into place an instant later, the components of its surface settling in a slightly different conformation. Harsh lines appeared where there had been fuzzy shielding eyebrows, her features were defined as with the amateur tightly-gripped pencil of a child where before they had grown into place from inside. Quickly she smiled but the mirror remained in its new pattern. The smile was drawn on also, black and straight-lined. Her head fell into her arms as the rain broke, and she wept.

The new day dawned with its own new color, obliterating yesterday. The blue of today's sky was not laid over the thunderclouds of yesterday, nor were those clouds rubbed out, leaving evidence of rubbing on the paper; there was absolutely nothing of yesterday's color glinting through to deaden or distort today's. No trace.

Gus telephoned at nine to say he would be home tonight, and by ten Lila had called six friends. They were coming to dinner. She chose her dress. She planned an all-goodie dinner (no stretchers, no fillers). She laughed and brushed her hair and watched it curl itself.

Mrs. ——— came by for coffee at eleven, and Lila jumped

to make it, laughed, and eagerly told her the menu. She tried to listen to her mother's suggestions, improvements. Her mother offered to make a mushroom soufflé, an epicurean side dish. Lila said, "That would be marvelous!" Everything was marvelous. "I feel alacritous," she said, and giggled. "Isn't that marvelous? Has anyone ever felt alacritous before?"

Mrs. ———'s eyes shone, and she smiled, because she knew her daughter was feeling this happiness from proper sources: in her relation to her husband and children. "Gus is good for you," she said. "Because you do like people—you really do—and he forces you to go out to them. He brings you out of yourself, and it is not natural to be shut up inside yourself, as you sometimes are."

"Yes, of course. You're right." Then she frowned. "Forces me?"

"Not really forces," her mother said. "But we all need to be forced a little bit, sometimes—I know I do. And there are very few people who have ever been able to force you, darling."

The day was so bright in the glass-dominant house that Lila's sudden feeling of dazzlement, of dream floating, seemed natural to a sunlight so strong that vision was impaired; one could see too well under the proper light for reading which the eye doctor suddenly demonstrated, and the print jumped forward so precisely detailed that it took on an existence of its own, and she could not read at all. Brilliant sunlight threw a haze of clarity over the room, and she could not see her mother. "Do you think I'm cold, Mother?"

Her mother's white, ringed hand covered hers where it crouched twisting a piece of paper napkin into a spiral—her mother's hand, harmonious pianist's bones, supple to the proper point, pushing back after. Even without manicure, the nails were narrow and of a fine pink grain. The knuckles were large, the veins decisive, flesh minimum. The hands had not changed in twenty years; her mother had grown into them. "I only meant that you sometimes hold back too much," her mother said. "You need only follow your natural instincts, darling. Don't be afraid to let what is inside come out."

It was ten-thirty and the dinner had been perfect. Lila felt stuffed with compliments. Her skin stretched tight over too many smiles. Her blood ran warmer and warmer from repeated thrusts of friendliness. Smiles and affirmations. She loved them all, and needed to seize and crush them before she burst and drowned them with her spewing love.

Everyone had left the table, left the strawberries in Kirsch and whipped cream blending with the rose and gold of dessert plates, left the table crumpled with used napkins looking, unfolded, like cuptowels, excessive linen; left the chairs erratically flung, cluttering the room patternless, left the mess —Lila insisted; she loved a mess in the morning. Loved it! Everyone stood about, tentatively happy, hesitating before sitting down again in the living room, waiting for someone to start an arrangement by settling the first position so that they could choose an optimum or a dutiful one. Gus offered brandy, and Lila got glasses. They would stand a while. The others stood, someone on pretext of looking through records. Two went to comb their hair, replace lipstick. Two more regarded a drawing on the wall, politely comparing.

Lila watched Gus, considering brandy. He was relaxed, handsome, looking always like himself. He smiled and waited for others to come to him; alternately saw them smile and went to them. Rhythm of ease. Her face melted and said, I love you. He smiled and said, I know that. She cried, But I love you! Don't you understand? Still he smiled. Love you! she insisted. Smiling. *LOVE!* The smile turned and offered a brandy to the two whose hair was combed, offered a record

suggestion to the searcher there. "Gus . . ." she was choking, breath bouncing out in wads sufficient to break her frame
like the disproportionate belch of a baby. "Do you want
me?" "Yes, of course." His eyes were smooth and open. His
arm went lightly around her shoulders and he said the dinner
was marvelous. Her hand on his waist clutched at the soft
fold above his belt, gripped his flesh. "Lila didn't hear you,"
he said to Max, turning to face him, rotating his fold away
from her fist, tugging slightly apart. "Max asked if you would
teach his wife to cook." She hadn't heard him but she felt the
pressure now of his alien face at the back of her cheek, his
hand ready to touch her shoulder. She whirled and grabbed
his arm. "Max! You love your wife!" His eyes were black
and sharp, and their quick touch licked the naked skin of her
breast tops and then smiled at her confusion. "You are un-
usually lovely tonight, Lila," he said. Gus's smile had turned
away; preened by his friend's praise, he looked for an aja-
cent wife whom he might fluff up. Lila felt the material of his
coat slip from her hand; she could grab a fold, hold tight, and
let a patch tear off in her fingers, hold that. She let go and
held the brandy. "I read a book last week that would interest you," Max said, in a formal sexless voice. He began to
describe the book. Lila forced down a swallow of brandy, set
down the glass, picked it up again, decided to take another
sip, changed her mind, inhaled, put the glass away from her.
She heard his voice, smooth, cynical, somewhere outside her
ears. She looked at the clipped hairs by *his* ears. As a child
she had drawn each tiny hair separately, sharpening and re-
sharpening her pencil a hundred times. She had tried to count
her own once, by a square-inch area. She recounted and got
a difference in the second hundred. She had taken tweezers
then, and pulled out a border, a square an inch on each side,
and then taken the hairs inside the plucked fence in her hand
and cut them off with scissors. These she had counted, sepa-

rating them into bunches of ten. She had forgotten how many there were—two thousand? less?—once they were counted it didn't matter. But her hair was fine; Max's was coarser, wasn't it? Or did it look coarser because it was black? There couldn't be two thousand in that inch by his ear. Scalp showed through.

"But it doesn't!" she interrupted suddenly. "It doesn't interest me at all!" She turned and walked quickly to the bedroom.

The morning hung with the humid promise of ninety degrees and possible showers. Lila sat—kind of sat, was sittingish—in a limp chair and pushed a spoon into one child's leftover bran flakes. She put a soggy bite in her mouth and swallowed it.

Gus was still asleep. Actually he was awake, because she had seen the pretending face turned to the daylight, flickering in the attempt to look relaxed; but he would stay in bed until she was through with the kitchen. He was angry, or disgusted—fed up with her. He didn't understand why she had to insult Max.

"What did he say? Do?"

"Nothing."

"Then why were you upset?"

"I don't know."

"*Try* to know."

"I felt he was playing games with me."

"Aha. You, the game-playingest child I know, objected to that?"

"Maybe that wasn't it. Gus, I'm sorry. I'm really sorry."

"That doesn't help."

"I'll try not to do it again."

"*Try?*"

Dinah sat on the couch reading a comic book, singing. Not

singing words, but da-da-da-ing a jerky popular tune. "Will you please be quiet?" She stopped with a blank look at Lila —for sixty seconds. Then, as she resumed reading, the da-da-da-ing came again. "I asked you to stop." Again, a sixty-second silence. Then da-da-da, with a few scattered words. "Shut up!" Lila stood over her, furious. *"SHUT UP SHUT UP SHUT UP!"* She slapped her hard on the nearest leg. "Goddam you, I told you to shut up. Now shut up!" Dinah's blank face looked back, motionless. *"GET OUT OF HERE!"* Lila crumpled to the couch as Dinah left the room. Neither cried.

Juni crawled into the open doorway, saw her, raised his hand with a smile and "Gaa!" and dropped back to all fours to scuttle rapidly across the floor to her. He pulled up on her leg, held up his hand again and repeated the smile and "Gaa!" She stared at him until the smile fell away. He clutched at her leg, trying to pull himself into her lap. With a dry sob she picked him up, held him fiercely, drinking deeply of his breath. He squirmed. She held him. He squirmed. The brittle smell of ammonia assaulted her nose and she put him abruptly on the floor and walked rapidly into the dining room, returning with dirty dishes. He started to cry, then crawled after her. She met him at the doorway; he stopped, changed course, and crawled after her to the sink. Before he reached her she had turned to go back to the dining room for another load. He changed course, met her again at the door-way, turned back. He took the middle of the path, so that as she turned again from the sink she had to change pace to avoid stepping on him. The third trip from the dining room she screamed, "Stop following me!" He followed her to the sink, turned back halfway as she met him on another trip to the dining room. She screamed again. "Go away!" He tried to crawl faster to keep up with her. She reached for him, held him in front of her at arm's length, carried him back to his

room with violent disgust and dropped him in his crib, shutting the door on his cries.

She filled the sink and began washing dinner plates, six of
them; each cost five dollars. I will throw them across the
room. Break five dollars at a time. Five, ten, fifteen, twenty,
twenty-five, thirty. Dessert plates, at fifteen dollars apiece.
Six of them. Fifteen, thirty, forty-five, sixty, seventy-five,
ninety. Goblets, six of them, at two-fifty. Too hard. Throw
them in pairs. Silverware won't break. Throw them at the
brick wall in a game of mumbletepeg and see.

Gus walked through the room, dressed, freshly shaved,
clean and combed. He paused on his way out the back door.
"Why is Juni crying?"

"I whipped him."

"Good for you," he said. "You're a natural mother, aren't
you?" He left. She heard him start the car on the first try,
back purposefully into the turnaround, and drive away.

She ate of the leftovers as she cleaned up—cold French
bread with congealed butter, acid mushrooms, soggy strawberries with alcoholic cream, salty tournedos—eating after
she was full. The exotic mess of flavors artificially combined
and cold in the morning made her stomach cry like a child's.
She finished a glass of wine. The sweat it produced hung in
her pores because the air was already saturated with its own
sweat. She reheated last night's coffee, drank a sip and spat it
out. Someone had put brandy in it.

Then the kitchen was spotless. It was immaculate. She
walked to a corner to look at all of it. It was perfectly clean.
She saw a twist of dust under the table and picked it up, rubbing up adjacent specks with her hands, picking them up on
damp fingers. She washed them down the sink, then dried the
sink. It was shining clean. She took a towel and polished off
finger smudges on the refrigerator handle, went back to the
corner and looked again. She took a cigarette from the pack-

age on the table, and lit it, careful to pick up the three bits of tobacco that fell out when she tapped it. She carried these and the match to the garbage can and dropped them in, then put the can in the recess under the sink and shut the door. She saw another tiny spread of dirt by this door, dampened a paper towel and wiped it up, and put the towel in the garbage can. She sat on the couch with a deep ashtray so no ashes would stray, a patterned one so ashes wouldn't scream messiness, and carefully smoked the cigarette, feasting on the room.

In the cool, all-white bathroom she took a thorough careful shower, then wiped up all traces of it. She dressed. She was thoroughly clean. She put her damp nightgown and robe into the hamper, shut it, and looked at the bathroom. It was spotless.

She went back to Juni's room. His screams after she had left him there had followed her back to the kitchen, had covered the background of her cleaning. She had tuned them out of the front half of her brain and had heard them as noise from someone else's house, rising and falling, changing amplitude and tone, screams of anger and despair. At some point they had stopped, and she had not been aware of the moment. She noticed only, in the middle of cleaning, that there was quiet, and that there had been for some time.

He lay now crosswise in the crib, the top of his head against the side ribs, pushing against it, the flesh of his head molded in grooves around the wood. His face was flushed, asleep, his thumb in his mouth, his body sprawled in the limp spread of exhaustion. The sheet was pulled away from the head of the mattress where his hands must have clawed at it, away from the bottom where his legs had kicked and pulled. The sheet and blanket, wet from urine, were bunched beneath him. His face lay on the flowered plastic in a puddle of sweat and tears, cheek flattened, stuck there. His thin white hair clung to his scalp in damp skinny ropes. The flesh of his thighs was red below the elastic of last night's rubber pants. She shuddered with a huge child-ache of pity and love, and gently moved his head away from the prisoning wood. Deep red dents divided his skull in three. He woke up, saw her, and immediately began to cry with the loud fury of before. The cheek he had lain on was red and blotched from the airless plastic, his stomach crossed in creases from the crumpled sheet. His breath came in gasps as he reached up for her, standing, trying to lift himself away from the crib. She took him into his bathroom, took off the amber-colored acid diaper. His buttocks and genitals were scarlet and he screamed as she tried to wipe him with oil. She tried to put him in the tub but he clutched her neck and would not let go. He cried, in sobs and gasps, aimless leftover tears, not loud. She took off her clothes, holding him while she undressed, gingerly holding him around his raw buttocks while he whimpered. She took him into the tub with her, on her lap, holding him there, softly dribbling water over his legs and belly, sending plastic ducks past his hands. In a few minutes he began to smile, reaching for her breasts, the ducks, the washrag, her hair, and laughing.

He had just finished lunch when the telephone rang.

"Can I give him some ice cream?" Alice said. "He likes ice cream."

"Not chocolate," Dinah said. "Chocolate gives him diarrhea."

"Yes, honey. Hello? Mother? No, not chocolate, Dinah's right. What? Alice, I said you could. Mother, what's the matter? *Mother.* I'll be right over."

The soft dead black of Francis' face met her, eyeless; he wouldn't look at her. "Francis," Alice said, "Can I give Juni some ice cream?" Lila shut the kitchen door behind her and went to her mother's bedroom.

Death, in the natural way, drew them all closer together: mother and daughter, Mrs. ——— and her husband, Lila and Gus, the children and Lila. It was several weeks before they received the body, or rather the Army box that contained his marked remains. By the time they could have the funeral, an unreality had seeped into their emotions. Four and a half weeks of grief, diluted with waiting for the body, waiting for the culminating ceremony, waiting for the burial after which they could weep freely and accept, cover with earth and mourn socially and go on—these long unfinished days of serving coffee and cakes, turkey sandwiches and highballs, sherry and lace napkins, to condolence callers, friends who came daily and stayed all morning or all afternoon, passing the slow suspended hours, pacing their talk to make it last, braking their sympathy for fear of causing a final explosion in the family before the final moment was here, the body which could be buried—the family, feeling the thread of their grief stretched thinner and thinner as the same days passed again and again, existed in a gray paralysis which caused the children to whine and bite their nails and the dogs to slink under the beds after breakfast and stay there most of the day, looking out only.

Their grief became unreal just as the war in which son and brother had been killed was unreal. Embarrassed visitors referred to the actual events of the combat in which Dick had lost his life as little as possible, to avoid making a distressing error of fact which would point up what everyone knew—that Dick's death was useless. "But I thought the war in Korea was over," someone would ask a friend, puzzled, outside the house. "This was a skirmish," the friend replied. "I think." The first callers, who had to come before the newspaper account of Dick's death clarified things for them, tried to research the facts from the morning's paper. It was there, although not on the front page; we were in truth engaged in sporadic guerrilla warfare with Communists somewhere in the Far East. "Why did Dick go?" someone else asked a husband or wife. "I thought he was at Stanford doing mathematics—teaching mathematics?" "He volunteered; a year ago." "Why did they take him?" an uncle asked a cousin. "He was thirty years old. Why would the Army take him as a private when he had a Ph.D. in mathematics?" "The Army." The uncle spat on the ground for the first time since his country boyhood.

Lila and her mother sought each other's arms, briefly, many times. There they would hold each other, and agree to cry on each other's shoulder, and there they would release each other a moment later, eyes barely damp; pull away from the other's soft and fluid body which pressed in obscenely where one gripped. They turned then each to her husband, where the hard chest provided comfort and a wall against which they could cry and push back tears until the time came when they could be let flow.

Four weeks. One of Gus's cousins had a baby during them, and her husband timidly brought the news. Four weeks. In the middle of them a distant relative died at ninety-two, and they had to go to a griefless, intermediate funeral. Lila had begun to laugh, high on deadening gin, when Juni absurdly kicked at a shaft of moonlight or frowned at a Gerber variation. She was out of her own philosophy, had used it up, and was angry and answerless at her mother's. Her mother had to fit this untimely senseless death into her belief that everything happens for the best, and Lila watched her struggle with it and wanted to scream because she knew that somehow her mother would succeed.

"She will do it," she told Gus, the night before the box was to arrive, when tension had been stretched so thin that one day's delay would cause them all to snap. "She'll find something, I know she will. She has already suggested that at least

he wasn't married, at least he didn't leave a widow and or-
phans. She is already looking for a fullness in his life to make
up for its shortness. She is searching, Gus, in her diabolical
need to make moral sense, and she'll find it, I know she will,
she'll find it," Lila shuddered. "Goddam her!"

Gus and William, the least involved, watching the two
women strained beyond endurance waiting for a regulation
Army box, sealed, whose contents they would not see, waiting for a mass-produced ordinary meaningless box printed
with identification only, had tried to persuade their wives to
have the funeral with a substitute box and let the undertakers
replace it with the real box when it arrived. Both women
screamed and called them inhuman. Now, with the box expected in the morning, with the funeral planned finally for tomorrow, Gus felt sufficiently inhuman (if that was what it
was) to know that if for some reason the box didn't arrive on
schedule he would make a box with his own hands and fill it
with his own body, if none other could be found, to provide a
corpse for tomorrow's ceremonial release.

The funeral came, and the box was there, and when it was
over the family found that there were no tears left to be shed.
The ground was dry and dusty in the newly opened section of
the cemetery where they had been forced to buy a lot (the
old plot was full), and the crowd was sparse. All afternoon
they sat in the ———'s living room, waiting for a sudden
burst of sobbing, silent. At five o'clock, Gus quietly fixed
everyone a highball. At six, Francis set food on the table.
Alice and Dinah looked up from their plates, tentatively,
wondering if conversation would begin again. After dinner,
Gus suggested that they were tired, that he would take Lila
home to bed. William agreed. They were tired. They would
go to bed early.

Through the increasingly warm days that followed, and all
the hot (controlled by air-conditioning in the ——— house)

weeks of summer, Lila and her mother talked. They were together daily—in the mornings, when Lila was involved with the house and the children, at her house; in the afternoons, with the children, at her mother's; and most evenings, with or without Gus or William, at whichever house was most convenient.

They saw hardly anyone else, because the only subject either of them wanted to talk about was Dick, and the only person either of them wanted to share the subject with was the other, not because either felt the other alone understood; on the contrary; their views about Dick diverged on many points, warmly debated—but because they each felt that only the other was experienced, damaged enough to be worthy of sharing the birth of a sudden insight, the return of a memory, the re-experience of a piece of his life.

It was the pieces they were trying to put together, carefully stitching square to square in the way of patient females who used to live by quilts and things. Every day they chose, cut, fitted, sewed, as slow and precise about each detail as if they thought they would live forever, and becoming as close to each other, as intimate and conscious of every speck of the other's being as women who were in fact immortal—a word which means that death has ceased to exist, and so a word which sucks the meaning from life also. Reverse that. If life is meaningless one is as immortal as a god. Old women, rocking between deaths. He is dead, we will die; let's get on with the quilt.

But this was different. As the days passed and the work progressed, two clear patterns could be seen on the patchwork surface. Mother and daughter working opposite ends would meet in the middle. Huddled together, their backs formed an arch which looked like the hump of despair; their whispers from outside sounded like sighs. By October, Gus became alarmed.

He had nothing to complain of concerning Lila's behavior except that she had become as close to her mother as if she would suffocate her. He asked her.

"She tells me things about Dick," Lila said. "At least she thinks she tells me things about Dick. Actually, of course, she is talking about herself, and how she felt about Dick, and me, but she doesn't know it."

"Stop."

"Don't be silly!"

He tried to listen, but the whispers died in the soft form opposite; he tried to see their faces, but they were shielded by a bent head and the back of the other's. Then he understood the purpose of the arch.

"Mrs. ————," he said. "I'm worried about Lila. What does she say, about Dick?"

Mrs. ———— stretched a limber, elongated hand, repositioning a ring when she was through. It was opal, surrounded by diamonds. "This will be Lila's," she said. "When I die. You see, she has built up a fantasy about her brother; she thinks he is perfect. Of course, no man is. But you know that!" She smiled at him, a smile that glowed and reached for him with such sudden warmth that he felt it had touched his flesh, burned him. "When she has talked enough, she will begin to see, gradually, and I will help her, what her brother was really like. That is essential for her—you see that, don't you? I know you do, because you love her. Then she will be free, to live a natural life." She gave a brief flash of a smile. "I mean, normal."

It was on a hot night in late October with a norther predicted for the morrow that Mrs. ———— had dinner with Lila and Gus. The room was close with compressed air stuffed into every space and hole. Lila poured coffee and Gus got up to open the door. Lila immediately began sneezing. He closed the door, passed coffee, and fixed a drink.

"Dick used to say that everyone should train his brain so that then when you drink you only lose your inhibitions, not your sense," Lila opened. "He was brilliant when he drank —he got high, not tight. Soared like a bird." She laughed. "I wrote a poem about him once—or more than once, but once about this. I called him Dicarus."

"Gus, you can fix me one, too, if you don't mind. A little bourbon on the rocks. A light bourbon in a short glass." Mrs. —— held out her predinner glass. "Use this. No sense in dirtying up more glasses. Don't be stingy, son. I've never fallen on my face yet, in spite of what Lila is implying."

Lila was up and had her arm around her mother's shoulders before imply had finished trailing out its suffix. "I didn't mean that, Mother, at all; you know I didn't. You get more affectionate when you drink, if anything; you get all warm and loving and forgive the world. I get clumsy. But Dick was inventive—but all I meant was that he said by *training* the brain you can relax it with alcohol and it will still function, automatically. You could say the same thing about the body —if it's trained then when it's playing it still works—dances —is beautiful."

"Well, I suppose in Dick's case the brain was all he *could* train, poor boy." Mrs. —— held the dark, full glass of bourbon and looked at the golden color in the light before she took a grateful sip. "He was never much of an athlete, God knows why, though—his father was, and I'll say this for Dickie, he tried. He just wasn't built for it, that's all. It was the way he was born."

"I remember a marvelous summer," Lila said. "He must have been nine; I was twelve. We were making a newspaper. It was his idea. His was the best of the two poems. His the comic-strip drawing. I was neatly filling in the lettering, and feeling like a machine, when Dick said, 'Your writing is so beautiful.' I cried then," she said. "Of course. His eyes were the color of gray Crayola, and his face looked so tiny, pointed, all the same dusty color as his hair, and just a minute before I'd wished I were him. His drawings were good, they made me laugh; everything he put on paper—words, lines—sparkled. And he was so thin, so tiny; I didn't understand what could be inside him, what there was room for. 'You could be an artist,' I said. He grinned, a huge face-obliterating grin of teeth and gaps. 'Could I? Could I really? Could I . . . draw you?' "

"And you let him," Mrs. ———— said.

"I adored it! He drew me over and over, all summer long, dozens of faces, sometimes just noses, or just one eye, over and over, until he got it right. It was like being tickled—his glance brushing my nose, his pencil then dabbing a light line on the paper, as if his look were made of a feather substance and connected my face to its image through him. The tiny gray touch on the picture touched me, was raised, he looked back at me, the paper, stroked, up." Lila stopped. "I just remembered; he said a funny thing. Just before school started that fall he took all the drawing things out to the trash can and burned them. He didn't ball them up, but lay them flat on top of the trash and set a match to papers underneath, so for an instant the fire licked the edges into a frame of flame, and suddenly the drawing on top looked beautiful, the heat and light made the clumsy painful pencil scratches *grow,* in the paper and up from it, and it was precious and I wanted to cry, 'Save it!' I think I said, *'NO!'* He looked at me, his own face growing *up* from itself in the firelight. He said, 'I'll draw in public when I'm a horse.' " Lila looked at Gus and insisted. "Isn't that odd? Isn't it? 'I'll draw in public when I'm a horse.' That moment it made sense, but the next day I no longer understood and decided that he just meant he never would. But at the time he didn't mean that at all. He meant he *would* draw in public when he was a horse."

Mrs. —— snorted. "I'm sorry to spoil your mystery or whatever it is, honey, but I think I can explain it. Your father told Dick that a boy would be a sissy if he drew pictures unless he was six feet two and squared off to a horse."

"Would *be* a sissy?" Gus said.

"Would be called a sissy. That's what he said," Mrs. —— firmly erased the erroneous statement. "Would be called a sissy, and that's what he meant. It was for Dick's own good."

"Of course it was," Lila answered quickly. "At least I'm sure that's what Daddy *meant*. Or thought he meant. Or meant to mean. But Dick *was* a sissy in some ways; I know because I used to try to teach him to be brave. I don't think he minded being a sissy, really . . ." That thought drifted off into the region of past disagreement. The next came back firmly. "But that doesn't invalidate the fact that what he was saying that night by the fire was that he intended to become a horse one day."

"Lila!" Mrs. ——'s snort this time lifted her from the table. She went to the bar. "You have gone absolutely out of your head," she said through her back.

"What do you mean, a horse?" Gus asked.

"A horse is a four-legged animal with hoofs and a mane and a tail, and marvelous eyes," Lila told him.

"Oh. You mean a horse."

"Yes."

"You don't mean a centaur, or a Yahoo, or an Indian with horse attributes?"

"The animal itself." Lila sucked at a piece of porous ice in the bottom of her glass. "I wanted to be a horse when I was a child."

"That's different from actually expecting to change into one."

Lila was silent.

"I could tell you a story about Dick's artistic pursuits that happened a year or two after that," Mrs. ———— said, rearranging herself, hands and glass, at the table. "And I think I will, because you seem to think that your father and I were against Dick or something. You see, darling," she reached to a brief clasp of her daughter's hand, crumpled into its twisting paper position, "you have a special feeling for Dick that is lovely, it really is, lovely, but because of it you sometimes don't see some things that are there. I know, because I'm the same way, and it's something you might just as well admit about yourself. If I love someone I just don't see things I don't want to see." Her dark eyes held her daughter, enfolded, by their conviction. That's the truth, Lila read. If you believe that, and you must, you are mine. Lila stared, motionless. It's the truth, the eyes demanded. Lila stared. Blink! she told herself. Blink!

Mrs. ———— withdrew her hand, began her story. Lila closed her eyes and let whisky seep underneath her lids, surround her eyeballs. Another sip softened the points of her frown and her brow slithered loose and relaxed. The image of her mother's jewelry fuzzed. She listened to the story as if she knew it by heart.

Francis had come upon Dick in the garage one afternoon. It was a gray, rainy afternoon. (That mattered.) It was also a Saturday. She was sure it was a Saturday because she had been playing golf, and Francis had to wait until she got back to tell her. What a long wait that must have been for him, with that thing hanging around. (And for Dick.) "Do you know what Dick had done?" she said, looking at Gus, her voice low. "Do you know what that child had done, out there in the garage that afternoon?" Pause. "He'd painted his body like a woman's! To look like a woman. He'd painted himself into the body of a woman!"

She thrust this information so squarely into Gus's face that he jumped. "Oh, come, now, Hannah," he said. "Surely all children decorate their bodies. It's the ancient tradition of the tattoo, isn't it?"

Lila smiled beneath closed eyes. As her mother described the horror of Dick's painting—drawn-on breasts (shaded), emphasized nipples, black-grass lines for pubic hair and his own equipment tied beneath out of sight—she saw only how crude the drawing must have been. "Lopsided breasts," she said, and laughed. "I'll bet the breasts were wildly uneven."

"*You* think it's funny," Mrs. ——— said. "All right. Think it's funny. But let me tell you, it wasn't. Francis' face went white when he told me about it." She thought she'd used an original image. "Francis! Imagine how Francis must have felt!"

Lila opened her eyes and leaned across the table. "Mother, I didn't mean that. It must have been awful for you. But I suspect the really awful part was that it was Francis who discovered him. Right? Such a thing between you and Francis! Christ yes, I can see what a funny position *that* would put you in, to share such a thing with Francis." She picked up her mother's glass and her own, and fixed them identical drinks. "But otherwise, Mother, nobody's shocked at all. Don't you see? Including you. It's just too common—and you know it." She kissed the top of her mother's head.

"Common is right," her mother said, but that was all.

"I think you're trying to persuade yourself or me that there was something so queer about Dick that maybe—just maybe—it's better that he didn't live." Lila said this very softly.

Mrs. ——— drew back. "If I thought he was like that, I certainly *might* think so."

"For the sake of the children," Lila said sardonically.

"For his own sake," Mrs. ——— snapped back. "Do you have any idea what life is like for—such people?"

"Oh, Mother, stop it. It's academic. That silly incident doesn't mean anything."

Mrs. ——— brought out her dark voice. "Well, of course, I wasn't finished with the story. There's another part—maybe I shouldn't even tell you. Another part that you won't be able to dismiss so lightly, I don't think. Your precious Dick. You think he hung the moon. I wonder what you'd say if I told you that three years later—three years later, mind you, and Dick was no child—why, he had shot up that summer until he was two inches taller than *me*. He was thirteen. This time *I* found him. He had painted the bodies of two of his friends to look like women—but painted their backs, upside down, so the buttocks were the bosom part and . . ." She stopped, and let them imagine for themselves. When she continued her voice trembled with an emotion which made Lila listen as if sound had suddenly replaced silence. "I found him—my own son, my child—and he was two inches taller than I was, and I stood there looking at him, looking *up* at him . . . I never felt so helpless. I'm glad your father wasn't alive to see it. *He* wouldn't have thought it was funny."

"I don't think it's *funny*, Mother. I . . ."

Mrs. ——— was looking over their heads, at the room's corner. "He was my own flesh; my flesh had outgrown *me*, and there was nothing I could do. You can't imagine how a mother feels at such a moment."

"I think I can," Lila said. "His flesh had outgrown yours?" She realized she was whispering.

Her mother's eyes turned to Lila. Yes, that's how it was, they said.

"That's something I never did to you, isn't it, Mother?" She was still whispering. "I never did outgrow you, did I?"

Gus said, loudly, "You never even came close. Now look, how much longer do you two good ladies intend to stay up, because I . . ."

Mrs. ———— put her glass decisively down on the table. "You can take me home now, Gus."

The sultry lingering summer split off at 1 A.M. as the predicted norther blew in. It was the next to last day of October. Lila and her mother did not speak to each other again, but no one noticed. They had enough previously recorded phrases to handle a year of days. The cold was bitter but the heat had been so cloying that relief, usurping everything, confused what little clarity of insight Gus might have had. He suffered from a nature made impotent by change.

Lila thrived on change, and grew like steel. Darts of cold organized the household into a northern box of efficiency. Crisp clothes shielded the children, polished glass froze the daylight for their use, hours were supervised and finished with a clean tick and the next one instantly met.

Reprieve came only at story time. After the children were bathed (and they were, this winter, every night) and clad in flannel nightclothes (without rips, the proper size), the hour from seven to eight was allowed to soften and fur into a teddy-bear time. Here Lila held them in pink and blue and yellow and told them plush-covered stories in a voice like milk. Gus was drinking more this winter, in an attempt to fix his own identity. This particular night, he brought a glass of Scotch and sat in the room with them, but in a chair, over by the window. He didn't sit on the bed with them, or on the other bed.

Lila held Juni in her cross-legged lap. Alice nestled up on one side in an h-curve, and Dinah lay, skeptical and face-up, along the bed's length, her feet by her mother's elbow.

"There once was a woman who lived in a shoe," Lila began. "But it wasn't an ordinary shoe that you buy in a Poll Parrot, it was really a whole country shaped like a shoe, like Italy. But they called it a shoe because . . ." She reached out to Dinah's bare foot and with her thumbnail gently scraped the arc of its bottom, arching it. Dinah cried out in surprise and pulled her foot back, tucking it beneath her nightgown. She laughed, though. "Because feet are terribly important."

"I don't like feet," Dinah said.

"I do," Alice said.

"They show us how long we are, for one thing. They stick us to the earth, most of the time, and they take us places, but they're so sensitive that we put shoes on them to protect them. But when this woman first came to live in the country which was shaped like a shoe, there were no people. There was just the shoe, and nothing inside it—except herself, of course, but she was only one, and filled about as much of the shoe as your littlest toe would a giant's boot. It was a helpless feeling, being no more than a little toe in an enormous shoe, and she didn't like it at all. I will have to grow, she thought. But there was no way to grow. She was already grown. So what could she do?"

"She could ask some heel in," Gus said, "and he could make her groan some more."

Alice giggled wildly.

"Didn't she have any friends or a mother or *anyone?*" Dinah said.

"Not a sole," Gus said.

"Hush, Daddy, you've heard this story before," Dinah said.

"I swear I haven't."

"Well, hush, anyway."

"Okay. Shhh. I'll be as quiet as a tiptoe."

Gus got unsteadily up and tiptoed out the door. He was going into the kitchen to get another drink. On the way, he stepped inside the slate blocks of the living-room floor, avoiding the cracks; let his hand aim for and then scoop over the candlestick on the hi-fi set; bent down and blew at a gray spider curled in his web behind the refrigerator, causing him to scurry aimlessly nowhere. He drank a shot straight. It burned his chest and let him hate. Nursery rimes. Damned old woman who lived in a shoe. Christ, don't all children hate nursery rimes? Having struggled to listen rationally to grown-ups when they talked to each other, he used to feel hopelessly defeated when they turned to him and began talking the mystical obscurity of nonsense, which they thought was *his* language. He took another drink and sat down. There was an assortment of dwelling places in nursery rimes such as to depress an architect for life. Shoes and pumpkins. Smelly things. The heat in this house came on and went off every three minutes. Like a throbbing noise. There had never been such a sensitive thermostat.

He drank that drink down and felt his head clear. Lila is on the point of exhaustion, he saw. She is just barely holding herself together, using the winter to harden and contract her surfaces, efficiency to steer time straight. She needs to rest, relax in sunshine. Everything was so clear to him that he felt a sudden flow of love. He called a friend and rented a house on the beach at Galveston for the summer. It was now February.

Back in the bedroom, the story was reaching its end. How did the woman fill her shoe? Why, she had children, of course. But not too many at all. She never had enough. When he reached the door, she was having her twenty-eighth.

"Imagine the bare, cold floor of a shoe, like this room," Lila said. "We line it with children, and then it's soft and warm and safe. We lay them down, side by side, leaving growing room between. They are all different sizes, like pieces of a puzzle. Then we line the living room. The kitchen. The whole house. By the time the woman was old, her shoe was filled . . ."

"It runneth over," Gus said, and started to walk over to his seat by the window.

"Be careful, Daddy!" Alice said. "You're stepping on the children."

He stopped. He picked his next foot up and felt gingerly in the air before he put it down. "Hey!" he mimicked a child's voice. "You poked my bottom!" At the next step, he used a girl's voice: "Ow, you pulled my hair!" He reached the chair, pulling his feet up as if hands held them, and put them on the desk.

Alice giggled wildly.

"Hush, Daddy," Dinah said.

". . . the whole country in the shape of a shoe was covered with her children," Lila said. "They were a soft growing field. They were so beautiful. But they were more than that. As long as they lay there, the country was safe. No soldiers or horsemen could come in, because they wouldn't for anything step on the children, and they couldn't step between them safely, they were growing too fast. The old woman had spread out all over the whole sunny land."

"Will you spread out on the bed for me?" Gus said later when they were alone in their room. He kissed the back of her neck and held her huge breasts and gently walked her toward the bed. In the middle of the soft excess of intercourse, she jumped, and tried to sit up.

"I left part of myself in the other room."

"No, you didn't. You're all here," he said, trying to continue.

"I'm not!"

He tried to ignore her, hold her, go on as if he hadn't heard.

"Gus!"

With a sigh, he rolled over and lay on the bed beside her.

"Go back and get it, then. Unfortunately, when you come back, I won't be all here."

She brought him a glass of milk and a brownie, and one for herself. She sat on the bed by him, her hand playing with the hairs on his chest, as she nibbled and talked.

"I want another child, that's what's the matter," she said.

"I was trying."

She patted him. "I'm sorry. I really am. I just suddenly . . . look, I was slipping away and all of me wasn't here to begin with, and it was frightening. I mean, I was becoming *you*. Do you understand?"

"Do you?"

"No. Not really." She finished her brownie and put her head on his shoulder, lying alongside him half-hugging him with her body, like a child. "I'm frigid, aren't I?"

"No," he said. "It's the weather." He shivered himself and pulled the covers closer around them. The latest norther butted against the senselessly large glass doors leading onto the balcony. He shifted his thigh away from the bone of her knee, which was denting it.

"I want another baby, though," she said.

"I rented a beach house for the summer," he said. "Galveston."

It was a day when the wind blew mightily. It pushed against the trees and turned their leaves over so that the flat finish of their under sides was uppermost. It lashed the high grasses on the dunes until they hugged the ground in strained arcs. It tossed and churned the ocean into a spray-heaving turmoil of cream.

All morning she sat by the window. Her fingers twisted paper and drummed the coffee can and her movements were quick and hectic like the sea's. By noon, agitation had become a monotony. Churning which never ceased even for an instant or changed its pace added to her own restlessness a dullness, and her constant movements left her with the same feeling of ennui, listlessness, as nonmovement would have done. Except that she was tired from the racing inside which she could not stop although it did nothing, got nowhere.

There was no contrast in opposites. Her skin was dry and wet at the same time—wet from the moisture which hung like a cloud through the air and yet dried immediately by the force of the wind which blew it off each second. She shut the window and felt she would drown. She opened it a tiny crack and the wind whipped through the room, swirling papers over everything.

Outside, it was impossible to stand unless one's back were to a wall and one could hold on. The beach was emptier than she had ever seen it. Cascading cardboard equipment from the merchandised world and uprooted growing things bounced across the sand; these objects as they spun and disappeared underlined the sense that nothing could stay on the beach and made emptiness dynamic.

Her ears were not left alone for a minute. Wind, in a meaningless shakeup of sound, usurped the entire air with its undertone of noise and made noise silence; any talking would have to take this as its background and begin with shouts. Shouts themselves could not exist. Emotional range was precluded.

There was no one to talk to anyway.

Smell? A volcano of air rushing into one's nose and lungs with the force of an assault paralyzed the sense of smell altogether.

Taste too was lost in a rape of wind. Eating was impossible.

"And yet," Lila said, "it must stop or climax. Soon, it must," she cried, running from window to window to see if a different view of the sky yielded a difference in the sky. If she looked up she was sure she was looking at the sky (although she was seeing only wind). If she looked down she was sure she was looking at sea (although she was seeing only wind). The middle was an ambiguous blur of wind. Another hour and her skin itself would scream—each pore acting like a window to receive ravaging needles of wind. She ran to her bed and got in, drawing the covers over her head, completely enclosing herself. I am safe, she said. You can't breathe. I am safe, she said. You are twisting the covers into a funnel. I am safe, she said. Her fingernails dug deeply into her flesh. They had pierced the sheets and laced them to her skin. Still there was a hole. She could feel it, a draft. There, coming in by her knee, from the window side of the bed. A huge cold bitter waft of air pushing in, now that her hands were fixed; a blow tempting her to lift the knee a bit and try to pinion the edge of the cover a little farther out to close out the hole, knowing that the attempt was more apt to enlarge the gap and let the whole width of the wind pour in. The knee moved quickly, struck out, and *down*. She crouched inside for a second, and waited. It was snug in here. It was tight. It was done. She relaxed then into a shiver. Shiver? There is no hole, no leak, no gap. She shivered again. Crouched there under the bedclothes the outer side of her body was warm because no wind blew into her cocoon; nevertheless a cold spasm began in her gut, swelled and broke in her chest cavity, receded, swelled, broke, as if her body were a diastole in the giant shiver of the island.

When the hurricane hit, she was sobbing. Gus found her. "Where are the children?" he shouted.

"I don't know."

"Where are the children?" he shouted again, and again. "Where are the children? Alice and Dinah, where are they?" He ran into the next room. "Where's Juni?" he shouted from there. "Juni's not in his crib. *LILA!*"

"I don't know."

"WHERE ARE THE CHILDREN?"

It was a shout louder than she would have thought possible, and yet she barely heard above the wind and through bedclothes. He forced her name through again; lunged forward and ripped back the covers; he seized her shoulders and pulled her up to face him. His mouth open to shout a new command, he stared at her face—a bleak gray wash of wind and rain, formless, depthless, a sheet of hurricane. He felt his breath sucked away and he could not speak; his hands were clammy and held nothing. "Gus," she wailed, "why do you look at me like that? I . . ." He dropped her as he turned and ran from the room.

Saturday morning the sun shone and Alice watched for rattlesnakes from the porch.

"There is an enormous black rattlesnake as big around as my arm and as long as this porch coming up the walk," she announced. "He has thirty rattles and all of them are rattling." She stood up and undulated her arms as if they were made of castanets, clicking her tongue in a rapid syncopated beat. It sounded jazzy. She switched to a burring noise. "It's a huge mother rattlesnake and she's coming for her children. She's big and she's mean and she's spitting wild with her tongue, and when she finds the man who chopped up her child with the hoe she's going to pound him with her rattles and stab him over and over and over again with her red pointy tongue until he's as full of holes as a strainer, until he's more holes than anything else, and then she's going to reach in his stomach and pull out her children and carry them home all in pieces and try to glue them together again. But they won't grow. She can stick them back together and look at them but they won't grow back together because they're dead, dead, dead." Alice forgot the castanets and began marching in a circle. "And behind her there's another mother, and another, and another—there's a whole army of huge black mother rattlesnakes marching up the sidewalk and all of them are spitting and all of them are looking for their children . . ."

Lila smiled. The day was balmy, the sky clear and blue except for bits of fluff moving softly with an unseen breeze. Her eyes, watching Alice, reflected the shining blue overhead; her face was soft and bright like the warming sun. She lay back in the deck chair, her body curving as lazily as the mild regular waves. The ocean showed no sign of the recent hurricane, except that the water seemed cleansed and harmonized by its violence. The littered twisted mess of the land was incongruous beside it. The day was bright, and Lila had smiled since morning, a peaceful background smile. She had hardly moved all day, except for her hands, which clenched and unclenched the rounded ends of her chair's arms. The action of her hands had not ceased since dawn. Their palms were red and sore and scratched, the veins on their tops were bulging and blue. They clenched and unclenched over the rounded ends of the chair's wooden arms now with the same unslackening intensity as when they had begun that morning.

Gus came out on the porch. He briefly touched one of the straining hands as he passed, avoiding looking at Lila's face. He stood by the rail. The touch of the hand made him shiver, as if he'd touched a hard repulsive thing in agony.

Dinah put the newspaper to one side, face up on the glider where she could still look at it. "It says here that there are rattlesnakes all over the island, in the streets, on the causeway—that the water drove them up from their homes and they're swarming all over the place—that no one ever knew there were so many of them . . ." She looked at Gus as if she had asked a question. Her face was pushed into a scowl because it was the strongest expression she had. She saw that she had not asked the question. "I mean, even if Juni managed to crawl into a hole somewhere and escape the hurricane, be safe from it, wouldn't they . . ."

"Get him?" Alice finished. "The rattlesnakes don't want Juni. What would they do with Juni?" Her laugh turned to a high cry, and she seized Gus's leg. "When are you going to find Juni? When are you going to find him, Daddy? *Find* him."

He pushed her head into his thigh and involuntarily turned to Lila. He had not meant to look at her, but once he did, his look hung there, fixed to the bland blue of her face, serene as noon, smiling like an idiot god at his physical world, demanding praise for the ever-renewing freshness of his sky and sea. God the esthetician.

"Get out of here!" he shouted at her. "Go to your room!"

Still she smiled, and her eyes shone with their innocent blue. "I could cry if it rained," she said. "But then they couldn't find Juni in the rain. He always laughs when the sun shines. He is running and singing because the sun is making him warm and his hair is white with light and he has found somewhere a tiny pink shell to put on his left little finger where it doesn't extend beyond the second knuckle to make it the same length as the one on the right hand. The shell will make him a nail and make him perfect and he will laugh because he has found just the right one, just the right size, and so pretty . . ."

"Get up," he said, and grabbed her shoulders and pulled her upright. Bodiless as a sapling she rose under his hands and swayed against him. He tried to pick her up but her hands would not release their grip on the chair arm. With his own he tried to pry them loose. Their touch made him shudder. He tugged at them and felt a sickly sweetness radiate in his throat, blackness make him dizzy. He pried with all his strength, getting a finger under one of her fingers, pushing against its wet broken skin, but if he raised one a fraction nine others gripped with double force. She leaned against him, sliding into him docile and bland like the day. A fly lit on her forehead, walked across her smooth brow to her eyelid, where he stopped to twist his wire legs together and please himself. She would not let go the chair arm to brush him off. Rage seized Gus and he swatted the fly with his hand as hard as he could. Her eye and adjacent brow and cheek rushed to red from his blow, one small tear escaped from the eye he had hit. "Why did you hit me?" she asked. A sob of pity for her caught him, and he pulled the chair arms free from the chair and picked her up and carried her back to the bedroom, her hands holding the torn-off pieces of wood with erratic nails and splinters sticking out from their other end, and put her in bed and covered her. He lowered the blinds and drew the curtains and tied a black scarf over her eyes. Over that he placed the edge of a quilt, leaving only her nose free. "It is dark; sleep, Lila. There is no sun. It is dark. Very dark. Sleep now. It is dark." He stroked her forehead.

She will die, he thought, as he closed the door behind him and walked away from the room. The darkness is complete. She will die.

Lila didn't die, however. Under the care of an expert doctor, in a little over three years her nightmares ceased. As he explained it to Gus: "Your wife feels guilty over the death of her son, you see. All parents do. Even in the case of parents who are far away from the scene of the tragedy, who are off on a vacation and have left the child in the care of someone else—even here we find that the parent often feels that if only he or she hadn't gone the tragedy wouldn't have happened. Of course it is worse in a case like your wife's—she *was* there and was the one who was looking after the child, so naturally we have to expect that she will feel guilty. Very guilty, in fact. Of course her emotional state was such that, at the time, it would have been very difficult for her, if not impossible, to be actively responsible for the care of young children. We understand that, and I have tried to explain that to your wife. The guilt is intensified, naturally, if there are already existing in the parent-child relationship any feelings of hostility or resentment on the part of the parent for the child. There often are, of course, *some*—but fortunately these do not usually go beyond feeling the burden, the very *realistic* burden, of being a mother to young children, particularly if there is more than one child. However, in your wife's case, there was a little more involved than that. If the—what can we call it?—*normal* hostility between parent and child is based not on the present daily relationship but stems from some deep-seated problem already present in the parent, then the guilt, of course, is very much intensified. I'm afraid this is the case with your wife. I wouldn't go so far as to say that there was an *active* death wish—unconscious, of course, and certainly your wife was very far from being aware of it (on the contrary, she expresses a high degree of affection for the child), nevertheless—(I hope you understand. I realize this is a lot to absorb from a layman's point of view)—it was her *son,* wasn't it? A *male* child?"

They moved to the country and Lila had another child, Bobby. She lived each day as easily as the grass. She grew placid and harmonious, and rolled with the seasons. She planted with the sun, watered with the moon. She slept at night, and grazed happily over the land in the daytime. Sometimes she read, in the same way—nibbling off the lines in a book patch by patch, occasionally stopping to chew over a section before going on.

Once he asked her, "What did you think of *Advertisements of Myself?*"

"I don't know," she said. "It's still in my second stomach."

And then one day she died. Quite accidentally. It just happened in the natural course of things.

Gus was halfway through plastering the fireplace wall when he stopped to rest and smoke a cigarette. This batch of plaster was almost used up. One more bucketful and the wall would be finished, the room finished. The wet plaster smelled like the underside of viaducts where he had sat by streams as a child and watched the sewage drift past. Plaster. A day of plastering had left him satiated and limp, had drawn the fire out of his insides like the smear of baking soda over a wasp sting or the mustard plaster on his chest had drawn him as a child. He was no longer swollen or congested and the room seemed suddenly unnecessary. It was simply empty. Four clean wet walls, furniture huddled together in the middle, a foolishly slanted floor. The richness he had imagined would be his, here, was stubbornly out of sight. He had planned to burst and fill each molecule of air with himself. Earlier he had wondered if the air would be disagreeably turgid; now he thought there may not be enough of him to go around.

He found the brandy bottle under a table and drank reasonably from it. Rationality regained control. He was experiencing the familiar depression which always came just as a project was about to be finished; that was all. If nothing else, life and analytic thinking had taught him this: that the moment when one knows, ah, this too will be the same, follows so close upon the moment of anticipation that, as one grows older and the end comes hard on the heels of the beginning as if they were in tandem, only alcohol serves to obstruct the system's highways sufficiently for there to be any time length at all. This he knew—that alcohol could postpone knowledge until it was meaningless. He was cheered. In a little while he could accept the emptiness of his room as a fact of reality. It had taken on another glow because of a child-learned habit of expectation, fantasy. Once its emptiness was firmly established, became the as-it-is, he could go forward and fill it with himself as planned. Density is a relative thing, after all; fullness a trick of the mind.

When he had first thought of the room, he had allowed himself not to remember that his own imagination had a wild and erratic quality. It was almost impossible for him to think of a thing without simultaneously conceiving of its limit. As a child, the moment he consciously realized that he loved ice cream, he wanted a bathtub full of it so he could sink down into it and eat as much as he possibly could without diminishing it in the least (the eye could not detect the diminution which made it not exist at that age). He was never after that satisfied with a dish of ice cream, or two dishes, or even a quart all to himself, although he often ate all three and was painfully full. He would buy a gallon container, and eat from it with a spoon. But no matter how large the container, before many bites had been taken he could see the telltale waxed-cardboard arc of the container's side slip furtively into view, hinting the bottom. Therefore the bottom was reachable; therefore it was already there.

An ice-cream-philia was no longer a tormenting concern of his, however. Since he had been adult (in the merely technical sense) food frustrations had slunk to the back corners of his psychic garage, overwhelmed by the problems of his interpeople emotions. For it was also true that his imagination could no sooner conceive of an emotion than it had instantly to try its limit. A single heartbeat of tenderness—if he concentrated on it for a few moments, if he relaxed and let himself fully feel it—immediately thundered into a total sixteen-year-old state of in-loveness which swept through his body and defined "lovesick." In the same way, a slight pique swelled into an overblown bellowing rage, an urge to hit a momentary opponent into a furious wish to kill everyone. Since he was a civilized man, he actually did little harm, but the *feeling* that he was murderous, that he held in himself the total of murderousness of which particular murders were interesting examples, so swamped him that no tiny flicker of "Look, you didn't kill, though, did you?" remained to him; he (the person, Gus) sunk and disappeared. Only a long stretch of sleep erased the mood and returned him to himself (or to his public container), only exhausted, spent, without the compensating contact or shakeup which the actual action might have given.

At first he dealt with this problem by laughing at himself. As he got up out of bed after a bout of needing to be loved, after days of feeling the giant welling loneliness of a child abandoned, he felt as if he had lost half his weight. Everything on him—hair, mouth corners, shoulders, belly—were slack and drooped comically toward the ground. In this mood, if his mother had come in and held him and told him he was wonderful, he would have perked upward like cartoon flowers watered by Mistress Mary. He was a model for Walt Disney.

Or if he felt spiteful, he would feel the whole green slimy flood of spitefulness surge through him; he would walk down the street with slitted eyes, curled fingers, feet rigidly demanding their path, where they stepped with pleasure on a cigarette butt, a torn candy wrapper, an unidentified bug if any were in the place his foot had chosen. He would not swerve a centimeter for this pleasure. He rode buses and stared at the drawn and wrinkled crotch of an old man opposite, drank coffee to watch the dark, dandruff-flaked roots of the waitress' cheaply dyed hair, read newspapers to pick out

the lie of the mother of three dead children who said she had
only stepped next door for a minute. He was a hideous man
who had to be turned into a caricature, stripped of human
identification. He was a quality only, a "such an one" that
Theophrastus would have written about, and the reader
could laugh because no one was really there.

But laughter was not possible within the feeling; it was
only an after-the-fact device, a way of framing what had happened so it could be hung on the wall and dimensioned. Besides, there was no one to laugh with.

Laughter was inefficient. He needed something to cut the
feeling itself with. He tried analysis, but since this usually
helpful science operates by looking at feelings, it simply rein-
forced his tendency to be swamped by them. But perhaps he
didn't stay with it long enough, or more likely something in
him didn't want to emerge. His doctor once said to him,
"You refuse to look at the surface of things, and that is almost as bad as never looking beyond the surface." He still
pondered that, sometimes: why he couldn't bear outsides.

He tried companions, and found that being with another
person allowed him to express the feeling itself. He was over-
joyed. When a trickle of tenderness expanded into a flood of
in-love, he could shower the other person with affection and
understanding. No need, now, to keep it enclosed within his
bursting skin. He felt alive. He was happy. He was neither
limp nor bulging. He could jump over mountains, laugh like
a child. Until the inevitable moment when the loved one
made him slightly angry. Anger! He could feel it begin to
swell. He raced to his house, up to his room, shut and locked
the door on his rage. His fist crashed through the wall, leaving a gaping hole in the sheetrock. Later he hung a picture
over the hole, and wondered if he could learn to give himself
in pieces—give just a part, not knock the person down with
his entire contents, but hold back most and send out threads
from time to time as other people do. He never did.

But there was the room—the room he had raced to with his exploding anger. There he could be alone, and no one would be hurt. But when he was alone he was insane.

It was true. When he was with people, he responded to them and kept his monolithic emotions inside. He *could* keep them in, if he made up his mind firmly in advance. And if he did not allow himself to be tempted by the thought that perhaps one of these people could share his burgeoning feeling. But when he was alone, he was the victim of violent somersaults of emotions and, no matter how quietly he lay on his bed and breathed, was sped along a wild roller-coaster of fantasy which was, simply, insanity. He grew weak and depressed.

That was why he had built the room in which he could burst, a room that was almost finished.

There was a knock and the door opened. His three children stood there—Dinah, Alice, and Bobby. They had something with them, ducked out of sight for the moment. He knew there was something; all three had giggles in their eyes, their feet. Alice said that they had a surprise for him; could they come in? Dinah thought that he was probably busy right now and they shouldn't bother him. Bobby jumped ahead, too full to wait.

"Daddy, I'm going to be six tomorrow, and we're having a birthday party for you, tonight. Okay?"

"It isn't my birthday," he said, and felt stupid. What's the difference about that? Come in, come in, he urged them. But first he must hide his eyes.

By the window overlooking the block's back yards, his back to the room and his hands cupping his eyes' periphery like blinders, he could see into the night, beyond the reflections in the glass. Bobby would be *six?* Then two and a half years had passed for Bobby while Gus had sat in his room proposing a project, occasionally building. Two and a half

years. What's the difference. He pressed his forehead against
the pane for its coolness.

"You're peeking." Bobby tugged his arm away to see.
"Are you peeking?"

"Don't peek, Daddy!"

"I'm not. I promise I'm not." He cupped his hands so
strictly they hurt his temples. From Pin-the-Tail-on-the-
Donkey and Blind Man's Bluff came the wish to be blind in
fact so as not to be accused. But so what that two and a half
years had passed. That's nothing. It was just a shock, that's
all, because he hadn't noticed, he hadn't seen them pass.

Looking into the distant darkness, he imagined that he was
a body traveling into space at the exact speed calculated to
paralyze time. He thought of Rip Van Winkle, that mealy old
man so boring to children, who spent forty years growing his
hair and beard. He felt his lower face and was not cheered by
its smoothness. Dinah must be almost eighteen! His hands
held his head more tightly. "Can I look now?" he said. Eighteen! And Alice . . . "Can I look now?"

"Not yet!"

"Just a minute!"

Alice twelve, going on thirteen. Those were the years in his
own life when things had been important: when spring was
full of furious restlessness, but so was summer and the rest;
fall bulging with promise, but so was winter and the rest. Because each day was slightly incomplete, with room for something to happen. But what's the difference.

"Now, Daddy!"

He turned around, and blinked to adjust his eyes to un-
blindered light. There was a cake for him, made like a room,
with a slanted floor—a room like those in doll houses, with
no top so the owner could reach inside. And there were
presents.

Tenderness rumbled in his gut in a random beginning; he

felt a kind of sick pleasure close to nausea. Then he noticed that the piece of cake which stood as one of the room's walls was not iced all over—a patch remained where cake showed through, with icing massed around it.

It was because his real room was not quite finished, Dinah explained. They wanted to have the party tonight because . . . well, they had a surprise for him which they would tell him later—but because he hadn't finished plastering the walls Alice thought they ought to duplicate that on the cake. But, Dinah peered anxiously, they hadn't got the patch quite right, had they? His unplastered wall was rectangular, and their cake showed a triangle.

Eighteen! She was taller than he. Inches taller. He touched her blonde shoulder gingerly.

"Alice must have been thinking about Eliza and her swan brothers," he said. "But what's the surprise? You all look like you have a marvelous secret."

"Later!" Alice said, a flash of bewitching diamond in her smile.

Bobby reached for his arm. "————— . . ." Alice's hand was solidly over his mouth and he stopped the sentence no one heard.

"You promised, Bobby," she said. His brown eyes were huge with surprise, then grew quiet with sudden maturity. He remembered. "You give Daddy his present first," she said, taking her hand away.

Bobby had made a rocket for him out of an old wax can. It had water inside, he explained, for fuel, and it was held up with sticks. There was a birthday candle which you lit, and after a while the water made steam and the rocket shot off. "What's that?" Gus asked. There was a skinny-legged man standing beside the rocket with his hand up. "That's the policeman saying, 'Stop,'" Bobby said. "He says, 'Stop,' until it's time for the rocket to go." Bobby studied the policeman.

"I couldn't make his legs very fat because then they'd be too close together."

Gus hugged Bobby, who stood as stiff as the stick-policeman until his father let go, but his eyes held his father with a naked, fundamental feeling that went deeper than love. Gus felt his gut tighten and melt, tighten and melt. He was utterly unlike Juni: solemn rather than frenetic, with the dignity of a city child who knows ugliness from the beginning.

"How did my mother die?" Bobby said.

"I told you, Bobby." Gus's hand reached for his shoulder, back, reached and touched. He was so tall so quickly. "It was an accident. She was climbing an apple tree one day, because it was summer. She fell."

He pulled free of Bobby. Like an exaggerated host, he took fast giant steps to the refrigerator he had had installed in a jut-in and produced three bottles of ginger ale. He held them up in a toast, as if they were a victory. He lowered his arms. "Dinah . . ." He stopped. Dinah was eighteen, practically. "Dinah, would you like wine instead?" he said quickly. She shook her head, and he searched for the opener and shook the bottles to make them spray and leaned his face over so it could receive the shower of ginger ale. He closed his eyes. Lila was a fool. A donkey, not a horse. A mule. Thirty-eight years old, and because it was summer she climbed apple trees. The summer before she had tried breathing under water and almost drowned. He wanted to shout: she was sick all her life, and then she got healthy and died. But Bobby would survive, if Gus stayed away from him. Bobby's health was threaded with sickness, in a thin intertwining pattern which would hold it together.

He handed Bobby the first bottle. "Thank you very much," Gus said.

"Now, you!" Alice said to Dinah. She was impatient to give her own.

Dinah reluctantly picked up a package and held it out to Gus.

"I don't think you'll like it," she said. "It's silly, really. But I didn't know . . ." She watched him open it. It was a pair of binoculars, the ones he had given her for her tenth birthday. "I thought if you were going to stay shut up in your room from now on, you might like to look out." Suddenly her face glowed. "I used to love to"—she turned to Alice—"remember the fun we used to have watching the people going into the laundermat? The mothers would take their clothes in at night, and the kids would sit outside reading comic books. And I could see right into the apartment across the street! They had a great baby! She stood up in her crib when they thought she was taking a nap, stood up and waved out the window. She could see me. I wonder what she thought I was doing with those funny things over my eyes?" Then, to Gus: "But you only have a back window here. You really need a street window."

"Dinah," he said. "I like them very much. I can look at the stars."

The child-face that had come while she was remembering the launderomat vanished, disappointed, and a serious college-student one came. "I might take astronomy next year. I remember how the thought of all that space and stars out there used to terrify me. Astronomy is interesting. But you need a telescope for that." She turned to the blind wall of the room in the direction of the front of the house, as if she were trying to see the street through it. "But the street's such fun!"

"Open mine now, Daddy!" Alice handed him her package, wrapped in pink, lavender, and yellow strips woven into a sheet, with a yellow rose tied on, and streamers saying *I love you.* She had wrapped presents and decorated letters in this way since she could do anything. He used to think, as he watched her, that if God had helpers Alice, in her prehuman past, would have been the one who made butterflies. "You can't guess what it is," she said. "I made it."

It was a clay sculpture which had been fired, painted, and glazed—two figures, a wolf and a lamb, lying on a mound of grass. The lamb was dead, and the wolf was eating it, had already eaten a portion out of its belly. Gus held it gingerly. A whirr of something nameless, a shock of harmony ran through him. He was appalled. He stared at the curve of love on the lamb, the soft ridge on the wolf's bent head that her fingers had made. A sense of the past, corrected, flooded him.

"You love them both!" he said. "You love them both."

She was shy with pleasure. "Can you see that, Daddy? Really? How can you see that?"

"It's *there*." He placed the gift on the table and held her head in his hands. She wanted to move, brush the moment off, step back (the emotion was almost too intense), but she stood still, letting pleasure ripple over her face like waves lapping a beach.

"Alice," he said. "It is so beautiful."

He did in fact sit looking at the stars, later, when the children had gone, but with his eyes simply. They had wanted to give a room-warming party for him, they had explained, but more than that. (That was enough, a dry voice said.) It was a celebration, too. They liked his idea of building a room inside his room, they liked the idea of bursting out—"It's like running naked on the beach," Dinah had translated for Bobby—and they had helped him with the rest of the plastering. The room was finished. Bobby's footprint was on the wall. Then they had left, suddenly, quickly. We have to go, was all they said.

"Wait! What was the secret?"

But "Come on, we have to go" was all they said. Alice lingered a moment at the door, and looked back at him, but Bobby tugged at her arm and told her she had to hurry. He heard Dinah's command from down the hall—"He can't know until tomorrow!"—and Alice left, too.

"Tomorrow!" she called back.

He stared at the stars. Thoughts were cascading through his head in torrent. They were trying to tell him something tonight, the children were, and it was something more than what he *had* seen: that now that the room was finished he didn't want it. They were saying that the reason he didn't want it was because it was empty. It *was* nothing; it didn't just *become* nothing because he finally had it.

But their faces, their intoxicating voices and presence had so stirred up the air in the room that Gus felt his blood dancing from the glow. He saw each one separately, in image, and as he focused on the first, he thought, Ah, that was it! It was the unshielded eyes of Bobby who could stand on pain and explore space—*that* had shocked him into life, that! Then he saw the pulse of Dinah and her street, the warm rhythm of her baby and her laundermat, and he thought, No, that was it! It was Dinah's joy that had waked him up with envy and desire. Joy! Then he saw Alice, her face glistening at his praise, and the sculpture which had overwhelmed him, and he knew *that* was it. Each in turn, and the circle of images whirled past again.

But what? *That* was—what? Agitation seized him. He turned abruptly from the placid stars. He paced the room erratically. His mind was spinning with such a richness of color that he lost a thought as soon as he reached for it. What else were they trying to tell him, telling him? There was a theme running through the party, if he could remember their glances, their expressions, he could track it down. It wasn't just that the room *was* empty . . . but go back to that. And it wasn't that it would still be empty after he had filled it with the pale molecules of himself. He knew that, but they didn't. Anemic air . . . and the contrast of *their* bursting vitality! The visual memory of the scene of them brought on a new spurt of whirling images and color, and his brain was taken over by the force of it. He sat down and let that swell subside.

He got up. *Bursting* vitality?

He knocked demandingly on Dinah's door.
"Who is it?"
"Daddy."
"Oh. Come in."

It was his own agitation, he was sure, that made him hear her voice differently; her voice which was strong and concentrated (it carried through crowds) seemed thin and diffuse in his present state. He opened the door.

"Dinah?" He could not see her.
"Yes, Daddy."
"Where are you?" He searched the room with his eyes. "Are you hiding?" A silly question; she was eighteen!
"No, Daddy. I'm right here."

There was nothing in the room except a haze, a denser light. Her voice was there, and her characteristic smell of cosmetic purée. Quickly he pulled shut the door, and held it. He stood in the hall, holding the door. With horror, he realized that bits of her must already have slipped through while he held it open, into the lower pressure area of the hall.

"Dinah!" he called through the door.

"What, Daddy?" Her voice was thinner and faint, now; the voice of someone very tired.

"Nothing, darling. Forget it. It's all right. I'm sorry I bothered you. Forget it. Okay?"

"Okay."

He ran downstairs to Alice's room, put his hand on the doorknob and instantly jerked it away. The other hand, raised to knock, froze. He knelt down and tried to see through the keyhole. His eye scrutinized that slit of the room as if sight were a rake and could scratch through air and uncover any telltale particles which did not usually exist there. The eye is hopeless. He could not even be sure that the air was denser, that density was not an illusion of his constricted view and unreliable eye.

"Alice?"

"Yes?" The monosyllable was stingy.

"Alice, listen. It's Daddy. Tell me, are you . . ." the words "inside your body" hung in his chest. "I mean are you all together?"

"Of course, Daddy!" He heard her high laugh, an Alice bird laugh, clear, even loud enough, but it seemed unfocused at its point of origin. "I'm all here. Every bit of me!"

He shivered. "I mean, are you inside . . ." He couldn't say, "your skin." He sobbed with the burning elemental need to touch her concentrated on his palms. "What are you doing?" he cried.

"Nothing, Daddy. Do you want to come in?"

"No! I mean . . ." He pressed his own head with his hands, instantly tore them away and looked at them stiffly. "I mean . . ." his voice was low and innocent. "I mean, yes, I do want to come in, but my hands are full. Could you open the door for me?" He was hardly breathing.

"Daddy." He heard her high fluted laugh, again, but no more words. The laugh spread, became a giggle, extended, thinned, until it was almost silence. Then there was nothing

except the sound of spring blowing against the windows.

He turned back to the hall and stared at the quiet closed door to Bobby's room.

"I AM LIZA!" he shouted.

I am Liza, am Liza, Liza, Liza, za, za, a, a, a, a . . . , said Echo.

JUNE ARNOLD was born in South Carolina in 1926, lived in Memphis during her childhood and later moved to Houston, Texas. She studied at Rice University in Houston where she earned a Masters Degree in Literature. Mrs. Arnold now lives in New York City with her children. *Applesauce* is her first published novel and she is presently finishing a second novel.